IN THE FLESH

ETHAN STONE

Dreamspinner Press

Published by
Dreamspinner Press
4760 Preston Road
Suite 244-149
Frisco, TX 75034
http://www.dreamspinnerpress.com/

In the Flesh

Cover Art by Justin James   http://www.wix.com/qpm2010/justinjames
Cover Design by Mara McKennen

ISBN: 978-1-61581-552-4

Printed in the United States of America
First Edition
August, 2010

eBook edition available
eBook ISBN: 978-1-61581-553-1

This book is dedicated to my parents. Without their love and support throughout the years, I wouldn't have accomplished half of what I have. Mom, I know you're watching me from Heaven, very pleased I have finally achieved this dream. Dad, I love you and appreciate everything you have done for me.

Acknowledgements

I OWE huge thanks to several people:

To Bobby and Teresa, for giving me the space and time to complete this novel.

To Amy, for all the advice and help you gave me and for pushing me to rewrite and rewrite and rewrite.

To Laura, Dawn and Julie for the words of confidence and support.

Chapter One

I LIVE my life by a strict set of rules. Some of the rules have been around since I was a kid; some are newer. For example, you have to know when to walk away, and you have to know when to run. I learned that from my dad, a big country music fan. Also, all the clothes in my closet have to be organized—pants together, shirts together. I learned that from my mom. The majority of the rules, and the most important, have to do with sex. Why so many? Because I like to have sex. A lot. As much as possible. In my mind sex is like money: you can never have too much. The rules have always guided my life, and I didn't break them for anybody. Wasn't even tempted. Until I met him. My life was already screwed up by then. Some of that was my own fault, but not all of it. He was tall, dark, and handsome. It's a cliché, I know, but for him it fits.

He straightened things out in my life while simultaneously tearing it apart. How did he do both? He got me out of the trouble I was in, but I also ended up breaking a few of my rules because of him. But breaking rules can be good, because some rules are made to be broken.

I'm a cop in Reno, Nevada. A detective, actually. No, we're not like the cops on that show *Reno 911!*.

It all started at the beginning of June, when my partner and I made a major bust.

My partner is a short but tough African-American woman named Alexandra Luther. Everybody calls her Lex. We're an odd pair. She's five-six and the slightest bit chubby. I'm six-two, skinny but built, and I have lily white skin that won't tan no matter what I do. Lex has a full head of dark hair that she always pulls up in a ponytail, and I keep my head shaved to the skin.

"Good job, Detectives." That was Chief Gary Brunson congratulating me and Lex on getting the arrest. We had just arrested a young white teen who had been running drugs for a local piece of scum named Anthony Zion. The boy was spilling his guts about Zion after we had promised he and his family would be protected.

"You guys did good. I'm surprised you got him to talk so quickly." Brunson always seemed to be surprised when we got results.

Well, more me than my partner. Lex has been a detective for years and has an excellent track record. She has a handsome hubby and two kids at home. She's been mentoring me for a while now. At twenty-five, I'm one of the youngest guys to ever make detective. What can I say? I'm dedicated. I wanted to be detective, so I did what I had to do to get it.

Brunson likes me well enough; I can't say the same for my fellow cops. There are a couple reasons for that. The first reason is my age. Other cops haven't been able to make detective despite more years on the force. They don't like it that I achieved it so quickly. In their mind it was easy for me, but it wasn't simple at all.

The other reason I'm not well-liked in the precinct is that I'm gay. Openly gay. I've never hid the fact that I'm homosexual, but I don't flaunt it, either. I'm not a fruity, dress-wearing, sashaying queer. I don't go around holding hands and kissing face with my boyfriend. First of all, I don't have a boyfriend, don't want one, but if I did, there wouldn't be any public displays of affection. PDAs, even between straight people, make me sick to the stomach.

After being congratulated by Brunson, Lex and I gave each other a high-five.

"You did good, Cris." Cris is short for Cristian, and Lex is the only one I allow to call me by the short version.

"You, too, Lex." We split up and headed for the locker rooms.

I was in the locker room drying off after taking a shower when I heard some whispering. I looked up to see three guys looking at me.

For some reason I didn't think they were talking about what good shape I was in at 220 pounds, or how good I looked with my head shaved, or how pretty my bright blue eyes were.

Still stark naked, I stood up and looked at the guys, meeting the ringleader square in the eyes. His name was Gus Curtis, a veteran cop of thirty years. Curtis was going bald and had a permanently red face—one of those faces that comes with drinking too much for way too many years. Curtis hated me for a number of reasons. The biggest reason was that I had a detective shield, and he didn't. He had never been able to pass the exam, and for some reason he thought it was my fault he was an idiot. With Curtis was his younger partner, a red-headed kid named Tim O'Reilly. He'd only been on the force for six months and was a legacy kid. Several family members on his mother's side, including his mother and grandfather, were cops. O'Reilly shared his hatred of me with Curtis but for different reasons.

"What's up?" I asked Curtis.

"We were just wondering how you made detective so fast, Flesh," he said. Flesh isn't some cutesy nickname; it's my last name. Not the one I was born with, but mine nonetheless. "Cuz I figure you must've sucked the right cocks."

I shrugged and turned away. Stupid shit like that isn't worth my time. Rule number seven: You don't have to fight to be a man.

"You wanna suck my cock?" Curtis asked.

"I don't do baby-boy cocks."

Curtis hopped over the bench between us and tried to tackle me. However, he was so fucking noisy about the whole thing that I knew he was coming and ducked out of the way. Curtis collided with the locker instead.

Rule number eight: Sometimes you have to fight whether you want to or not. I spun around, struck out my right hand, my fist connecting with Curtis's cheek, knocking him to the ground.

Curtis recovered quickly and jumped to his feet. "Fucking queer. I'm gonna kick your ass."

"Go ahead." I let Curtis take a punch at me, which I ducked easily. He swung at me a few more times before I connected to his solar plexus. His breath was knocked out of him, but he kept swinging, getting sloppier with each one.

When I decided I was done, I gave a one-two punch to his gut and his face, knocking him to the floor. He lay on the floor, blood oozing from his nose and breathing heavily in and out. I kneeled down on one knee. "I hope this settled at least one fact. This is one queer who can kick your ass any day."

I stood up and offered my hand to Curtis. He looked at me in astonishment but grabbed my hand, and I helped him up. I turned away, walked back to my locker, and continued getting dressed.

As I pulled on my pants I looked at Curtis and caught O'Reilly staring at me with ice-cold green eyes. It was the red hair and green eyes that had attracted me to O'Reilly when I first met him—at a gay bar.

It was before O'Reilly had joined the force, before I knew he was a cop. I saw him sitting at a table alone and couldn't keep my eyes off of him. A few guys were hitting on him and asking him to dance, but he brushed them all off. After watching him for close to an hour, I finally approached him. He looked at me like he was expecting another lame pick-up line about his looks. I always like to skip that bullshit and knew it wouldn't work on him anyway.

"Wanna fuck me, Red?" I asked him as I sat down.

"Where?"

"In the ass," I answered.

He laughed at my little joke. "I was asking for that one. I hate clichés and didn't want to use the old 'My place or yours?' line."

"My place," I said.

"Lead the way."

We drove to my place in separate cars. We screwed for hours, and when we were done, he dressed and left. We didn't exchange names or numbers, which was just how I liked it.

A month or so later, I ran into O'Reilly at the precinct. He was as shocked as I was. He was afraid I would out him as queer because I was open about it.

"You don't have to worry about that, Red," I told him. "I won't tell a soul that you're queer."

"I'm no fag. I was drunk."

"Tell yourself whatever you need to so you can sleep at night. I really don't give a shit about who you screw."

O'Reilly and I had hardly exchanged words since then, but he seemed to hate me because I knew his secret.

ON THE drive home, I considered heading to a bar and trying to pick someone up, but decided I was too tired to play the game so I went home to my third-floor apartment instead. The Courtyard Apartments aren't the best apartments in Reno, but they're nowhere near the worst.

I don't have much in my apartment, but I don't need much, either. I have an older thirty-two inch TV with a cheap thirty-dollar DVD player. The newest piece of furniture I own is a recliner, a dark brown La-Z-Boy. It occasionally doubles as my bed, so I spent a lot of money on it.

The DVD player gets quite a bit of use, but the only movies ever played in it are gay porn, which I own a lot of.

For a long time the recliner was the only furniture I had in the living room, but Lex insisted I needed a couch for company. I tried to tell her I didn't have company, and if I did we were in the bedroom, but she didn't listen. When she bought new furniture, she gave me her old couch, a simple tan one with big, soft cushions. I would never admit this to her, but I loved the couch.

My apartment door opens to a small hallway where I always hang my coat and leave my shoes. The TV sits on the wall the living room shares with my only bedroom. The kitchen is connected to the living room and has an island between them.

It's not much, but it's all I need.

I pulled a Guinness out of my fridge, grabbed one of the several newspapers piled up on the kitchen counter, and sat down in my recliner. I got half the Guinness drank and two articles read before I was asleep in the chair.

Chapter Two

My CELL phone woke me up at six o'clock Monday morning, earlier than I expected to be waking up. Lex and I usually didn't report 'til ten or so. It was a good thing I hadn't gone to the bar last night.

I looked at the caller ID: Lex. "Yeah," I mumbled.

"Cris, get your ass out of bed and get dressed; we got a new case."

"What about Zion?"

"Chief wants us on this one. Going to be high profile."

"What is it?"

"Joseph Pryor has been stabbed. He almost died."

Pryor was one of them Bible thumpers with a TV show. He was a minister at some local church. On his show, *Pryor Sins*, he talked a lot about all the sinning people do and how they all need to repent and allow God into their lives.

A bunch of crap, if you ask me, but then again, I'm one of those sinners he's always pounding on his pulpit about. Pryor tended to talk a lot about homosexuals and their evil actions and how they'll rot in Hell if they don't change their ways.

I know the man is a hypocrite.

Renown Regional Medical Center was only five minutes from my apartment, so I got there before Lex did. I waited in the parking lot in my vehicle, a faded blue 2005 Jeep Liberty Sport. I bought it a few years ago, when my 1992 Toyota Camry stopped working. I don't do any off-roading but needed a four-by-four for those winters when the snow hits Reno hard, and I have business in some of the outskirts.

Lex finally showed up, and I met her at the front door. The medical center was a huge building with something to meet every medical need.

Lex handed me the file, and we took the elevator to the third floor and found Pryor's room. A large, Hispanic nurse was fussing with Pryor's IV drip, but she stepped out when we flashed our badges.

Pryor was in his early forties and in decent shape for his age. He still had a full head of hair, but it was totally gray. He was just under six feet tall with only a slight paunch on his belly. His face was thin, and he had a long, pointy nose. He couldn't have been mistaken for an Abercrombie & Fitch model, but I figured maybe he could've when he was younger.

Pryor wasn't looking very well. According to the report, he had been stabbed several times. Surgery took care of most of the wounds, but he was pale from having lost so much blood.

Lex and I introduced ourselves.

"So what happened, Mr. Pryor?" I asked.

He looked at me for a moment before speaking.

"I was home writing a sermon. My wife Madeline and sons, Joseph Junior and Mark, were all gone for the night."

"So you were alone?" Lex asked.

"Yes."

"Were you expecting any company?" I asked. Lex looked at me, somewhat surprised. She usually did the questioning while I took notes. She had a better manner than I did. For some reason I tend to upset people. I call it being straightforward. She calls it rude.

Pryor hesitated and looked me in the eyes for several moments before answering.

"No, I wasn't expecting anyone."

I spoke up again. "Absolutely no one? Someone from your church or your show? Maybe a friend?"

He looked me in the eyes again before answering. "No, I already told you. I wasn't expecting anyone. I was home alone working on a sermon."

Lex looked at me for a moment, waiting for me to ask another question, before she spoke. "Tell us what happened."

"I was in my office, listening to some music, when I heard an odd noise coming from the living room. I went out there thinking the family had returned early. But it wasn't them. I saw a guy going through my wallet.

"I wasn't going to confront him. I tried to be quiet and go back to my office and lock the door, but he saw me. He told me not to move, but I started to run. He chased me and dragged me back to the living room.

"He made me lie on my back, and he was sitting on top of me. That's when he pulled out a knife."

"Can you describe the knife at all?"

"Uh, no. Just looked like a knife."

I spoke up again. "Hunting knife? Kitchen knife?"

He glared at me. "I guess it was some kind of hunting knife." I knew most hunting knives have serrated edges. I flipped through the report—the wounds hadn't appeared to have any jagged edges.

"Then what happened?" Lex asked.

"He put the blade to my throat and asked me if I was some rich bitch. I was too scared to talk and that made him angry. He was shaking like he was on drugs, totally tripping, you know what I mean? I told him that God could take care of him. He started screaming and saying that God had never done anything but spit on him.

"I told him 1 John 1:9 said if we admit that we have sinned and confess our sins, He is faithful and just and will forgive our sins and cleanse us from all unrighteousness. He went crazy and stabbed me again and again. I blacked out and didn't wake up until I was in the ambulance."

"Can you describe your attacker?"

"He was a little shorter than me, maybe five-ten. Pretty skinny. He was white, and he had long, brown hair. Looked like he hadn't shaved his face in a couple days, though."

"Eye color?"

"Um… I'm not sure. Brown or hazel."

"How old would you guess he was?"

"Real young. Seventeen or eighteen. No older than twenty."

"Anything else you can remember?"

"No, that's it."

"Okay, Mr. Pryor. We'll send a police sketch artist down so he can do a drawing of your attacker. I promise we'll do our best to find this guy," Lex said.

Pryor nodded back at her.

I pulled my card out of my pocket and handed it to him. He reluctantly reached out and took it. "Call me if you remember anything else."

He nodded again.

"He's hiding something," I said when we were in the elevator.

Lex looked at me. "How do you know?"

"I just do." Lex shook her head but didn't say anything else. She knew by the tone in my voice that I wasn't going to say more.

Chapter Three

I HAD been at work a few hours on Tuesday morning when my cell rang. The caller ID said "Renown Regional."

"Flesh," I answered.

"It's Pryor. I need to talk to you, without your partner. Be here in fifteen minutes."

"I'll be there in an hour," I replied and hung up before he could say anything else.

AN HOUR and fifteen minutes later, I was at Renown and walking into Pryor's room. His wife, a short, blonde woman with caked-on makeup, was sitting by his side and holding his hand. I introduced myself and asked if I could talk to Pryor alone. She stepped out of the room.

"What do you want, Pryor?"

"Have you found the guy who stabbed me?"

"You know we haven't."

"I need to know what you're doing to find him."

"You don't need to know anything other than that I'm doing my job. And for the record, if you want me to find him, then you need to tell me the truth."

"I gave you my statement."

"Your statement was bullshit. I know you're hiding something, Pryor. Or should I call you Daddy Joe?" Daddy Joe. That's what I called Joseph Pryor when we got together for sex. And we did that fairly often.

"Keep your voice down!" he hissed at me. "My wife can't hear you call me that."

"Of course not. Why would you want her to know your secret?"

I HAD first met Pryor more than four years ago at a private party a mutual friend had organized. Well, less of a party and more of an orgy. I didn't know who Pryor was at that point. What I did know was that he was hung, and he knew how to use what God gave him.

We both wanted the same thing—great, no-strings-attached sex. He liked to fuck, and I liked to get fucked. He liked to dominate, and I needed to submit. I had been having sex with Pryor for several months before I learned about his Bible-thumping sermons. I was curious enough to actually pay a visit to his church. When he started expounding on the sins of homosexuals, I had to leave.

I wasn't the only young man who visited Pryor often. I knew of several guys who saw Daddy Joe on a regular basis. I hated the man for being a hypocrite, but I figured that was his business. How he never got exposed by any of the guys he screwed, I don't know. I have ideas. I've heard of a few guys who have suddenly come into a large amount of cash, enough cash for them to leave town and start over somewhere else.

"So are you going to tell me the truth, Pryor?"

He looked at me for a minute. "Yeah, I will."

I took a seat next to his bed and said nothing, waiting for him to start talking.

"I know the guy who stabbed me. His name is Ricardo Sanchez. He and I were best friends growing up. We started the normal fooling-around thing when we hit puberty. You know, jacking off together and touching. But I wanted more, so I took it. I gave him a blow job, and he was hooked.

"We explored everything together. Blow jobs, anal, everything. I cared for him a great deal, but didn't know what I wanted from the future. I really believed it was just an exploration thing and that we would both grow out of it."

"But you didn't, did you?"

"I tried to leave Ric several times, but I couldn't stay away from him."

"True love, huh?"

"No, not for me anyway."

"It was love for him?"

He didn't answer the question. "I had opportunities and planned on college. Ric didn't have the brains or the money for college, but he talked about following me wherever I went. We weren't sure what we were going to do. But then our future, or at least his future, was decided.

"We were using this old house in town as a place to screw around. The Harbridge house had been empty for a while, so we figured it was safe. But Mrs. Harbridge showed up one time and caught us together. Ric got into an argument with Mrs. Harbridge. They were at the top of the stairs. He pushed her, and she fell down and died."

"Was he arrested?"

"He confessed to the crime. He was seventeen, but he was certified as adult, and sentenced to twenty years. He sent me letters, and I wrote back a few times but eventually stopped."

"You decided you didn't want to have anything to do with your fag inmate boyfriend?"

He ignored my sarcasm. "I moved on, went to college, met Madeline, got married, and started my new life."

"When did Sanchez contact you again?"

"He called me when he was released a year or so ago. I told him I had a different life now and didn't want anything to do with him. He was very hurt and said he still loved me. I said I never loved him and told him to move on."

"Then what happened?"

"The night of the attack, he called me and said he was in Reno. He said he needed to see me. I said no, but he said he knew about my secrets. He even called me Daddy Joe and said my secrets would be exposed if I didn't meet with him.

"My family was going to be out that night so I invited him over. I tried to pay him off. I offered him twenty-five thousand dollars to leave town and forget he ever knew me."

"It had worked before, huh, Pryor?"

He looked at me, nodding slightly to acknowledge I was right on that count.

"Go on," I told him.

"Ric was furious that I wanted to pay him off. He insisted he loved me and knew I loved him too. I tried to convince him that I had moved on a long time ago.

"We were arguing when he suddenly pulled me into a kiss. I pushed him away and told him to do what he had to do. I said I wasn't going back to him, so if he wanted to hurt me he could do it."

"Bet that didn't make him very happy."

"No. Ric started raving that I was evil for denying my love for him. He said I would regret it. He came at me with a knife and stabbed me several times. He stared at me for a minute like he hadn't known what he was doing. Then he took off."

"You think Sanchez is still in town?"

"I know he is." Pryor looked at me, and I realized what he was saying.

"He's contacted you since the attack," I said matter-of-factly.

"He's got pictures of me with men. He's blackmailing me."

"So pay him and get him out of town."

"I plan on it. But I need someone to make sure that if he takes the money he really does leave town."

We were both silent for a minute.

"You have to make this go away, Flesh."

"Me? You want me to make this go away? Why would I risk my job to help you?"

"Because if the truth comes out and I get in trouble, I will never fuck you again."

"You think you're that good?"

"I know I am."

"You might be a good lay, but it isn't worth me risking my job," I said, laughing.

"If you don't help me out, I will tell everyone about the things we've done."

I laughed again. "I'm not in the closet, Pryor."

"You want everyone to know what a whoring, little, bottom-boy slut you are? That being humiliated turns you on?"

"Get on your knees, boy." I was completely naked, but Daddy Joe was wearing a short silk bathrobe. The robe was tied around his waist, but his erection hung below the hem.

"Yes, sir." I got on my knees in front of him. He slapped me across the face. "You're a worthless piece of shit; do you know that?"

"Yes, sir!" I was rock hard as he slapped me again.

I stared Pryor right in the eye. "Do whatever you want, Pryor. But I am not helping you scare this guy away."

I left the room without saying another word.

WHEN I got back to the precinct, I pulled Lex aside.

"We need to get off the Pryor case," I told her.

"Why?"

"I met Joseph Pryor before this case. I've known him for years. I know him very well."

"What do you mean you know him 'very well'?" She paused as she realized what I was talking about. "No way. You don't mean…?"

I nodded my head. "Yeah, Pryor and I have been having sex for years."

"You've been having an affair with Pryor?"

"I wouldn't call it an affair. That would insinuate there were feelings involved. We meet occasionally and have sex. Just sex. And I'm not the only guy he does it with, either."

Lex was genuinely shocked that such a supposed man of God would be, not just cheating on his wife, but cheating on her with men.

"Why didn't you say something before?"

"I didn't think it would matter. But I just visited Pryor. He admitted he knew the guy who stabbed him, and he wanted me to pay him off and scare him into leaving town."

"What did you say?"

"I told him to go to hell. That's why I'm telling you."

"You know we have to tell Brunson?"

"Yeah, I know."

"When?"

"Now," I said as I walked to Brunson's office.

"WHAT the hell do you mean you've slept with Joseph Pryor?" Brunson wasn't at all happy with the news.

"You want details, Boss?"

"Shut up, smart ass. Of course I don't want details."

"There's more," I said.

"What?"

"Pryor admitted to me this morning that he knows his attacker. He attempted to force me to pay the guy off and scare him into leaving town."

"How was he going to force you?" Brunson asked.

"He threatened to tell everyone the details of our sexual liaisons."

"He was going to blackmail you?"

"Yeah," I answered. "I told him I wasn't going to risk my job for him."

"Okay," Brunson said. "I'll put Curtis and O'Reilly on this case. You guys are off it."

"Thank you, sir," I said.

Lex and I were the only detectives in the Reno Police Department, but other cops often took over investigations when the detectives were working on other cases.

"Is it possible Pryor could face charges for attempted blackmail, Chief?" Lex asked.

"It's possible, but not likely," he answered honestly. Lex and I turned to leave the office.

"Good job, Flesh," Brunson said as I left. I met his eyes for a moment, nodded, and left.

Brunson called O'Reilly and Curtis into his office.

I could hear Curtis yelling even though the office door was closed.

"Why the hell do we gotta take over this case?"

"Because I say so, Curtis," Brunson yelled back. "Now lower your goddamn voice because I do not like to be screamed at by my officers."

The conversation was quieter after that, and I couldn't hear what was said. A few minutes later, Curtis and O'Reilly stormed out of Brunson's office, giving me the evil eye as they left.

AFTER work, I made myself a dinner of tacos and Spanish rice. I watched television for a bit before deciding to go out for a couple hours. I showered and shaved and splashed a small amount of cologne on my face.

Reno had a few gay bars to choose from, and I decided to go to a bar called Quest. Quest was noisy with dancing and stripping. Guys there weren't looking for anything other than some fun.

When I got to Quest, I walked around checking out the guys. There were a lot of good-looking guys, but nothing that I was craving that night. I didn't actually know what I wanted, but I figured I'd know when I saw him.

I have varied tastes when it comes to men. I like all shapes, sizes and colors. Quest had several young men with perfect bodies as well as some silver foxes, older, good-looking men. I'd been with my fair share of both of those types, but that's not what I wanted right then.

When I first saw him, he was staring at me from across the room. A Hispanic man probably in his early forties. He wasn't very tall, around five-seven, and on the skinny side. He had dark hair that hadn't been cut in a while. He was good-looking, with a lean face and no facial hair. He had a hungry look on his face—hungry for raw, animalistic sex.

He followed me with his eyes as I walked around the bar. Whenever I looked his way, he was staring at me. He nodded, indicating he wanted me to come his way.

I walked toward him, and he looked me up and down, stopping to notice the bulge in my tight jeans. I sat down next to him at the bar.

"What're you drinking?" he asked me.

"Whatever you give me."

He nodded and ordered me a beer. I took the beer bottle and seductively tongued the tip before taking a long swig. He never took his eyes off of me.

"What's your name?" he asked me when I set the bottle down.

I shook my head. "Don't matter."

"What?"

"You don't need to know my name, and I don't need to know yours. We both want to have fun. Why waste time with names?" He smiled at me, reached over, and grabbed my crotch.

"You like getting right to the point, huh?" I said.

"When I see what I want, I go for it. You up for it?"

"Hell yeah."

He stood up. "I got a room at the Aloha Inn on McCarran. Room 212."

"Let's go." I stood and walked to the door. He smiled a small grin, threw a twenty on the bar to pay for the drinks, and followed me.

"Meet you there," he said.

I drove to the motel and got there right after him. He got to the door a few steps before me, unlocked and opened it, and walked in, leaving the door open for me.

He was sitting on the bed holding a manila envelope. "I've been expecting this," he told me.

I walked up to him and stood there. The envelope had a dozen or so stamps on it and was taped all over. He was having a hard time trying to rip it open. I reached into my pocket, pulled out a pocket knife, and handed it to him.

"Careful, it's sharp. Brand new." I walked into the bathroom to take a leak. My stream had just started when I heard the guy curse.

"What happened?" I called out.

"Nothing, man. Just cut myself."

"You okay?" I finished, flushed, and stepped out of the bathroom. He had a hand towel wrapped around his hand.

"Yeah. Got some blood on the sheets, but nothing major." He folded my knife closed and handed it to me. I stuck it in my pocket.

"Let's not worry about me," he said as he stepped up to me. He slid my jacket off, unbuttoned my shirt, and slid his hands across my chest.

"Nice."

He stepped back and pulled his T-shirt over his head. He turned as he tossed the shirt into a corner. He had tattoos covering most of his back and his arms as well as a one-inch scar on his lower back. I finished taking off my shirt and gazed at his built body.

When he had his pants off, I stepped up to him and dropped to my knees, burying my face in his boxer briefs. I traced the outline of his shaft with my tongue. His hands went to the back of my head and pushed me harder against him.

I pulled down his underwear and freed his cock. It was long, skinny, and uncut. I gripped it and pulled the skin back, revealing a glistening head. I licked around the head, drinking in the taste of wetness. Pulling the skin back over the head, I stuck my tongue in under the skin.

He arched against me. "You do that too much, and I'm gonna come right away."

"Don't tell me you're a one-and-done guy?"

"No, I can come as many times as you want me to."

"Then don't worry about it."

I started sucking on his cock like it was the last one I would ever see. He grabbed the back of my head and shoved his prick down my throat. I sucked harder, and he started grunting and moaning. "I'm gonna shoot," he warned me. But I didn't let go. He let loose with several sprays, and I swallowed it down.

When his cock softened, he pulled me up and pushed me over on the bed. He kneeled in front of me and stuck his face into my jeans, licking the outline of my cock.

He unzipped my pants, and I lifted my hips so he could slide the pants down to my ankles.

"Nice cock, man." He started slurping up and down my dick. And this guy was an expert cock sucker. I didn't feel a single tooth scrape as he deep-throated my meat.

"You keep doing that, and I'm gonna come," I said, repeating his earlier statement.

"But I know you can come more than once."

After just a few minutes of sucking, I knew I was going to explode. "Go-nn-a commmmmme," I grunted. He pulled off just as I shot and several loads of sperm landed on him and the floor.

He walked into the bathroom, and I heard him pissing, then washing his hands. When he came out, he slipped off his socks. I pulled up my pants and walked into the bathroom, where I pissed again and washed out my mouth.

When I walked out of the bathroom, he was lying on the bed, stroking an erect penis. I smiled and quickly stripped off all my clothes so I was totally naked.

Climbing onto the bed, I dove between his legs and started licking his balls. He had a wonderful manly smell, and I took in the scent as I took turns taking his testicles in my mouth one at a time.

"Flip around, guy," he told me.

We flipped into a side-by-side sixty-nine position. I swallowed his length as he licked my shaft and buried his face in my testicles.

"I want this big cock in my ass," he said.

Fuck. I thought we were on the same page.

"I don't top," I said.

"What?"

Damn it. I hate when this happens. "I don't top," I repeated.

"Never?"

Why is this always so hard to figure out? "No."

"I just figured with a cock this size…."

I quickly stood up and started grabbing my clothes.

"I guess this isn't gonna work out," I said.

He sat up quickly and scooted to the end of the bed. "Wow, hold up, man. It's cool."

"No, I think we're looking for different things."

"I don't need to be fucked. I'm okay with fucking you. You got a cute ass."

I didn't stop getting dressed, but he grabbed me and pulled me onto the bed. He lay on top of me, pressing his cock against mine.

"You know you want it," he said. He was right; I did want it. I relaxed and started pressing myself against him.

He rolled off of me. "Take those clothes off, and let's fuck."

"I play safe," I said.

"Of course," he said. He got off the bed and walked to the dresser. He pulled out a condom and lube. As I got naked again, he opened the rubber, slid it on, and lubed it up.

I got on the edge of the bed on my hands and knees. He walked up to me and started rubbing his cock against my hole. He teased me for a while, driving me crazy.

"C'mon, put it in me," I begged.

He started to push it in, I forced my ass to relax, and his head popped in.

"Oh, damn," I moaned.

He didn't move for a minute then slowly started to slide in. He stopped halfway in, pulled most of the way out, slid in, pulled out.

"Oh, man. That's good. So freakin' tight," he said. Dirty talk turned me on.

"Yeah, you got a hot cock, man."

He continued slipping in and out of me. I wanted the entire length, so I pushed back.

"You want the whole thing, you got it." His whole shaft slid into me in one quick movement, and I felt his balls pressed against my ass. My body was on fire as I played with my own prick, fisting it slowly so I wouldn't come too soon.

"Damn, that feels good. So hot. You can pound me. Give it to me hard."

"Just the way I like it. Your hole is incredible, man. One of the hottest, tightest fucks I've ever had."

He started slamming into me, and I couldn't hold back any longer. I fisted my cock hard and felt the eruption getting close.

"I'm gonna shoot my load, man. I can't hold it back."

"Let it go, man. Shoot your load while I'm buried in you. Tighten your ass around my dick."

I quickened the stroke and started to come. "OHHHHH," I grunted as I shot onto the bed.

"Yeah, fucking yeah." He pounded me even harder and moaned

as he buried himself as deep as he could go. I could feel his cock flexing as it unloaded into the condom.

He pulled out, and I lay down on the bed, letting my body relax. He pulled off the condom and threw it into the garbage can.

"Thanks, man. That was hot. I always wanted to fuck a cop."

How the hell did he know I was a cop? I stood up and walked over to him.

"How'd you know I was a cop?"

He paused as he looked into my eyes. "It ain't a big deal. I noticed your badge in your coat." I wasn't sure I believed him. "What would your cop buddies think if they knew what we just did?"

"They wouldn't care. I'm not in the closet."

He looked at me like I was crazy. "You're out?"

"Yeah, I don't hide who I am."

"Well, thanks, man. That was fun. Come by if you feel like doing it again."

"Yeah, maybe I will."

He went into the bathroom and closed the door. I heard the shower going. That was my cue to leave. I sat on the bed and grabbed my clothes. I pulled on my underwear, socks and pants, but couldn't find my shirt. I got on my hands and knees and looked under the bed. I saw the shirt and pulled it out. Part of the packaging was stuck to it. As I pulled the packaging off my shirt I noticed the return address. No name, but it was from Pioche, a small Nevada town not far from Las Vegas. I finished getting dressed and left.

Chapter Four

I WOKE up Wednesday morning around eight. I didn't have to go to work until ten. And, of course, I was horny. I couldn't stop thinking about the guy at the Aloha Inn. I figured I could meet him for a quickie before I went to work.

I knocked on the room of door 212 and noticed it wasn't totally shut. There was no answer when I knocked, so I pushed the door open with one hand, while the other hand instinctively went to my revolver.

"Hello. Anyone here?" I stepped into the room, slowly surveying everything. I was a few steps into the room when I saw a pair of legs sticking out from behind the end of the bed. I stepped forward and saw a body. I stooped down to feel for a pulse on his neck. None—he was dead.

A pair of boxer briefs was the only piece of clothing he had on. His face and stomach were bruised and bloody. If I had had to identify him by his face it would have been difficult. It was the tattoos and other markings on his body that I recognized. There wasn't any doubt in my mind it was the man I had slept with the previous night. The floor was covered in his blood. After making sure no one was hiding in the bedroom, I pulled out my cell.

"This is Detective Cristian Flesh," I said when the 911 operator answered. "I need an ambulance and police at the Aloha Inn on McCarran. Room 212. Hurry."

I punched another number into my cell.

"What's up, Cris?" Lex answered.

"Lex, I need you."

"Where?"

"Aloha Inn."

"I'll be right there." That's one reason I loved Lex; I knew whenever I needed her she'd be there.

The ambulance and two police units arrived in five minutes. I stepped out of the room to let the officers step in, but stayed right there.

"What happened?" the responding officer, Mike Gray, asked me.

"I came to visit him. I noticed the door was open so I came in. That's when I found the body."

"What's the vic's name?"

"I don't know his name."

"You were visiting him, but you don't know his name?"

"Yeah."

"Can you explain that?"

"Sure, Gray, I can explain that. I spent a few hours with him last night, but didn't catch his name. I was coming back for more when I found the body."

He finally realized what I was saying.

"Don't go anywhere," he said.

"I won't."

Lex arrived and ran up to me.

"Cris, what's going on? Are you okay?"

"I'm fine."

"What's going on here?" she asked as she peeked into the motel room.

"There's a dead guy in there. I picked him up last night, and we came back here for a couple hours."

I looked at her to make sure she understood what I was saying.

"I came by this morning to see him again. The door was open, so I came in and found the body."

"Damn, Cris. You got some kind of bad luck, huh?"

"Yeah, I guess so. I wasn't sure what to do. I almost ran, but I stopped myself."

"You did the right thing, Cris. We'll figure it out." The Crime Scene Unit officers arrived and started going through the motel room. "Let's get out of here," Lex said. She spoke to Gray and had me get in her car. "Gray says he'll have an officer get your car to the precinct," she said. We drove to the precinct, where we immediately went in to see Brunson.

"What the hell, Flesh?" Brunson yelled. He wasn't any happier about this than he was when he learned about my relationship with Pryor. "First you fuck a stabbing victim then you fuck a guy who gets killed. Your next screw better be careful."

I just sat there and nodded, looking remorseful.

"Cris has been honest about both incidents," Lex said. "He hasn't tried to lie or hide anything."

"I know that, Lex," Brunson said. "But we have to be careful so it doesn't look like we're trying to cover up anything."

"I'll do whatever you want me to do, Chief."

"I need to keep you isolated so there's no way anyone can accuse us of anything. I'm gonna have you hang out in an interrogation room."

"You want him to sit in there like a criminal? Come on, Chief!" Lex exclaimed.

I stopped her. "No, Lex. He's right. I'm not hiding anything, and I don't want it to look like I am. I'll stay in a room until everything is figured out."

Brunson walked me to an interrogation room and left me. Being there as a suspect was very different than being there as a cop. Now it was dark and intimidating. I sat in the chair, put my feet on the table and waited.

An hour later, Lex, Brunson, and a female CSU tech came into the room.

"We found semen at the murder scene," Brunson said.

"It'll probably be mine," I said.

"They need to verify that," Lex said.

The CSU tech stepped up to me with a swab. I opened my mouth; she rubbed it on the inside of my cheek, then closed the swab in a plastic container.

"I need those results ASAP," Brunson told the tech.

"Yes, sir," she replied.

Then I was alone again.

EVENTUALLY Gray came in to interview me, and I gave him my official statement.

"I met him at Quest. We were both looking for sex, and he invited me to join him at his motel room. I did, and we had sexual relations."

"What kind of sexual relations?"

"I performed oral sex on him, and he did the same to me. Then we had anal intercourse."

"Were you the…?" He paused, looking for the right words.

"I was on the receiving end," I answered to spare him further embarrassment.

"When the intercourse was over what did you do?"

"He got into the shower. I got dressed and left."

"And what happened this morning?"

"I wanted to visit him again."

"Why?"

I looked at Gray like he had just asked the stupidest question ever. "Why? Because I wanted to be on the receiving end of anal intercourse again."

"What happened when you got there?"

"I knocked on the door and noticed it wasn't shut. I pushed it open and called out. There wasn't an answer, so I stepped in. That's when I noticed him. I checked his pulse and didn't find one."

"Is that when you called?"

"I checked the bathroom to make sure it was empty, then called."

"And you never got his name?"

"No. I didn't need his name."

Gray was silent for a moment.

"You got anything else to say, Flesh? Now's the time. If this was some accident during sex or if you wanted something he didn't want. Or the other way around. Come clean now."

"I didn't kill him. I got no reason to kill him. He was just a fuck, nothing more."

"That's all for now," Gray said, and he stepped out of the room.

Twenty minutes later, Lex stepped in.

"The semen at the scene matched your DNA," she said.

"I said it was mine."

"It corroborates your story. That's a good thing. Brunson's deciding what to do with you."

Brunson stepped in.

"You're free to go, Flesh. You're not an official suspect, but you haven't been totally ruled out, either. So don't be leaving town or anything."

"Yes, sir."

"Keep your nose out of the case, Flesh."

"Yes, sir."

I sat at my desk, trying to keep my mind off the murder, but I couldn't. It wasn't grief; after all I didn't even know the guy. But I couldn't stop thinking about the few hours we spent together. Less than a half a day ago we were having sex, really great sex. And now he was dead. I was one of the last people to see him alive, to talk to him. I wondered if his murder had been a crime of passion. A former lover, maybe? Had the killer been nearby the whole time? Had he been waiting for me to leave? Maybe I'd have been the victim if I hadn't left when I did.

Would that have been how I wanted to spend my last hours? In bed with a stranger. Sharing my body with a man whose name I hadn't known. Even though anonymous sex had always been what I sought, I wondered if there was something I had been missing.

A couple hours later, I heard Gray and a few other officers getting excited about something. I wandered over trying to hear what was going on.

"What're you doing?" Lex asked me.

"Umm...."

"Get back to your desk, Cris. I'll find out what's going on and fill you in."

I went back to my desk and sat, not-so-patiently waiting for Lex to come back.

"We got a name on the vic," she told me when she came back. "Ricardo Sanchez. He's an ex-con."

"What did you say his name was?"

"Sanchez. Ricardo Sanchez."

"Damn it!"

"What is it Cris?"

"The guy who stabbed Pryor, his ex-boyfriend, his name was Ricardo Sanchez."

"Holy shit, Cris. I need to tell Gray. He'll have to talk to Curtis and O'Reilly."

Lex took off, and a few seconds later I was in my car heading to Renown Regional.

I STORMED into Pryor's room, slamming the door behind me.

"What the hell are you doing, Flesh?"

I grabbed Pryor by his hospital gown and pulled him to just inches from my face.

"Did you do it?"

"Do what? What are you talking about?"

I let go and pushed him back down. He winced in pain.

I winced in pain as Daddy Joe gagged me with his prick. His hands gripped either side of my head as he made it go all the way down my throat. Tears began to stream down my face as I fought for a gasp of air. He slapped my face. "Suck it, you queer cocksucker."

"He's dead."

"Who?"

"You know damn well who. Sanchez."

"Ric? He's dead?" I wish I could say that Pryor was lying, and I could read his face, but I couldn't. He seemed genuinely surprised at the news and maybe even the littlest bit sad. "Did you do it?" he asked me.

"Fuck no, I didn't. Why the hell would you even ask me that?"

"Are you investigating the case?"

"I'm a fuckin' suspect!"

"A suspect?"

"I was with your boyfriend last night. He picked me up at a bar, and we went to his motel room."

Pryor started laughing. "He fucks pretty good, doesn't he?"

"Yeah, he did. Past tense, Pryor." Pryor stopped smiling.

"I don't suppose you had anything to do with him picking me up?"

"Why would I do that? I wanted Ric out of town, not hanging around screwing one of my boys."

"I ain't one of your boys, Pryor."

"Whatever you need to tell yourself. So do they know who killed Ric?"

"I was thinking you did, Pryor."

"Me?" he asked, astonished. "I didn't leave the hospital all night. I haven't even left my room for days."

"I hope you're telling me the truth, Pryor. Because if you set me up, you won't only hang for murder; I'll make you regret ever knowing me."

I left Pryor's room and paid a visit to the hospital administrator, a strikingly tall woman with short black hair. Her name was Patrice Norman, and she was single. I knew that because she told me, more than once.

I spent more than an hour talking to Patty, as she insisted I call her, during which she dropped plenty of hints that she would love to go out to dinner with me sometime. Too bad she was wasting her time, but I didn't want to tell her that until I got what I wanted—the security tapes.

She eventually took me to the security room, where she showed me where all the cameras were in and out of the hospital. In addition to cameras mounted on all entrance and exit doors, there were some cameras located on the outside of patient rooms.

"We use those if the patient is high profile," she explained.

"Is Joseph Pryor one of those patients?"

"Yes, he is."

She cued up the video from the camera placed outside of Pryor's door. We started with my visit there at the beginning of the day and then began to quickly fast forward through more than twenty-four hours of footage.

Pryor was telling the truth; he never left his room.

I thanked Patty for her time.

"If you think of anything else that might help, feel free to call." I handed her my card. She seemed pleased to have a way to contact me, and I knew one way or another, she would be calling me.

"WHERE'VE you been?" Lex asked me when I sat down at my desk.

"Nowhere."

"You can't lie to me, Cris. Now tell me where you went."

She was right, and I knew she would get the truth out of me

sooner or later. "I went to see Pryor."

"Brunson told you to stay out of the case."

I looked her right in the eyes. "C'mon, Lex, if you were the one in trouble would you be sitting on your ass letting everyone else do the work?"

"Of course not. So why did you visit Pryor?"

"I thought maybe he killed Sanchez."

"And?"

"He's got a rock-solid alibi. Renown has rooms with cameras outside the door. They use them for high-profile patients like Pryor. I saw the security tapes. Pryor didn't leave his room all night."

"So he didn't do it," Lex said.

"Not personally, anyway. He could've arranged for someone else to do it."

"Is it possible Pryor had Sanchez pick you up?"

"I thought of that, but I don't see what the reason would've been."

"That's true." After a few moments of silence, Lex spoke again. "Don't worry. It'll all work out."

"I hope so, but I don't have a good feeling about this."

LATER that day, Patty called me, just like I knew she would.

"I don't know if this will help or not," she said, "but I have a list of all the numbers Mr. Pryor called recently. I'm not supposed to let this information out, but I figured I'd make an exception… for you."

I gave her my e-mail address and tried to get off the phone quickly. I wasn't quick enough.

"Detective Flesh…." She paused, waiting for me to say something. When I didn't, she continued, "I was hoping I could take you out to dinner sometime."

"I'd love that, Patty. As soon as this case is over, I'll give you a call."

"You promise?"

Damn, I hate making promises, especially ones I knew I wouldn't keep.

"I'll do my best." She giggled without realizing I hadn't actually promised and said good-bye. A few minutes later, I got the e-mail.

"Hey, Lex, I just got a list of the phone numbers Pryor's called since he's been in the hospital."

"How did you get those?"

"Don't ask," I answered. "You want to turn these over to Gray, or do you want to help me go through them?"

"What do you think, Cris?"

I grinned at her. "I think you want to help me go through the numbers."

"You're right." She smiled at me.

I printed out the numbers and gave half to Lex. We started using a reverse directory to put names to the numbers. Most of them were easily identified—his home, his church, his family and several members of his congregation. But one number, a cell phone, was harder to ID.

"I know someone who can help," Lex said.

"Who?"

"My dear hubby, Kenny. He's quite the computer geek."

"Well, give him a call."

She picked up her cell and dialed a number. "Hey, babe. What's up? I need a favor. I got a number I need to put a name to. No, I can't use police resources, this is something more personal. Great, thanks, babe." She gave him the number and hung up.

Kenny called back fifteen minutes later. "Thanks, honey. I'll pay you back tonight."

"Lex, you naughty girl."

"You think I don't like sex, Cris?"

"You got a name?" I asked, changing the subject as quickly as possible.

"Yeah, Gabriel Vargas. I'm running his name through the system right now."

I walked around so I could see what Lex found out. Her computer pulled up a file on Vargas. He was twenty years old and basically a street kid.

"He's had six arrests for thefts," Lex said. "Started when he was seventeen with simple shoplifting, and it's progressed since then. He had a joyriding charge a few months ago."

"He running with a gang?" I asked.

"Yeah," she answered. "The Kings. But it doesn't look like he's gotten in too deep. He's had a few fights with rival gangbangers. His street name is Tejon, which means badger. They call him that because he fights like one."

"What's his connection to Pryor?" Lex wondered.

I had an idea, but I didn't say anything. I knew from personal experience that scared, young men were drawn to rich and powerful men.

"We need to find this kid and talk to him," I said.

"I don't know how we're going to do that, Cris. Gray needs this info. If we bring him in first, Brunson will explode."

"Yeah, but if we let Gray bring him in we won't be able to talk to him ourselves," I said.

"We can track him down, have a talk with him, then turn the info over to Gray," Lex stated.

"But he'll tell Gray we already talked to him," I said. "Unless we can convince him not to say anything."

"I don't know if this is a good idea, Cris."

"Of course it isn't a good idea. But that doesn't mean you don't want to do it. You know you want to, Lex."

"Fine, let's do it."

"How do we track him down?" I asked.

"Simple, we arrange a meeting."

"And what're we gonna tell him so he meets with us?"

"Not us. You. You're going to call him and tell him you're a friend of Pryor's and need to talk to him."

I smiled at her deviousness, something I didn't always see.

I dialed the cell number. "Yeah," he answered.

"My name is Will Singer," I said. "I'm a friend of Joseph Pryor. He thought we should meet."

"Where you wanna meet?"

"Sparks Marina Park," I answered. "Sit at a picnic table. I know what you look like. I'll find you." I hung up.

"He went for it," I said. "What do you think he's expecting from me?"

"Drugs would be my guess," Lex replied.

"Maybe," I said, but I didn't think so. I thought the kid had something else in mind.

I GOT to Marina Park and saw the kid sitting at a picnic table. He was looking around and saw me coming. He stared at me the entire way. I sat at the table.

"Will?" he asked.

"Yeah. You Tejon?"

"You said Pryor sent you?" he asked.

"Yeah."

"You're a goddamn liar, man." He stood up and started to leave.

"Wait, what do you mean I'm lying?"

"Pryor don't know my street name."

Fuck, he was gonna get away. I was afraid we might have to do a foot chase if he ran. Lex solved the dilemma by stepping in front of him. She flashed her badge.

"Have a seat, young man," she told him.

He turned to me, and I flashed my badge.

"Shit, I should've known."

"This ain't a big deal; we just need to ask a few questions."

Vargas sat down at the picnic table. I took a seat next to him, and Lex sat across from us.

I got a good look at the kid. He wasn't very tall, five-six or so. He had short, spiky black hair and light-brown eyes. He didn't have the usual characteristics of a gangbanger: he wasn't covered in tattoos or wearing a colored bandana. The only facial hair he had was a small soul patch under his bottom lip.

"How do you know Joseph Pryor?" Lex asked.

"I go to his church," he said, smirking.

"We have proof that you have been talking to Joseph Pryor every day for the last several days."

"I don't know what you're talking about, man."

"Look, Gabriel." Lex switched to his real name. She was playing good cop to my bad cop. "We're investigating a murder here, and unless you come clean, you could get the rap for this."

"I don't know nothing 'bout no murder."

I stood up, slammed the table with my fist and got right in his face. "I'm gonna pin this fuckin' murder on you if you don't tell me everything, you little cocksucker."

"Don't call me a cocksucker. I ain't no goddamn fag."

Way too much protest in that statement. I sat down and looked at Lex, then at Vargas.

"You know Daddy Joe, don't you?"

He looked at me, shocked that I knew Pryor's other name. Lex also looked amazed.

"Come on, Vargas," I said. "Tell us the truth."

"If my homies ever learn that I'm... that I...."

"Your private actions have nothing to do with this case, Gabriel,"

Lex said. "If you tell us what you know, we promise your friends will never learn about your sexuality."

"I ain't gay," Gabriel said. "But sometimes I—"

"It's okay," I said. "You don't have to explain to me. I know exactly how you feel."

Gabriel met my gaze and knew what I was talking about.

"You can trust me," I said, and I meant it.

"Yeah, I've known Daddy Joe... I mean Pryor, for a couple years. We get together every once in a while to... you know."

"Yeah, I know."

"I hadn't talked to him for a while when I heard he had been stabbed. I visited him in the hospital and said that he could call me if he needed anything. He called me the next day. He said he might need someone killed and asked if I could help him."

"Help him how?" Lex asked.

"He figured I had plenty of contacts on the streets and thought maybe I could put him in touch with someone."

"A hit man?" I asked.

Vargas nodded. "I said I'd start looking around."

"How often was he calling you?" I was letting Lex ask the questions so I could concentrate on Gabriel's face. He seemed to find it easier to talk while he met me in the eyes.

"Like, every day. I was letting him know the different guys I'd talked to, the different prices."

"Did he ever decide who to hire?"

"No. He kept saying he wasn't even sure if he wanted to hire anyone or not."

"Did he ever make a decision?"

"Yeah, he called me the other day. He said he had decided not to hire anyone. He said he was feeling better and was looking forward to getting together with me again. We talked for a while."

"Talked about what?" Lex asked.

"You know… dirty talk. Phone sex." He couldn't meet Lex in the eyes but stared into mine.

"Where were you two nights ago?" Lex asked.

"I was hanging out at home with my baby mama and our little boy. Her family was there too."

"If that's true you got nothing to worry about, kid," I told him.

"It's the truth, man. I swear it." I believed him.

"Lex, I need to talk to him alone," I said. She stood and walked to the car. "Listen, kid. You need to talk to another cop; tell him what you told us."

"Why do I gotta talk to another cop?"

"My partner and I are breaking a few rules by talking to you. We aren't officially on the case, and we could get in trouble if they knew we talked to you."

"Why should I do anything to help you out, man. I don't owe you nothin'."

"You're right, kid. You don't owe me anything." I paused for a moment. "Look, I'll be honest with you. I could be in trouble if this shit doesn't get cleared up. I'm trying to save my own life here. If you tell anyone else I talked to you, it could make me look guilty. I'm not guilty. You ever been accused of doing something you didn't do?"

"Yeah," he said, chuckling. "All the time. I ain't done half the shit I been accused of."

"So you know what it's like. So help me out here, kid."

"Okay, man. You got it. I won't say nothing. When I talk to this other cop, do I gotta tell him how I know Pryor?"

"That's up to you. But your sex life doesn't really have much to do with the case. Maybe you know Pryor some other way, maybe you got some family who go to his church. Maybe he knew you were a gangbanger and called you because he'd figured you had street contacts."

He looked at me for a second. "Thanks, man. That's pretty cool."

I handed him my card and smiled at him. "If you ever need

anything, feel free to call me… anytime.”

"Hey, thanks, man." He took my card and stuck it in his pocket. I knew he'd be calling me.

LEX and I returned to the precinct. She talked to Gray and learned O'Reilly and Curtis had taken over the Sanchez murder since it was now connected to Pryor's stabbing

Twenty minutes later, O'Reilly was standing at my desk. I took my time acknowledging he was there. Curtis was standing a few feet away from my desk, and even from that distance I could smell the stink of whiskey.

"What's up, Red?"

"You need to keep your nose out of this case, Flesh."

"What're you talking about?"

He slammed his fist on my desk. "You goddamn know what I'm talking about. We just talked to Patty Norman at Renown. She told me about the security tapes that proved Pryor didn't leave his room all night. She also told us she already gave this information to you."

"Red, you can't blame me for trying to save my own ass."

He smiled. "I don't give a shit about your ass."

"That's not what you said the first time we met."

The smile disappeared from his face. "Shut the hell up. What I'm telling you is that you better stay away from my investigation, or I'll have your ass in trouble for obstruction of justice. You got me?"

I met his eyes and gave him an icy stare. "Yeah, Red. I got you."

"Anything else you know that I should know?"

"Did Patty tell you about the phone numbers?"

"Yeah. We haven't run any of the numbers yet."

"Most of the numbers are easily identified." I pulled out the printout of the numbers and the names we matched them to. I pointed to Gabe's number. "You'll probably want to talk to this kid.

Gangbanger named Gabriel Vargas, street name is Tejon."

"You already talked to him?"

I shook my head. He looked at me like he was trying to figure out if I was lying or not. He turned and started to walk away, but stopped and faced me again.

"I mean it, Flesh. Don't interfere again, or I go to Brunson."

"Yes, sir." I mocked him with a salute.

He walked off.

A short while later, Gabe was in the precinct heading to an interrogation room with Curtis and O'Reilly. He saw me and gave me a slight smile. I nodded back. Lex convinced Brunson to let her watch the interrogation from the observation room on the other side of the two-way mirror. I used the opportunity to slip out. I wanted to talk to Pryor again.

WHEN I arrived at Pryor's room, he had a visitor—a young man who probably looked like Pryor did when he was twenty-two. He was about my height, with bright green eyes and high cheek bones. For sure he could have been a model for Abercrombie & Fitch. He had a little stubble on his head, like he had just shaved his head a few days ago.

"Detective Flesh," Pryor said. "This is my son, Joseph Junior."

"Detective," he said as he gripped my hand firmly. He had an iron grip and held on a second longer than most guys do. He met my eyes for longer than normal too.

"Nice haircut," I told Junior as I rubbed my own clean-shaven noggin.

He rubbed his head. "It was an experiment. I don't like it, think it makes me look scummy." I wasn't sure what he meant by that. "Are you the officer investigating the case?" Junior asked.

"No," I answered. "I have other matters to discuss with your father... alone."

"Whatever you need to say to my father, you can say to me."

"Please, Son," Pryor said. "I need to talk to Detective Flesh in private."

Junior wasn't very happy, but he obeyed and left the room.

"I hope this is all resolved soon," Pryor said.

"I'm hoping the same thing."

"So why are you here?"

"I have a list of phone numbers you've been calling from your hospital room."

"That's private information!"

"Whatever. It's information I have, and you're gonna answer my questions."

"I don't think—"

"You don't have to think; just listen."

I threw a copy of the phone numbers on his bed. Gabe's number had been circled.

"Whose number is that?"

"I don't have to tell you anything, boy."

"Yeah, boy, you're a nasty piece of filth. You like having your butt rammed, don't you?" Daddy Joe called out as he slammed into me. I was face down on the floor; he was over me, basically doing pushups as he screwed me. He slapped my ass.

"Yeah, Daddy Joe. Use my ass."

"That's all you're good for, boy, isn't it?"

"Don't ever call me boy again," I ordered as I glared into his eyes.

"You always liked being called boy before."

"And you liked being called Daddy Joe."

We had a stare down for a minute before Pryor glanced away.

"Whose number is that?" I repeated my question.

"It's a member of my congregation. He's been having personal issues with his wife, and I've been counseling him."

"What's his name?"

"I'm sorry. I can't give you his name. Confidentiality."

"You sure are being tight-lipped and rude to someone who's keeping your secrets."

"I don't think you want this information to come out any more than I do. After all, you don't want anyone knowing what a pussy, little, bottom-boy, cumslut you are, do you?"

"I told you before. I don't care what comes out about me. You have more to lose than I do. Everyone knows I'm gay. If everyone learned you were a fag, your entire world would be turned upside down."

His face turned a deep shade of purple. "I am not a fag!"

I chuckled. "Sorry, you're a straight man who likes his dick sucked by guys and likes to poke their asses. But that's not a fag." He glared at me. "I already talked to Gabriel Vargas."

"You found my Mexican cocksucker, huh? Why did you pretend you didn't know who the number belonged to?"

"I wanted to be sure about what a lying hypocrite you are."

"Keep up this attitude of yours, and I won't be inviting you over again."

"I'd be happy if I never saw you again. I want you out of my life for good." I turned and left.

Junior was in the hallway and walked straight up to me and got right in my face.

"You need to stop harassing my father, Flesh. He needs to recover."

I looked at the young man.

"Listen, Junior, I'm not doing anything. I got nothing to do with this case."

"You do have something to do with the case. I know it. And I know you're out to hurt my father. I won't let you do it. Do you understand me?"

I pushed him away from me with a hard shove.

"Yeah, Junior, I understand you." I turned and walked away.

"Stay away from my father, Flesh. You'll regret it if you don't." I wondered what the hell the boy was all upset about and turned around to find out. Junior had already stepped out of the hallway and back into his father's room.

Before I got to Pryor's room, I heard loud voices coming from the room.

"You make me sick, you know that, Father?"

"Don't talk to me like that, Son. I am your father—"

Junior cut him off. "Your whoring and perverted ways are going to ruin this family. I've had enough of it. I won't stand for it anymore."

"You don't know what you're talking about."

"Yes, I do, Father. I know all about you and your... your... homosexual lovers. I've known for years."

"What?" Pryor sounded shocked.

"Since I was a teenager. I came home early one night and caught you. I saw you... I saw you... sucking some guy's penis. I was disgusted. But I didn't say anything out of respect for you. But your indiscretions have increased, and it's going to ruin our lives."

"How much do you know?"

"I know Sanchez was a teenage fling, and he was here to blackmail you. I know Flesh is one of your... indiscretions."

That was why Junior had been in my face. I had heard enough, so I left.

AT THE precinct, Lex told me Gabe had been released. "His alibi checked out," she said.

"O'Reilly give him any trouble?"

"Nothing major."

"Glad to hear it. He's a good kid."

"Why are you being so nice to him?" she asked.

"I know how easy it is for kids like him to be taken advantage of."

"How do you know?"

"Never mind." Rule number six: I don't talk about my past.

I WAS at home in my boxers drinking a Bud when my phone rang. I didn't recognize the number, but answered it anyway.

"Detective Flesh?" a timid voice asked.

"Yeah, who's this?"

"This is Gabe Vargas… Tejon."

"Hey, kid. What's up?"

"I was hoping you have time to… talk."

"Sure, do you want to meet somewhere?"

"Do you think I could come to your place? I mean, if not, that's okay too."

"Sure. My place is fine."

I gave him my address, and he said he'd be there in about forty-five minutes. I knew giving my address to a gangbanger might not have been a good idea, but I knew what he wanted, and it wasn't to rob the place. I took a quick shower before Gabriel got there, and sat on the couch wearing a pair of boxers and playing with myself. By the time Gabriel arrived, I was already hard. His eyes glanced downward when I opened the door.

"Come in, Tejon." I sat down in my recliner. He walked in, shutting the door behind him.

"My friends call me Gabe." He stood in front of me and started making small talk. "You like being a cop?"

"Yeah, it ain't bad."

He slipped off his coat, and I noticed the outline of a pistol in a pocket. Most gangbangers carry guns, and if law enforcement tried to bust every kid carrying one we'd be doing nothing but that.

"Look, kid. I understand you think you need protection on the streets. But you don't need it in here, not that kind of protection, anyway."

He smiled. "Sorry. I always carry."

"I don't want to have to choose between busting you or looking the other way and bending the law. I don't suppose it's licensed."

"Of course it is," he said sarcastically.

"Next time, make sure you leave it in the car. Okay, kid?"

"Got it."

It was a minute before Gabe spoke again.

"You ever shot anyone?" he asked.

"Sure. You?"

"Shot a guy in the leg once, but it was an accident."

He had his hands thrust into his pockets, and he was nervously bouncing on his toes.

"So." He looked around the place. "You watch football? Cuz I like—"

I interrupted him. "Look, kid. If you're here to talk, that's fine—we can talk." I stood up and was only inches from his face. "But if you want to do something else, I'd rather just get down to it."

He dropped to his knees, pulled my boxers down and took my cock in his hand, slowly stroking it.

"Damn," he said. He rubbed it for several minutes before swirling his tongue around my head. He stuck his face down in my balls and sucked them in one at a time.

After concentrating on my testicles for several minutes, he trailed his tongue up my cock and then began to swallow. I prepared for some teeth, but there weren't any. I moaned as I put my hands on his head and pressed him to go down further. He bobbed on my dick for a while, expertly deep-throating me in a way that doesn't happen very often.

He pulled off, and while still stroking me, asked me "So what else do you like to do?"

"Anal," I answered.

"You a pitcher or a catcher?"

"Catcher," I answered with a smile. "You?"

"I'm versimile, or versevica or whatever."

"Versatile?"

"Yeah. I can catch or pitch."

"Good," I said. "Let's go to the bedroom."

He stood up, and I could see his pants had a very visible tent in them.

Gabe lay down on my bed, and I sat next to him. I unzipped his pants, reached into his underwear and fished out a decent-sized cock that was already leaking precome.

I licked off the tasty liquid and began sucking on his cock. I pulled down his pants as he pulled off his shirt. He lay there naked, and I stared at the young gorgeous body for a moment.

He was almost totally hairless except for a small patch of hair on his pubes. I rubbed his beautiful chest, stopping to play with, then suck, his nipples. I trailed my tongue down his chest and stomach and took his prick into my mouth again.

Then I traveled down and covered his balls with my tongue. He had a wonderful, sweet taste that I hadn't tasted before. As I played with him, he leaked more precome, which I continued to lick up.

"God, I want you to fuck my ass," I said.

He smiled and stood up, fishing a condom out of his pants pockets. He stood at the end of the bed and threw the condom at me.

"Put in on," he ordered.

I slid to the end of the bed, tore open the foil wrapper, and pulled out the rubber. I put the condom on the tip of his head, placed my mouth on his cock and rolled the condom down his prick with my mouth.

I sucked him in deep. He grunted and grabbed my head and shoved his dick down my throat. I pulled off, grabbed some lube, putting it on his prick and my hole.

I lay down on my back and put my legs in the air. Gabe grabbed his cock and positioned it against my hole and started to push in. It doesn't matter how often I get fucked, it always hurts trying to get the head in. I tried to relax and allow myself to loosen up, but it wasn't happening.

Then, suddenly, it did happen and his head was in me.

"Ohhh, fuck. Stay right there," I said. I could tell he wanted to push in further, but he didn't.

After a few moments, my ass relaxed and the pain was gone, replaced with a wonderful, tingling feeling.

"Okay, kid. You can fuck me, but go slow at first."

He slowly slid his entire length into me. He buried his shaft all the way in me and didn't move. With his hands holding my legs up, he looked at me and smiled. He had a very cute smile.

"You like that?"

"Hell yeah."

"I thought so."

He pulled out most of his cock, leaving just the head in, and then slid back in 'til his balls were pressed against my ass. He did it again, going faster each time he slid in. This kid was a master pitcher.

I moaned as he pounded into me, his length caressing my prostate again and again. He let go of one leg and started stroking my cock as he pushed into me.

I swear it seemed like he fucked me forever. I wanted to explode, but I also didn't want it to end.

With him stroking me and slamming me at the same time, I knew I would come before I was really ready. I pushed his hand away from my shaft so I could stroke it myself, easing back when I needed to. I lay there stroking myself as he slid in and out of me.

"You feel so good," he moaned.

"Damn, kid, you're good at this," I said.

He smiled at me. I had closed my eyes, trying to stop myself from coming too soon, when I felt his hot breath on my face. I opened my eyes and saw him leaning down to kiss me. I turned my head, and his lips landed on my ear instead.

He stood back up, looking at me with surprise and hurt in his eyes.

"I don't kiss." Rule number two.

He said nothing, just continued fucking me.

After a while, I knew I wasn't going to last much longer.

"I'm gonna come," I cried out.

He continued fucking me and slammed into me harder than he had yet. The rough pounding sent me over the edge, and I shot a load all over my stomach.

He pulled out of me, pulled off the condom and started stroking himself. He grunted a few times, then shot a load with amazing distance, with shots hitting my stomach and my chest, a few even landed on my face.

Breathing heavy, Gabe lay down on the bed next to me. We stayed there for a few minutes.

"Can I ask you a question, kid?"

"Shoot."

"You don't look like the typical gangbanger."

"That ain't a question."

"Smart ass," I laughed.

"No, I ain't the typical gangbanger. I been able to avoid most of that shit awhile. I only been runnin' for a couple years and been lucky enough not to get anything too heavy."

"Why'd you start runnin'?"

"My girl."

"Women ain't nothing but trouble."

"Violet's great, great bod, a blast in the sack. What more could I ask for?"

"A dick?"

Gabe laughed. "Yeah, well, I like a little of both. I sleep with a lot of chicks. I'm cheating on Violet all the time. I can't help myself. We been together for a couple years now. When we hooked up, her brothers started pushing me to join in with them. I didn't really want to, but when I knocked her up I wasn't given much choice. I was basically told to either join, or I was gonna disappear."

"How have you avoided getting in trouble?"

"Well, I done mostly small-time shit, a few robberies, some fights. I been trying to convince Violet to leave town with me so we can get out of this shit. But she won't, so I figured I was stuck for good. I been able to avoid the heavy shit mostly by making arrangements for other people to do it. Making the arrangements for Pryor would've scored me some major points. And I knew the person getting whacked was a piece of shit."

"Are you sure about that?"

"About what?"

"That Sanchez was a piece of shit."

"Pryor said he was."

"You believe everything Pryor tells you?"

"Got no reason not to."

"Be careful, kid. Pryor's only out for number one."

"Maybe, but he got one hell of a cock." Gabe laughed.

"You pitch or catch with Pryor?"

"Both. Depends on what he wanted. But he always liked it rough and nasty."

"He liked to be roughed up?" That surprised me.

"Yup, loved it."

"You been with a lot of guys?" I asked him.

"Not that many. Mostly business arrangements."

"Hustling?"

"Yeah, I guess you could call it that. I was sixteen the first time. I was wandering the streets, and this old guy said he'd pay me to let him suck my cock. I figured it was just a blow job. So I let him, and he paid me a hundred bucks. I thought it was good money so I started doing it more."

"That's pretty dangerous."

"Yeah, I know. I didn't mind getting sucked off, and the first time I sucked somebody off I found I liked it. Fucking another guy was no problem, either. But there was this one guy with a big cock who wanted to fuck me. I said no, and he tried to force me."

"What happened?"

"I beat the shit out of him. But later, a guy with a smaller cock wanted to fuck me, so I let him. It wasn't that bad, so I started letting guys with bigger ones do me, and found it actually felt pretty good. But I don't do nothing I don't want to."

"How'd you meet Pryor?"

"There was this older guy named Lane who was paying me to show up at his house every week. He convinced me to let him throw this party, and I was the party favor." He chuckled a low laugh.

"A gangbang?"

"Yeah, but they all wore condoms. Wasn't nothing happening without the glove. And I got over two grand for the night."

"Pryor was there?"

"Yeah. He was the best-looking guy there. And he fucked me the best too. He asked me for my number and said he would call me. He did, and we had a blast."

"He pays you every time?"

"When I ask for money, he gives me some. It's a mutual thing. I can call him when I'm feeling the need, and he obliges."

"You ever hook up with other guys just for the fun of it?"

"No, you the first guy I really wanted just because you made me hot."

"Thanks."

"I mean it. I wanted you the minute I saw you. And when you called Pryor 'Daddy Joe' I thought I might actually have a chance. This was hot, man. I mean it."

"Yeah, kid, it was good for me too."

"Mind if I take a shower?" he asked.

"Sure."

"You wanna join me?"

"No thanks." Rule number four: No sharing showers.

"Suit yourself."

He walked into the shower, and I admired his cute ass. He showered quickly, and I stepped in as he stepped out. I was hoping he'd be gone when I got out.

He was not only still there, he was asleep—in my bed. I wanted to shake him awake and get him to leave, but he looked so peaceful; I couldn't do it. Doing that violated a rule—rule number three: No sleepovers. I figured it didn't count if we didn't sleep in the same bed.

I grabbed some blankets and sat in my recliner, putting the footrest up. As exhausted as I was, it didn't take long to fall asleep.

CHAPTER FIVE

I WAS having a sexy dream where a gorgeous young man was sucking my cock. I felt myself coming and woke up to find it wasn't a dream. I was coming in Gabe's mouth, and he was swallowing it all.

"What a way to wake up," I said, smirking.

He smiled. "I gotta get going. Just wanted to say good-bye."

"I like the way you say good-bye, kid."

He slipped on his clothes.

"Wanna hook up tonight?" he asked.

"Sorry, kid, I have a rule about hooking up two nights in a row." Rule number eleven.

"Okay, give me a call when you wanna hook up."

"I will, kid. Believe me."

"See ya, Flesh."

"Bye, kid."

He walked out. I was relieved he hadn't been upset about not getting together again so soon.

I think there are certain things that lead up to a relationship. One of those is sleeping over. I never let that happen, but I let him stay anyway, and I'm glad he didn't take that the wrong way. Another thing that leads to a relationship is getting together two nights in a row.

I went to my closet and saw I only had a few more pairs of clean clothes. I hadn't done laundry in almost a week, and the dirty clothes were piled up. I had time to do one load of laundry before work, so I had to choose between washing clothes and washing my sheets.

I chose the sheets. I stripped my bed and took the sheets and pillow cases to the basement laundry room and got the load started. I went back to my place and made two more trips to the laundry room to first put the sheets in the dryer and then to bring the sheets back to my place.

By the time I had made my bed up, it was time to leave. I pushed the dirty clothes to one side before leaving.

THE day at work was relatively quiet, for me, anyway. I saw O'Reilly and Curtis storming around the office cursing each other.

"What's up with Beavis and Butthead?" I asked Lex.

"They lost a bag of evidence in the Sanchez murder."

"What's missing?"

"Sanchez had a duffle bag of personal belongings. They can't find it."

"Dumb asses," I said, chuckling.

"Curtis is blaming O'Reilly, and O'Reilly is blaming Curtis. I heard O'Reilly tell Curtis he better lay off the whiskey."

"You think Curtis has been drinking on the job?"

"I know he drinks about every second off the job. I hope he has the sense not to come to work drunk or hung over, but I don't know. "

Lex and I got called to respond to a report of domestic violence. As we were leaving, I saw Curtis talking to a woman who was obviously a prostitute. I wondered what she might have to do with the case.

WHEN Lex and I returned from the domestic violence call, I was floored to see Pryor at the station.

"Hello, Detective Flesh," he said to me.

"What are you doing here?" I asked.

"I'm here to see if the man found murdered at the Aloha Inn was the man who stabbed me."

"We both know it is. How are you going to explain that the official description you gave me and my partner doesn't match Sanchez at all?"

"I was in shock. I had lost a lot of blood. I was confused."

O'Reilly walked up to us. "Leave my witness alone, Flesh."

"Relax, Red. I was just leaving."

"This way, Mr. Pryor. The morgue is downstairs."

"After you, Timothy."

It caught me as very strange that Pryor used O'Reilly's first name. There was also something in the way he said his name. It was the same tone he used when he called me boy.

I was about to follow them downstairs when Lex stopped me.

"Stay out of it, Cris. O'Reilly and Curtis may be pigs, but they'll solve the case. Don't get yourself in anymore trouble."

I reluctantly went to my desk, keeping an eye on the stairwell.

PRYOR and O'Reilly exited the stairwell ten minutes later. O'Reilly said something to Pryor and then walked into Brunson's office. Pryor walked up to me. I ignored him.

"I've decided to forgive your insolence, Flesh. When all this is over, we'll have to arrange a personal meeting."

I snorted. "You've decided to forgive me? You make me sick. I'd rather fuck a woman than ever lower myself to being with you again."

"I know that's not true. You love lowering yourself and being degraded."

"Not with you. Not anymore."

"We'll see about that," Pryor said as he turned and left the precinct.

I walked into Brunson's office and interrupted Brunson's discussion with O'Reilly.

"Is Pryor a suspect in Sanchez's murder?" I asked O'Reilly.

"What do you mean?"

"It seems to me he would have the most to gain from Sanchez's death."

"He's got a rock solid alibi and no motive."

"No motive?" I laughed. "I'd say blackmail is a pretty big motive."

"And his alibi?" O'Reilly asked.

"I'm not saying he did it himself. Vargas said Pryor was considering hiring a hit man."

"Pryor admitted to that. Both he and the gangbanger said he decided not to have Sanchez killed."

"Maybe he found someone else."

"You're stumbling in the dark here, Flesh," O'Reilly told me.

"Damn it." I stood, getting into Red's face.

Brunson got in the middle of us.

"Knock it off, both of you. Flesh, this is O'Reilly's case, and you will stay out of it. Do I make myself clear?"

"Yes, sir," I said as I sat down.

O'Reilly glared at me for a moment before he walked away.

I GOT home early and was about to start working on the massive piles of laundry when there was a knock on my door. I looked through the peephole—it was Gabe. I opened the door and could see he was upset.

"Look, man," he started off. "I'm sorry. I know what you said about a second night and all that but I just—"

"Come in," I said. He stepped in, and I shut the door behind him.

He turned to me, and I saw his eye was bruised, and he had a bloody lip.

"What happened, kid?" I reached out to touch his eye. He flinched, and I pulled my hand back.

"What happened?" I repeated with more emphasis.

"A guy picked me up to…." He paused.

"Picked you up for sex?"

"Yeah. He said he just wanted to suck me off. So we went to his place. He started sucking me, then said he wanted to tie me up. I told him I wasn't into that, and he lost it. Started screaming at me and calling me a cheap slut. I told him to fuck off and grabbed my stuff to leave. He grabbed my hair and punched me in the face. He got a couple more hits in before I kicked him in the nuts and took off."

"You okay, kid?"

"Yeah, I'm fine. I think he would've raped me if I didn't get out of there. I saw handcuffs and whips. A shitload of S and M shit."

I was furious for what had happened to Gabe. Not just for him, but for all the other abused young men who had been abandoned by their families and were left to fend for themselves. Young men who were forced to do whatever it took to survive.

I grabbed my coat but left behind my gun and my badge. "Tell me where he lives."

"Why?"

"Just tell me."

"I ain't gonna tell you unless you tell me what you're gonna do," Gabe said.

"I'm going to pay a visit to this guy and teach him a lesson about hurting young men."

"You serious?"

"Hell yeah, I'm serious. Now tell me."

"How about I show you?"

"No, you need to stay here."

"I go with you or nothing."

"Fine, let's go."

He directed me to a large house on Mountaingate Drive on the edge of the city. The guy was obviously loaded; the entrance to the house was decorated with marble statues.

I walked to the front door and knocked hard. "Stay out of sight for a minute," I told Gabe. He ducked behind a corner.

A short, chunky man answered the door wearing a pair of sweats and a grungy T-shirt. "Who the hell are you?"

"A friend of the boy you just tried to rape."

"What the hell are you talking about?"

I grabbed the guy by his shirt, pushed him into his house, and forced him to the floor. I sat on top of him. "You sick bastard, you think you can take whatever you want. Bastards like you deserve to die." I heard Gabe step inside and close the front door.

I punched the guy in the gut and stood up, pulling him with me.

"You?" the guy said when he saw Gabe. "You're behind this, you little whore."

I slapped the guy across the face—a bitch slap. "Don't talk to him like that."

"Why the fuck do you care about a cheap hustler like him?"

I slapped him again, spun him around, and slammed him against the wall.

"He's a decent young man. And you will apologize to him."

"Fuck you," the guy spat. "I ain't apologizing to no one."

I slammed him against the wall again. "You're a lowlife piece of scum, you know that? What you choose to do in your bedroom is your business. I don't care if you like to use handcuffs or whips or whatever. But there are plenty of guys out there who are into that thing; you don't need to force nobody into it."

"He's a whore. No one cares what happens to him."

"I care," I whispered into his ear. "I think maybe you need to be taught a lesson."

"What're you doing?" Gabe asked me.

"I'm gonna teach him how it feels to be the victim, instead of the victimizer."

"You're going to pay for this," the guy said.

"Shut the hell up," I yelled in his ear.

With one hand pushing him against the wall, I pulled down his sweats, revealing a hairy ass. Then I opened my pants, pulling out my cock. I rubbed my dick against his ass.

"I'm gonna rape you like you were gonna do to my friend."

"What? No, please don't," the guy begged. He started crying, blubbering like a baby.

I started to press myself against him, and he cried even louder.

"Please, don't do that. Please, please, please."

"Apologize."

"What?" he said between sobs.

"Apologize. To. My. Friend."

"I'm sorry, so sorry."

"Beg for his forgiveness," I ordered. "Grovel like the pig you are." I threw him to the ground, and he crawled to Gabe's feet.

"I'm sorry. I really am. Please forgive me. I won't ever do anything like that again."

Gabe stood there with a look of half-amusement, half-shock.

"You good, kid?" I asked as I zipped my pants up.

"Umm… yeah."

"Good, let's go." As I walked by the sobbing pile of blubber, I knelt down so I could whisper in his ear. "Say one of word of this to anyone, and I will be back."

Gabe and I got in my car and drove to my place in silence.

WE WERE back at my place for a few minutes before Gabe said anything.

"That was freaking unbelicvable, Flesh."

"He had it coming," I said.

"I don't get it."

"Get what?"

"Why you did that for me."

"I know what it's like to be made to do something you don't want to do. I couldn't let that guy get away with it."

"I still don't get it, but I appreciate it. What can I do to repay you?" He reached out and rubbed my crotch.

I walked away. "I didn't do it so you'd sleep with me, kid. I wouldn't do that. When we have sex again, it'll because we both want it. Not out of some warped sense of gratitude."

"I just ain't used to people doing things for no reason," he said.

"It happens, kid."

"Can I ask something, Flesh?"

"No."

"No?"

"No, I wouldn't have raped him."

He smiled. "That's what I figured."

"I might've killed him," I admitted. "That's why I left my gun here. I wasn't sure I'd be able to hold back."

He looked at me for a minute before I broke eye contact. "You think I can crash here? I don't feel like going home yet."

"Sure thing, kid. You can have the couch."

I grabbed a pillow off my bed and two blankets from a closet and tossed them at him. He nodded his appreciation.

"G'nite," I told him as I walked into my bedroom.

"See ya."

I was asleep a minute after my head hit the pillow.

Chapter Six

GABE was gone when I got up in the morning. Part of me was glad he was gone, but I had also halfway hoped he would still be there so we could play again.

When I walked into the station, other officers were looking at me in an odd way, and I suddenly had the feeling that it was going to be a very bad day. Lex wasn't there yet, but the chief ordered me into his office.

I could tell he was pissed, so pissed that he wasn't saying a word.

"What's up, Chief?"

"Just sit there and shut up. Don't speak unless I tell you to. You got it?"

"Yes, sir." Fuck!

Lex came in a few minutes later. She was looking just as freaked out as I was.

"What's going on, Chief?"

"Sit down, Lex." She sat next to me and put her hand on my leg.

Brunson sat there for a second before looking at us.

"New evidence has come in on the Sanchez murder," he said.

"That's good news," Lex exclaimed.

"Hold on." The way he said it, I knew it wasn't good news.

"Curtis and O'Reilly have found the evidence that had been misplaced. It got misfiled. We also have a prostitute who was at the Aloha the night of the murder."

"And?"

"The evidence was a personal journal of Sanchez's with information about a suspect. The prostitute's statement leads to the same suspect."

"Who?" Lex asked. The way Brunson looked at me told me what I feared. The suspect was me.

"I'm the suspect, Lex."

She looked at me. "No way."

"He's right," Brunson said.

"What? Chief, you can't be serious."

"Sanchez's journal mentioned Flesh by name," Brunson answered. "Sanchez knew Flesh was gay and had specifics about the... somewhat kinky stuff he likes. Sanchez was planning on blackmailing you, Flesh."

"How could he blackmail me? I don't hide my sexuality."

"Maybe you didn't want it brought out that you like to be dominated sexually," Brunson said.

"Of course I wouldn't want the details of my sex life broadcast. Nobody would. But it's not something I would kill for. I didn't know anything about his plan to blackmail me."

"He didn't mention it when you were at his motel room?" Lex asked me.

"He knew I was a cop," I answered. "He claimed he saw my badge, but he must've known when he picked me up at the bar. He probably knew about my connection to Pryor. Sanchez made some comment about me not wanting my cop buddies to know about my sex life. I told him I was out and didn't hide in the closet."

"But he never mentioned blackmail?"

"No. Does he think I'm rich or something?"

"He was planning on using you to hide evidence of crimes," Brunson said.

"What does the prostitute say?" Lex asked.

"Her name is Kismet," Brunson replied. "She saw Flesh go into the vic's motel room."

"I never denied going, sir."

"You never said you went back that night."

"What? I didn't go back that night."

"The witness says she saw you come back, knock on the door and go in. Wearing the same clothes."

"I didn't go back, Boss. I went home and stayed there."

"Do you have anyone who can corroborate your story about going and staying home?"

"Yeah, I was having tea with my old auntie. No, I was all by myself. Now I'm wishing I had picked up another guy and sucked his cock so I had an alibi."

"Me too," the chief said.

He motioned to someone outside the door, and O'Reilly and Curtis came in. O'Reilly was grinning like a Cheshire cat, but Curtis looked slightly more reserved.

"I need you to turn in your badge and gun," Brunson said.

"Chief, what the hell is going on?" Lex demanded.

"Relax, Lex," I said. I stood, pulled out my gun and badge and put them on Brunson's desk. O' Reilly and Curtis stepped up behind me.

"You're under arrest, Flesh," O'Reilly growled. He pulled out a set of cuffs and slapped them on my wrist hard.

"O'Reilly, you don't got to be so rough," Curtis said. I could smell the whiskey on Curtis's breath.

"He's just another killer, as far as I'm concerned," O'Reilly responded.

Brunson stepped in. "He's not convicted yet, O'Reilly. And he's still a cop. You will give him respect."

"Yes, sir," O'Reilly said.

Once we were out of Brunson's office, O'Reilly continued

manhandling me. I didn't push back; maybe it helped him feel better about himself. O'Reilly took me through all the booking procedures: fingerprints, picture, and all that. I was amazed at how humiliating it all felt.

After that was done, O'Reilly escorted me into a private cell. Giving me another glare, he shut the door. Damn, the slamming of the cell door seemed really loud. Even though the room had bars and was open, I felt closed in and totally alone. I'm used to being alone, but this was different.

Twenty minutes later, Lex showed up. I was still sitting on the bed and looked up to see her sad, but angry face.

"Damn, Cris, you really screwed yourself good. I have no idea how you're going to get out of this."

"You aren't going to ask me?"

"Ask what?"

"If I did it? If I killed Sanchez?"

"Are you kidding me? I know you, Cris. Maybe better than you know yourself. I know you didn't kill this guy, but the case is pretty strong. But you can beat it. As long as there isn't anything else. There isn't, is there?"

"No, I'm not hiding anything. But I don't know who was at Sanchez's room the second time. I didn't go back. I promise you, Lex."

"We'll figure it out, Cris. Have faith."

"Have faith? In what? God? Myself?"

"How about justice? You swore an oath to preserve justice, and justice is what will triumph."

"I wish I could believe that, Lex."

TWO hours later, Lex was back. The look on her face wasn't a good one.

"What now?"

"They searched your apartment." I had a sudden vision of Curtis and O'Reilly going through my gay porn collection and finding the box of sex toys under my bed.

"And?"

"They found blood on your pocket knife and some of your clothes."

"Blood?"

"Yes, Sanchez's blood."

"Damn, I forgot about that."

"I thought you said you weren't hiding anything else."

"I wasn't hiding anything. I forgot about it."

"What?" she asked.

"When we got back to the motel room Sanchez had a package. He used my knife to open it and cut himself on his hand."

"The cut on his hand looks like a defensive wound, Cris."

"Of course. What about the package he got? His blood's on it, and that could back up my story."

"There's no package, Cris."

"What? There has to be. It was under the bed."

"I've looked at every piece of evidence, including the journal. There was no package."

"What the hell happened to it?"

"I don't know. It looks like you're being set up, Cris."

"Yeah. But why? And by who?"

"You need to get yourself a good lawyer, Cris."

"Yeah, right. I've pissed off every lawyer in the city by arresting their clients. They'd all love nothing more than to get me in jail. I'll stick with Reno's finest public defender."

"Good luck with that."

"Any word on bail, Lex?"

"No. Judge Barrett got your case. He says he has to take the matter under deep consideration."

"Barrett? Fuck, the last time I was in court with him, he nearly threw me out. He'd rather see me rot in jail than go free. He's gonna slow play it for as long as he can."

"I'm pushing to get you a quick prelim and maybe you can get bail at the same time."

"Thanks, Lex."

The night in jail was horrible. Extremely uncomfortable bed, thin-ass blanket. I finally fell asleep around midnight.

CHAPTER SEVEN

I WAS startled awake at six a.m. by a visitor—Joseph Pryor.

"What do you want?" I asked him.

"I heard about you getting arrested for Ric's murder."

"Yeah. It's been loads of fun."

"Did you do it?"

I laughed. "No. Not that it matters to me what you think."

"Are you going to go public... about me?"

"Always think of yourself first, huh, Pryor?"

"Please don't say anything about me, Flesh. I could lose everything. My family, my job, my reputation. Everything."

I guess it didn't matter to him that I had a lot to lose myself. Like my freedom.

"Get the hell out of here, Pryor."

"Are you going to expose me or not?"

"I guess you'll have to wait. Because I don't know yet. So get the fuck out of here and leave me alone."

Pryor stood there for a moment without saying a word. I lay down on the bed and turned to face the wall. Finally, I heard Pryor leave. A few minutes later, I heard footsteps coming back.

"I told you to leave me alone, Pryor."

"Cris, it's me."

I flipped around.

"Lex, it's great to see you. Any news?"

"Not good news, I'm afraid. You have to stay here over the weekend. I couldn't get your prelim scheduled until Monday morning."

"Shit."

"There's more. Giles was the PD assigned to your case."

"Peter Giles? Is that the guy who stammers through his questions?"

"Yeah, that's him. I told you to hire a lawyer."

"No, I'll take my luck with Giles. He can't be that bad."

I was wrong. Giles really was that bad.

GILES met with me Saturday afternoon. I'd witnessed Giles in court, stammering through his questions to witnesses and judges, but I didn't realize he was like that outside of the courtroom as well—he stammered through our entire meeting. There were so many umms and aaahs as we were talking I couldn't understand what he was asking me. I had forgotten the first words in each sentence by the time he got to the last words.

"I'm pleading not guilty," I told him. He tried to talk me into a plea bargain, but I said there was no way I was taking the hit for anything other than messing around with a guy who was killed.

The pronouncement of my sexuality changed Giles a bit. He still stammered, but was suddenly playing with himself. No fucking way that was gonna happen. I could just picture him in bed: *Ummmm, yeah, suck my uhhh cock. Ohh, ummm, that, um, feels good, uumm.*

Going into my prelim with Giles as my lawyer didn't fill me with confidence, but I was determined to make the best of it.

MY PRELIM took place first thing Monday morning. A preliminary hearing is just used to determine if there is enough evidence to proceed with a trial. Cases almost always move forward to a trial.

Washoe County District Attorney Richard Cahill was a good lawyer, and he presented a good case for the judge. Cahill didn't have to present too much evidence to make his case. Curtis, O'Reilly, and Kismet were called to the stand. Curtis and O'Reilly talked about the evidence they had gathered, including the blood found at my place and Sanchez's journal indicating his plan to blackmail me.

It seemed to me it would've been easy to discredit Curtis and O'Reilly, but Giles didn't even try. I thought of a thousand questions to ask them, but Giles insisted it wasn't needed.

It was during Kismet's testimony that I lost it. Cahill's questioning was strong, and Giles was pathetic. Absolutely fucking pathetic.

"That's it." I stood up.

"Mr. Flesh, sit down." Judge Barrett ordered.

"No, I don't want this idiot as my lawyer. You're fired, Giles."

"Mr. Flesh, that is not a good idea. You know what they say about a man who represents himself," Judge Barrett said.

"I'd rather be a fool than have that fool represent me," I said, pointing a finger at Giles.

"Mr. Giles, I suggest you talk to your client."

Giles sat down at the table. "This ummm isn't a good ahhh umm idea," he said.

"I don't care. You're horrible at this, man. You should consider a total career change, really."

"Now, ummm, Mr. Flesh. Aaaahhhh. I can... ummm... handle your... umm case... uhhh... fine."

"Forget it, Giles. You're fired. I wouldn't want you as my lawyer if I was accused of jaywalking, and there was proof that I was in another country at the time. You are pathetic. It's really sad. Honestly, man."

Giles slammed his hand on the table and stood up. "I'm done, your honor. Mr. Flesh can take care of himself." He grabbed his briefcase and walked out of the door. Now he didn't stammer.

Cahill stood up. "Your honor, I do not object to Mr. Flesh defending himself."

"Very well, Mr. Flesh," Judge Barrett said. "If you want to represent yourself, I will allow it."

"Thank you, your honor."

"Proceed with the questioning of Miss... Kismet."

I did proceed. I proceeded to tear the happy hooker to shreds on the stand. I don't know how much it did to help my case, but it still felt pretty good.

Kismet had a high, squeaky voice with a thick New Jersey accent. On the stand, she admitted to not seeing the face of whoever came to see Sanchez the second time. She said he was wearing the same clothes I had been wearing, was approximately my height and build and had a shaved head. She also admitted to having been with a lot of johns that night and to smoking pot. Cahill was not at all happy to have that come out.

When it was all done, Judge Barrett did what I expected him to do. He held the case over for trial. However, he also denied me bail, calling me a high flight-risk. He refused to hear what I had to say, and he eventually ordered me removed from the courtroom and the bailiffs had to drag me out.

I know, not a good decision to lose my temper. But it happened and now all I could do was damage control.

I HAD a few visitors that afternoon: Lex, who chewed me out for losing my temper in the courtroom, and a few cops who told me they loved what I did in court. One visitor, however, was an unknown to me. He was a tall, built black man. An officer opened the cell door, and the big guy stepped in.

"Detective Flesh, my name is Colby Maddox." We shook hands. He had a strong, firm grip. He was actually the same height as me, but he seemed a lot bigger. He was wider than me and the muscles underneath his Armani suit and tie seemed to bulge out. He was light-skinned for a black guy, with bright brown eyes. His hair was perfectly styled, black with a few signs of gray coming in.

"What can I do for you?" I asked him.

"It's more about what I can do for you," he answered. "I'm your new lawyer."

"Oh. Sorry for wasting your time, but I don't need another public defender. I can take care of myself."

"I'm not a PD. I work for McMillan, McPhee here in town. I was hired to take your case."

"Hired by who?" As soon as I asked the question, I already knew the answer. "It was Lex, right?"

He nodded with a small smile.

"I'm sure Lex meant well, but I didn't want her to hire a lawyer for me."

"Lex was quite insistent. I'm sure you know how she is."

"Yeah, I know." I chuckled. "I don't think I can let her do this."

"You're assuming you have a choice, Cristian. You don't. As a matter of fact, I don't really have a choice, either. Lex didn't ask me to defend you as much as she told me I was going to defend you."

I could just picture Lex talking to the big guy and getting him to agree to help her out. I knew trying to refuse her help wouldn't do any good. It was either give in now or argue with her, and give in later. "Okay, you got yourself a client, but I can't let Lex pay my bill."

"I'm sorry. She absolutely insisted that she pay my fees and to not accept a cent from you. Don't worry. I'm giving her a discount. She's a good friend."

"How do you know her?" I asked.

"I was college roommates with Kenny at UNLV. He helped me get the job at McMillan, McPhee when they were looking for an associate."

"What did Lex tell you about the case?"

"She told me everything."

"She told you I slept with the vic the night he was murdered?"

"Yes."

"And about the victim's past with Joseph Pryor?"

"Yes, she told me."

"And about my relationship with Pryor."

"Yes, Cristian. I said she told me everything."

"None of that bothers you?"

"Why would it bother me?

"I don't know. I just wanted to make sure me being gay wasn't an issue."

"Your sexuality isn't a concern of mine at all," he assured me.

"Good," I responded. "I just wanted to make sure we're on the same page. Where do we start?"

"We start with bail."

"Judge Barrett already decided on bail. I don't think he's going to change his mind after what happened today."

Colby smiled. "I heard about your little tirade. Pretty funny. And your cross examination of the hooker was excellent. If you hadn't become a cop you might have had a career as a lawyer."

"I never could've made it through law school."

"I've already scheduled a meeting with Judge Barrett to discuss the issue of bail again. I'll be back afterward with the good news."

"I hope it'll be good news, but I'm not betting on it."

"Trust me, Cristian."

LESS than an hour later, Colby was back, and Lex was at his side.

"Ready to go, Cristian?" Colby asked me.

"Go? You got bail?"

"Of course I did." He didn't come off sounding cocky, just very self-confident. Everything about him radiated self-assurance—his posture, his speech. Yeah, he wore expensive clothes and top-of-the-line cologne, but you almost didn't notice those things. It was the way he carried himself that you noticed.

As a young man, I spent a lot of time with older, wealthy men who not only wore the best of everything, they also had me wearing the best. I knew what an Armani suit cost, I knew what silk boxers felt like against my skin, and I knew what Clive Christian No. 1—one of the most expensive men's colognes—smelled like. I hated all those things on me, and I usually hated the men who did wear those things. I didn't hate Colby, but I wasn't sure why.

"How much was the bail?" I asked him.

"I got you released on your own recognizance."

"You got OR? How the hell did you do that?"

"I'm the best at what I do."

I smiled because that line was close to one of my rules. Rule number seventeen: Do it right, or don't do it at all. I like to be the best at everything I do. I want to be the best cop, the best fuck, the best cocksucker.

Lex opened the door, and we walked to the front, where I got my personal items back. Lots of officers were there to shake my hand and wish me luck. I wondered how many of them were being genuine. Across the precinct, I saw O'Reilly and Curtis staring at me. O'Reilly glared at me like he always did, but it was Curtis's expression that really struck me as odd. He didn't appear to be angry; he seemed to be sad, almost remorseful.

"Thank you for helping Cris, Colby. Thank you so much," Lex told Colby as she gave him a big hug. I smiled at the site of the two hugging. It was like a Pomeranian hugging a grizzly bear.

Brunson walked up to me. "Good luck with your case, Flesh. I really am sorry about this."

"I understand, Boss."

"I'm sure you understand that you're not allowed at the precinct until this is over."

"Yes, sir."

Lex hugged me good-bye. "Bye, Cris. I'll stop by your place soon."

"You and I are going to be spending a lot of time together for awhile," Maddox told me as we walked out of the building. That was something I could easily live with. "We're both going to eat, sleep and breathe this case, Cristian."

"I got it, big guy. I'm yours whenever you need me." There was a sexual double meaning to my words that I was sure Maddox wasn't going to get. My gaydar was not going off at all around him, unfortunately. However, he gave me a sly smile that made me think for a split second that he got my meaning and wanted to take me up on it.

"Want to meet for dinner?" he asked.

"I guess. But first I need to get home. I feel filthy after being in that cell, and I need to shower and get cleaned up. Want to meet at seven or so?"

He glanced at his watch. "That will work fine. I'll pick you up at your place." I started to give him my address, but he stopped me. "I know your address, Cristian." Of course he did. He already seemed to know a lot about me.

I WAS shocked when I opened the door to my apartment, but I should've been expecting it. My apartment had been ransacked, just like I had done to other suspects hundreds of times. I don't know why I thought it would be different for me.

The couch cushions had been thrown off and the couch tipped over. Everything in the closet had been tossed on the floor. Every movie I owned had been individually gone through. The DVDs were tossed on the floor and the cover art removed from the slipcase. They had been looking for a blackmail letter from Sanchez. I guess they thought I might've hid it in the porn.

Every appliance was unplugged and sitting on the floor. All the pots and pans in the kitchen were in the sink, everything was out of the cupboards. In my bedroom, the sheets were thrown off the bed. My books and sex toys were thrown on the bed.

Every room was a mess. I sat on my bed and couldn't decide where to start cleaning up. I felt so violated, every private thing I had was no longer private. My fellow officers had touched everything I owned.

I finally decided to start with cleaning myself up. I took off my dirty clothes and threw them into a pile on the floor. I put the things away in the bathroom that had been messed up, turned on the hot water and stepped into it. The water was scalding, just like I like it. I stood under that hot stream for at least twenty minutes before I grabbed the soap and started scrubbing myself.

I washed myself from head to toe, rinsed off, and then did it again. I was in the shower until the water turned from hot to lukewarm to freezing cold. I stayed in even after the water was cold. I'm not sure why I did, but for some reason the cold water felt as good as the hot water.

Finally, I got out, dried myself off, and threw on a pair of sweat pants.

I started cleaning in the bedroom. I took all my sheets, all my clothes, and started doing laundry. I didn't feel like anything I owned would be clean, not after it had all been touched and gone through. I put the drawers back in my dresser, put my books and sex toys away, and my bedroom was somewhat clean.

Not paying attention to the time, I ignored the living room, which was the biggest mess, and started in the kitchen. I stopped cleaning only to go back and forth from the laundry room to put the loads into dryers. I was lucky because the laundry room wasn't being used, and I had access to three machines.

I put all my food back where it belonged and organized the pots and pans in my cupboards. When the kitchen was done, I realized I had to work on the living room. I righted the couch and replaced the cushions, then put all the appliances back in the correct spots. I had just finished putting things back in the closet when there was a knock on the door.

Colby. Fuck, I totally forgot.

I opened the door. Colby looked at me in my sweats questioningly.

"I forgot, big guy. I got busy cleaning up."

He stepped in. "You still got some work to do, huh?"

"Yeah."

"Well, get dressed. Let's have dinner, and you can finish this afterward."

"That's gonna be a problem. Everything I own that's even halfway decent is in the washing machine."

"I'll order a pizza, and I can help you take care of this mess." He already had his cell phone out. He ordered the meat lover's special, no veggies, just like I like it.

He started to pick up the movies and blushed when he saw the title *Horse Hung Homos*. He didn't say anything, just handed me the movie. "They made quite a mess, didn't they?"

"We always do."

We started collecting the DVDs, cover art, and slipcases. We were sliding the cover art into the cases when the pizza arrived. I turned on the TV and found an old movie, *Young Frankenstein*, one of my favorites.

Maddox recognized it immediately and quoted from the movie. "It's Fronkensteen." We sat down to eat the pizza directly from the box, using our shirts as napkins.

We started talking about the case and our defense plans. "Our best defense is to create reasonable doubt by pointing out who else could've killed Sanchez," Colby said.

"That would mean going public about Pryor's past with Sanchez, as well as my own connection to Pryor, right?"

"Yes, we can easily point out that Pryor had more reason to kill Sanchez than you did."

"No," I said.

"What?"

"Find another way to defend me. I don't want the details of my sex life broadcast for the world to hear."

"You're not in the closet, Cristian. So what if everyone knows you slept with Pryor and the victim? Being gay isn't a crime."

"I know being queer isn't a crime. Pryor tried to blackmail me into helping him get rid of Sanchez, and I told him to go to hell. I wouldn't commit a crime to stop everyone from learning about my sex life, but that doesn't mean I want it to happen."

"What's the big deal? What is it that you find embarrassing?"

"I just don't want to deal with the media. It's one thing to be openly gay. It's another to have the details of my private life broadcast on every TV station and printed in every newspaper, which is exactly what would happen in this case. I just think there's got to be a different way to defend me."

He looked into my eyes. He knew I hadn't answered his question and thankfully didn't push me further. I don't know why I didn't want to tell him how I liked to be dominated and humiliated during sex. Maybe it was a fear that he would think less of me or maybe it was a fear that he would ask why I liked those sex acts.

"Any defense suggestions?"

"You're the hotshot lawyer, big guy."

"That's true. But you're also very smart, and I'm sure you have a few ideas."

"We can start with motive," I replied. "I don't have one."

"What about the blackmail?"

"I didn't know anything about any blackmail until Brunson told me about Sanchez's journal. I think I ruined his plans when I told him I was out."

"His blood on your clothes and knife doesn't look good."

"That can be explained. He had a package."

"No package was found at the scene."

"Then we need to learn where it went."

"My firm uses an excellent investigator named Phil Hunter. Former Vegas cop. I already have him working on the case."

We finished off the pizza and started organizing the movies while still talking about the case.

"I've got *Do Me, Daddy. Do Me Hard*," Maddox said.

"I've got the cover for *Raw Las Vegas Action*."

"I just saw that one. Here it is." He handed me the movie, and I slipped it into the case.

"You sure do have a lot of these." He said it without judgment, just as a matter of fact.

"Yeah." What else could I say?

"Porn doesn't do much for me," he said. "Never has. Bad acting, shallow plots."

"I love the gorgeous bodies."

He chuckled, but didn't say anything else.

He helped me clean up my place, even stayed to vacuum. It was midnight before we realized how late it had gotten. We were both yawning and could barely keep our eyes open. By that time my sheets had been washed and dried. He helped me make my bed before saying it was time to go.

"You sure you can make it home? Feel free to crash here. On the couch, I mean." *No, I mean my bed. Come on, big guy, share my bed with me.*

"Thanks for the offer, Cristian, but I need to go home."

"Somebody waiting for you at home?"

"No."

"Then why not just stay here?" I couldn't believe I asked him to stay, not once, but twice.

"That wouldn't be a good idea." He grabbed his stuff, waved good-bye, and left. What did he mean it wouldn't be a good idea?

I lay down in my bed, so thankful not to be sleeping in a cell again. I considered jacking off, but was asleep before I could even finish the thought.

CHAPTER EIGHT

MY INTERNAL alarm clock woke me at the usual time, and it took me a moment to realize I didn't have anywhere to go or anything to do. It was a weird feeling. I hadn't realized how much I had invested in my job, in my career. It wasn't like I was wishing I had a husband and kids, living in a house with a white picket fence and an outrageous mortgage, but I was thinking I should want more than I had.

I had been up a couple hours when Lex called.

"How are you doing, Cris?"

"Well, I'm not in jail."

She laughed. "Take this time to enjoy the quiet. I know this is all going to work out. Colby is an excellent lawyer. If anybody can get you off, it's him."

I chuckled inwardly at her use of the words "get off." I was picturing something very different than she was.

"I can't just sit on my ass and do nothing, Lex. You have to help me out."

"No way," she said. "What we did was bad enough. I'm not going to risk my job or yours. It could end up making you look guilty, when I know you're not. O'Reilly and Curtis may be assholes, but they're good cops."

"I don't know if I can put my life in their hands, Lex."

"You don't have much choice. Promise me you'll stay out of it. Let Colby take care of your case and let the cops handle the investigation."

"I don't know—"

Lex cut me off. "Promise me, Cris. Promise me you will stay out of this."

"Okay, Lex. I got it."

"Say the words." She knew I hated to break promises. Honesty is important to me.

"Fine. I promise I will stay out of it."

"I mean it, Cris. Take the time to be by yourself. Figure out some things about yourself."

"Thanks, Lex. Talk to you later."

Be by myself? Figure out myself? I didn't want to do that. Too many things running around in my head. Too many memories I had worked too hard to forget. I tried to sit and watch TV, but I couldn't concentrate on anything. I put in a porn flick, but couldn't even focus on that. When I managed to push the case out of my mind, other images, other memories came flooding in. Memories I didn't want to recall. Screaming, fighting, hitting. An older man with no shirt on hovering over me with a whiskey bottle in one hand and an evil smile on his face.

When I pushed that memory away, another came in. Old men in their sixties wearing expensive suits and stinking of marijuana and cognac standing in a circle staring down at me.

I needed something to occupy my mind. Anything to stop those thoughts.

I decided to go out for a run. I went to the Sparks Marina. At one point it was just a quiet lake with nothing but a water park and a motel near it. Now the motel, the Western Village Inn, had grown to include a casino. A sprawling mall had crept up around the Marina as well. Target, Best Buy and a movie theater were just a few of the places there. The marina still had a running track around it, and it was one of my favorite places to run because it was quiet and serene.

I turned up my iPod and tried to drown out the thoughts in my head with head-banging music. But the thoughts in my head were loud and the images were bright.

I ran for more than an hour, and it helped clear some of the things out of my mind, but not all. I sat down at a picnic table, quickly remembering it was the same one where Lex and I had talked to Gabe.

Gabe. I hadn't thought of him much since being arrested. He had contacts on the street, and I wondered if they would be able to get information on the murder. I rationalized that calling Gabe and asking for his help wasn't me interfering in the case. That wasn't breaking my promise to Lex.

I dialed Gabe's number. He answered on the second ring.

"Hello."

"Hey, kid. It's Flesh."

"Flesh, how ya doing?" he asked cheerfully.

"Not bad but not good."

"Yeah, I heard about you being arrested. It's bullshit."

"You busy, kid?"

"Not really. Why?"

"Can you meet me?"

"Sure. Where?"

"Marina Park. Where we met the first time."

"See ya soon."

IT ONLY took Gabe twenty minutes to get to the marina. He drove up in a battered station wagon. He stepped out, saw me, and smiled.

"Hey, kid," I said when he sat down on the table. I was sitting on the bench. He sat on the table top on the same side. He spread his legs wide, and I could see the outline of an erection.

"I need a favor, kid."

"Anything you want, Flesh. I'm all yours."

We both smiled, understanding the double meaning in his statement.

"Can you ask around and see what the word on the street is about the Sanchez murder?"

"Sure," he answered. "I got friends all over the place. I'll see what I find out and give you a call."

"Thanks, kid," I said. "I appreciate it."

"I was hoping we could get together again," he said.

"That'd be cool, kid. Maybe in a couple days. You been getting any lately?"

"Not with a guy, not since that guy you scared the shit out of. I been getting pussy, though."

"You thought about hooking up with a guy without getting paid for it?"

"I thought 'bout it, but been afraid. I'm not real good with figuring out who's gay and who's not. Afraid of hitting on the wrong guy and getting my ass beat."

"You'll figure it out, kid." I told him.

"I hope so."

WHEN I got home, I decided to call Colby to ask him if he had anything new on my case. I was about to pick up the phone when there was a knock on the door. A peek through the peephole made me smile—it was Colby.

I tried to squash the smile when I opened the door.

"Hey, big guy, what's up?" I tried to sound as nonchalant as possible.

Colby smiled a big, broad smile. "You got plans for today?"

"Let me check my date book." I pulled my cell and ran through my calendar. "Let's see. No job. Nope, nothing to do. Oh, except try to figure out how to make sure I don't get sent away for murder."

Colby smiled. "I got people working on that. We can do something else. Let's go."

"Where we goin'?"

"An old theater in Carson City is playing a marathon of Errol Flynn movies."

"You want me to go see a bunch of old black and white flicks?"

"I love *Captain Blood*. Most people prefer *The Adventures of Robin Hood*. They're playing both of those plus a few more."

"I've never seen a Flynn flick," I said.

"You haven't seen any of them?" he asked, astonished.

I shook my head.

"I promise you'll love them," he said as he grabbed my coat and threw it at me. I gave in. I knew that if I stayed home, I'd either be obsessing about the case or trying to ignore the images in my head. I hadn't realized how much I had used the job to keep those memories away. Considering my choices, I figured going with Colby was the best option.

I was instantly impressed with Colby's choice of vehicle. I had figured he would be driving the most expensive, most fashionable car of the times. Something like a Beemer or one of those ugly Hummers.

No, he drove a classic. I could tell it was a Corvette, but was unsure of the year. I walked around the car, admiring its pristine beauty. It was white and didn't appear to have a dent or even a speck of dirt on it. Of course, Colby was walking around the vehicle rubbing off any dirt he saw.

"What year?" I asked him.

"1956," he answered.

"It looks awesome, big guy." He smiled and nodded.

We climbed into the car and started driving. I admired the interior; it was spotless as well.

"I restored her myself," Colby said.

"It's all authentic?"

"For the most part. I added some high-tech electronics in the trunk. I've got a GPS system back there that's tied to my cell phone."

"What about a decent music system?" I pointed at the AM radio in the dashboard.

He laughed. "No, I never upgraded the music system. I mostly listen to talk radio, anyway."

"The GPS was more important? You got a habit of getting lost a lot?"

"No. I always find my way to what I want." He looked me right in the eye when he said that. I wondered what he meant but was too chicken to ask.

AT THE theater, Colby insisted on paying my way in as well as for the snacks. He ordered an extra large popcorn with extra butter, Red Vines, Milk Duds, and an extra large Diet Pepsi—all for himself.

"I don't think the Diet Pepsi is gonna do much good with the rest of that crap," I teased.

He smiled sheepishly. "It's one of my indulgences. I'll be working out extra hard for the next week to make up for it."

I got a medium popcorn, no butter, and a bottle of water.

"Come on, Cristian," Colby told me. "Don't make me look like a pig here."

I added a bag of Skittles to my order.

Colby insisted on sitting in the very front row, even though it meant craning our necks to be able to see the movie. The first movie was *Captain Blood*, and I admit I was in love with Errol Flynn from the very beginning. *Robin Hood* was good, but I loved *Captain Blood* more. I also enjoyed *The Sea Hawk*.

It didn't take long for me to get in the movie mood, and I pigged out like Colby did, returning to the concession stand for popcorn, this time with butter, as well as more Skittles, Starbursts, and a Snickers.

After the fourth movie, my ass was killing me, and I was stuffed from the popcorn and candy, as well as the nachos and a footlong hot dog.

"You ready to go?" Colby asked me. I wanted to see more of the movies, but I didn't think I could sit on those hard theater chairs any longer.

As we left, Colby half-joked that we should go get a pizza. I knew I couldn't eat another bite, but I wasn't ready for the day to end.

"How about Starbucks?" I suggested.

"Sounds great."

"YOU find a table; I'll order," Colby said. "What do you want?"

"Espresso macchiato."

"Wow. That's strong."

"I'd have them hook me up to a caffeine IV if it was on the menu. But an espresso will do."

Colby laughed as he walked up to the counter.

I found a small table in the corner, and Colby returned with my macchiato. He had a hazelnut latte.

We slowly sipped our coffees and talked. There seemed to be an unspoken agreement not to talk about the case.

"So you and Kenny Luther were friends in college?" I asked. "You guys seem like total opposites."

He laughed. "You're right. We were. He was shy, and I was outgoing. But once I got him to come out of his shell, we got along great. Our freshman year, we partied so much we almost got kicked out of school!"

"Really?" I asked, hardly believing him. Kenny just didn't seem the party-boy type.

"Really." He shook his head, remembering. "We straightened up our sophomore year, though. Learned how to balance schoolwork with the fun stuff."

"And after that?"

"We were roommates all through my undergrad years. Then I headed off for Stanford, and he came home to Reno."

"You stayed in touch, obviously?"

"Off and on. It wasn't until our reunion last year that we really got back in touch. It was a blast seeing him again and catching up. I was looking for a new job, and the technology company Kenny works for had just put in a new network for McMillan, McPhee. He found out the firm was looking for a new associate. He e-mailed me, and I had one of the first applications in."

"And they hired you, apparently?"

"They could tell I was the best," he said with a grin.

"Your car must've cost quite a bit," I said.

"Not so much to buy it originally. It was pretty beat up. But I've put a lot of money into it to get it restored."

"You got a lot of money?"

He smiled. "Right to the point, huh? Do you mean am I a rich boy?"

"Yeah, that's what I mean."

"Yes, my family is wealthy. But I earned my law degree on my own. My family may have paid the tuition, but I did the work." He said it with a hint of defensiveness.

"Calm down, big guy. I didn't mean anything by it. I got no doubt you've earned everything you have."

"Sorry, Cristian. I'm used to having to defend myself. I get a lot of crap for being a spoiled, little rich boy. I used the money to get an education and not start my career in debt, but everything since then I've bought with my own money. There've been other lawyers who are wallowing in debt who get angry at me."

"That isn't fair," I said. "If they had been in your position they would've done the same thing."

"Exactly. I also get crap because of my race. Other black people say I've turned into a white man just because I'm a professional."

"You don't use the term African-American?"

"I wasn't born in Africa. I was born in America."

After three cups of coffee, we both had to piss badly we went to the men's room. I sidled up to one urinal, and Colby took the one next to me. There was a partition between us, and I tried to get a peek at his cock, but he was angled away from me. That's a classic straight guy move, I sadly realized. Gay guys will whip out their weenie and stand back while they piss so anyone who wants to get a look can do so.

Colby took me home, and I invited him up to my place, but he declined. We said good-bye, and I tried not to look back as he drove away. I gave in and looked back. He was looking at me too. He shot me a smile and drove off.

IT WAS still early, only eight p.m. I didn't feel like hanging out by myself in my apartment, so I decided to head for Steve's, the gay bathhouse. It was always a good place to get fucked or sucked once or twice or seven times in a night. Twenty-two bucks for a small room for six hours.

I showered and shaved and headed out to Steve's on West Second Street.

Gino, a sexy young twenty-four-year-old, was on duty that night. I'd fooled around with Gino a few times, but knew tonight wouldn't be one of those times. Gino had told me that he was strictly prohibited from playing while on duty. However, one of the perks of the job was that he got to come in for free three nights a week when he wasn't working.

"How's it going, Flesh?" Gino asked with a thick Italian accent. Gino had come to America from Italy on a school visa when he was eighteen. He had been going to college since then, six years total, and was working on his second degree. The first was in journalism; the one he was currently working on was business.

Gino's parents still lived in Italy and were filthy rich. He had told me he planned on going to college as long as he could. His parents didn't know he was gay, and if they knew he would be cut off, which was one of the reasons he had come to the U.S.

"Busy tonight, Gino?" I asked.

"'Bout fifteen guys here now," he said. "Not sure if any are your type, Flesh."

I laughed. "I usually only require a big dick and a pulse."

He smiled. "A few of them almost don't have a pulse and most of them don't meet your size requirement."

"Trolls?" I asked, using the slang term for old, fat bald men who didn't take no for an answer.

"Yeah. Trolls with one foot in the grave and another on a banana peel." He laughed at his joke as he handed me a towel and a key to my private room.

The room was small, no more than ten feet long and four feet wide. It had a cot-sized bed with a thin mattress and sheet, a small pillow and a table at the far end. There was also an ash tray, a trash can, and a large mirror on the wall.

I stripped off my clothes, wrapped the towel around my waist, and began to stroll.

I walked around the hall of rooms looking for open doors with men who interested me. There were a few open doors, but none of those guys interested me. Most of them were lying on their stomach, a signal that they were bottoms and wanted to be fucked.

Steve's had several glory hole rooms, and they were all open. I figured if nothing else I could come back there later. I headed downstairs, past the showers and steam room, the outside patio and into the video room.

Three flat-panel televisions were up on the wall playing your standard queer-fuck flick. Currently, the scene was two guys sitting in a chaise lounge by a pool. One guy, a young dude, was sucking on the very large cock of a much older man.

There were four guys in the video room. Only one even remotely interested me—a black guy with dark, shiny, ebony skin and a six-inch cock he was rapidly stroking.

I sat down next to the black dude, and we began making eyes at each other. I reached over and started stroking his cock, and he did the same to me. Due to the confusion that happens so often with me, I like to make it clear what I want. I leaned over and whispered in his ear, "I want you to fuck me with that thing." He withdrew his hand and shook his head.

"Sorry, dude," he whispered. "Bottom."

I grabbed my towel and left the room. The evening wasn't starting off on a good note.

I decided to head to the steam room. When I stepped in, I could make out the shapes of four guys. I put my towel on the bench and sat down. My eyes focused, and I could make out all four guys there.

One guy was young with spiky brown hair and a pierced eyebrow. He was the definition of a stud—gorgeous face and incredible body. He was slowly stroking a semi-erect cock. His eyes caught mine and locked on.

The stud stood, his cock hardening as he walked toward me. He stood in front of me, holding his erection with one hand. His other hand reached out and went to the back of my head, pulling me toward him. I opened my mouth and took his shaft in my mouth.

"Yeah, suck my cock," the stud told me. "You do that so good."

I slid his dick in and out of my mouth, tonguing him as I did so. He started slamming into my throat harder, and I took it, fighting back the urge to gag. He paid no attention to me, he was being completely selfish. Just the way I like it.

I had sucked him for a few minutes when he stood me up and spun me around. He grabbed a condom off a box on the wall, opened the package with his teeth and slid it on his member.

The stud spit on his hand and wiped it on his shaft. He spit in his hand again, this time rubbing it on my hole. I looked back as he slid into me.

He pushed on my back, indicating he wanted me to bend over more, and I did so. I felt his cock trying to push in, forced myself to relax, and he slid in. He stopped for only a second, and then drove it all the way in without any care of the pain it caused me.

It did hurt, a lot. The pain lasted a minute or so longer than normal, but soon it was gone and the wonderful feeling of his length rubbing my prostate was there. He had a firm grip on my hips as he pulled in and out.

"You got a tight hole, man. Perfect for my cock."

Just like when I was sucking him, I knew he had no concern for how I was feeling. He didn't bother with a reach-around or to ask me if getting fucked felt good. That's the way I like it, usually.

There was even the mix of pain and pleasure, which usually got my endorphins revving. But it wasn't the same. I'm not saying it didn't feel good, because it did. It was everything I usually liked in a sexual encounter, but it wasn't giving me the same rush it usually did.

The stud slammed into me harder and harder, and I could tell he was going to come. He pulled out, slipped off the condom and shot his load onto my back. Without saying another word, he grabbed his towel and walked out of the steam room. I used my towel to clean his come off of my back and stepped out of the steam room. The showers were right outside the steam room. The stud was already showering, but he didn't acknowledge me. I turned on the hot water and rinsed off.

I returned to my room, lay down on the bed with the door open, and watched the traffic walk by. I went through a mental checklist of the things I like in a sexual encounter, comparing it to what I had just done with the stud. No names. Check. Pain and pleasure. Check and check. No concern for my own enjoyment. Check. No emotions. Check.

That last item—no emotions—stuck in my mind. It had been a long time since I had sex with a guy where there were emotions, even one-sided emotions, involved. I wondered what it would be like to have sex with a guy I cared for and maybe even cared for me back.

I shut my door so I would have privacy. It was the lack of caring that had made the encounter with the stud not as fulfilling as I had expected. I could figure that out easy enough, but what I couldn't figure out was why I was suddenly craving some kind of emotional connection.

I thought about Colby and the day we spent watching movies. Honestly, it was one of the best days I'd ever had in my life. I was attracted to Colby, but the day together had also made me like him as a person. I had to admit it. I liked him, and I cared for him. What that meant, I didn't know.

I heard the door next to me open and shut. I heard the voices of two men. Only a few words were spoken before I heard the obvious sounds of oral sex. The slurping sounds and accompanying moans went on for almost ten minutes. I was trying to picture the scene in my mind so I could get hard, but it wasn't happening. I could see what was happening, but it wasn't turning me on.

"I want you to fuck me," I heard one guy say. "Get a rubber." I could distinguish between the two voices who was the top and who was the bottom. I could hear the sounds of the package opening, then the sound of the cap of a lube bottle being flipped open.

"Yeah, man. You got a nice prick man," the bottom said.

"You ready?" the top asked.

"Hell yeah."

There were no sounds for a minute or two, and then I heard the bottom moan. "Oh, yeah."

They both started grunting, and I could hear the sound of skin slapping skin. I closed my eyes and tried to block out the sounds of the guys having sex. I tried to concentrate on the beat of the techno music, which was pumping throughout the building. But no matter how hard I tried, I couldn't drown out the noise coming from the room next door.

It seemed they fucked for hours, but it was actually only fifteen minutes or so. I heard them both moan as they came. They were silent for a minute before I heard the other guy talk. "Thanks, man. That was fun," the top said. The door opened and shut.

A few minutes later, I heard the bottom leave the room. I knew it was useless to stay there; I wasn't going to find what I wanted.

I turned in my key, got my ID back and left.

My apartment seemed very lonely, but I didn't know what I could do to change it.

I climbed into bed and started flipping through the channels and came across *The Sea Hawk* on Turner Classic Movies. I fell asleep to Errol Flynn.

CHAPTER NINE

THE next several days passed slowly. Colby was busy on other cases, but we talked on the phone occasionally, and he assured me he was working on my case and communicating with the investigator.

Lex called me as well, but she was busy with her kids and their sports games. When we first started working together, Lex had invited me over to her place on a regular basis. I accepted less than half the time. I got along with Kenny and their two kids, and Lex made killer spaghetti. But it was weird for me to be around a family that was so… different from my own. Lex's family was always laughing, always joking and having fun. The love they all shared was nice to see, but difficult because it contrasted so sharply with my own experiences of family.

I started making excuses about why I couldn't come for dinner, and the invitations stopped coming. I'm sure she just got tired of me turning her down. Now I was wishing she would invite me again because I would accept.

I had never thought of my life as being a lonely one, but I realized it was. I was doing the same things I had been doing for years, sitting in my apartment, reading, watching TV, but now it seemed so empty.

I decided I had to do something. My new loneliness was connected to Colby and my feelings for him. I had to find out if Colby cared for me in the same way. Of course, I had to find out if Colby was gay or straight, or straight but still interested.

How I was going to do that, I didn't know.

THURSDAY was a dreary day spent watching TV court shows. Judge Judy was caustic. Judge Joe was endearing, but my favorite was *The People's Court* with Judge Marilyn Milan. She had a straight-forward attitude that didn't turn into bitchiness.

I also spent a lot of time trying to figure out what I was going to do about Colby.

My cell rang around three in the afternoon. It was Colby. I tried to suppress a smile.

I failed.

"Hey, big guy."

"Cristian, we need to discuss your case. Can you come to my office?" His tone was very different than it had been the day of our Errol Flynn marathon. Now it was more business, less personal.

"How about you come to my place?"

"Umm. No, that won't work for me. Starbucks?"

"There's a nice quiet bar down on Keystone. We can meet there if you want?"

"Sure, yeah. Yes, that'll work," Colby said.

"It's called Gin Works." I gave him the address, and we agreed to meet there at six.

I stripped and jumped into the shower. I scrubbed my body more than I should've for a business meeting, but I had to admit I was hoping it might become more than a business meeting. I shaved not just my face, but my privates as well. I'm a fan of being clean shaven almost all over. I don't like hair on my cock, balls, or my ass. I don't grow much body hair, and what little I do grow is so blond it's almost white. I do have hair on my chest and arms, but not much.

I especially don't like any kind of hair on my pubes, but while staying home the last couple days I hadn't done any of my usual body work. I took extra time to make sure there wasn't a single hair down there.

I also shaved my head to the skin again.

Out of the shower, I slathered my body with lotion, giving it a nice sheen. I try not to be too narcissistic, but looking at my naked body in the mirror I had to admit I was damn good-looking and, I hoped, irresistible.

I spent an hour trying to find the best clothes to wear. I tried on every pair of pants and shirt I owned, hoping to find just the right combination that would make Colby want me even the tiniest bit as much as I wanted him.

I ended up going with a classic look: a pair of slightly distressed blue jeans that were almost too tight on me. For a shirt, I chose a simple white wife-beater underneath an unbuttoned tan seersucker shirt.

By the time I was dressed, it was time to leave.

I PULLED in front of Gin Works and walked in, nodding to Donny, the bartender. There weren't many customers; something that I hoped would work to my advantage. I was determined to find out tonight what Colby thought of me. I chose a small table with two chairs instead of a larger booth. The table would bring Colby and me physically closer. A glance at my watch told me I had arrived ten minutes early, which ended up being thirty minutes earlier than Colby.

When he finally got there, he was obviously stressed. He was wearing the same outfit he had worn the first time I met him, but he had lost the sport coat and his tie was undone. He walked in with a briefcase in one hand and his cell phone to his ear.

He looked around briefly before spotting me and walking over. He set the briefcase down, nodding at me as he sat down. He remained on the phone.

"Can you get me a Jack and Coke?" he asked me.

First he's late, and then he treats me like a fucking waiter. Nice.

But I did it, getting a Jack and Coke for him and a screwdriver for me. I was halfway finished with my drink before he finally got off the phone.

"Sorry," he said in a half-assed sort of way.

I shrugged my shoulders like I didn't care.

The small table had the desired results. Our legs had no choice but to occasionally brush up against each other. He was trying to stay still, but I was taking advantage of every opportunity for our legs to touch. The music was pretty loud, and we had to lean in close so we could hear each other.

He started talking about my case, and I sat there and listened. Well, pretended to listen. Actually, I was using the time to look into Colby's eyes, meeting them straight on and not looking away. I hoped the look I was giving him was telling him I wanted him to fuck me so bad I could scream.

He folded his hands on the table, and I did the same, occasionally allowing our skin to brush together. Colby suddenly pulled back and sat up straight in his chair, even sliding back a bit so our legs didn't touch.

"You doing anything tomorrow night?" I asked. "I thought we could go see a movie."

"No, I'm busy. I'm attending a fundraiser at the convention center for The Children's Defense Fund. We need to come up with a definite strategy for your case. I still think we need to point the finger at Pryor as a possible suspect."

It was obvious we were out for different things that night. I was trying to make it personal; he was trying to keep it all business.

"I was reading about Errol Flynn's rape trial in 1943. It's amazing his career didn't suffer at all after that," I said.

"Damn it, Cristian. We need to concentrate on your case. We don't have time for fun and games."

"Fuck it, big guy. I'm the one whose life is on the line. Not you."

"I know exactly who and what is at risk here, Cristian." Something in his tone told me he was talking about more than the case, but I didn't know for sure.

We sat silent for a moment, and I was the one who spoke first.

"Do you know how Pryor and I know each other?" I asked.

"Yes, I do."

"You do, huh? Well, tell me. How do Pryor and I know each other?"

"You and he are lovers," he answered very matter-of-factly.

"Actually, I wouldn't call it lovers. Fuck buddies would be a better description."

Colby's face blanched.

"And it was in the past, not the present."

"It doesn't matter to me."

"I'm not some twink, boy toy," I said. "And it's not like we cared about each other."

"But you two were involved. There must have been feelings of some kind."

I snorted. "Feelings? Yeah, I guess there were feelings involved. The feeling of him sliding his big cock up my ass. The feeling of my mouth around his cock."

"Damn it, Cristian, I don't need the fucking details." He was speaking in a loud whisper, afraid that the people around us would hear something.

"I just want you to know that what I had with Pryor was just sex."

"I repeat: it doesn't matter."

"Well, it goddamn fucking matters to me. It matters what you think."

"What I think?"

"What do you think of my relationship with Pryor? Do you find that sort of thing sickening? Does it disgust you?" I reached across the table and grabbed his hand, gripping it tightly. "Or does it turn you on?"

Colby met my hard stare with one of his own before he jerked away. "I don't give a shit what you do in your personal life, or who you do it with. What we have is a strictly professional relationship."

"Do you take all your clients to Errol Flynn marathons?"

"That was a business move. I needed you to relax and learn to trust me."

That comment was like a slap across the face. It hadn't felt strictly business to me. That day had felt very personal.

He stood up. "I think it's time to go. I think any future meetings should take place at the courthouse or my office."

I stood up too. The outline of my hard cock was apparent, and Colby's eyes went right to it. He lingered there for a second before darting his eyes away.

I walked up to him. "I can't figure you out, big guy. And I'm usually pretty good at things like that." I kept going until I was very much in his personal space. Our noses were almost touching, and I could feel him tense as he prepared for me to punch him. But that's not what I did, though I did make a move.

I grabbed him by the waist and pulled him to me so we were crotch to crotch. I rubbed against him. He was too shocked to resist at first but then pulled away.

"What the fuck, Cristian! Why the hell did you do that? And why in a place like this?"

I laughed. "What better place than a gay bar?"

"A what?" Colby looked around and for the first time actually saw everyone else in the bar. Several men were holding hands and talking, others were dancing, and others were making out. "Go to hell," he told me as he turned and left. I wanted to stop him and ask him not to leave. I wanted to apologize but wasn't sure what I needed to apologize for. For tricking him into coming to a gay bar?

Or should I say I'm sorry for grabbing him? That one would be a lie—I wasn't sorry for the grope. I wasn't happy with the outcome, but even if I never got any physically closer to him again, I did have that brief moment. He had been hard when I did it. I was sure of it. At least I told myself I was sure of it.

I bought a bottle of tequila to go and headed home. I threw my coat on the couch and the rest of my clothes to the floor. I sat naked on top of my bed leafing through some fag mags as I finished off the tequila.

I don't know when I passed out.

CHAPTER TEN

I DIDN'T wake up until noon Friday. My cell phone beeped, telling me that I had a message. I actually had five: one from Lex, one from Colby and three from Gabe. Gabe sounded scared in all the messages.

"Flesh. You gotta call me. We gotta talk right away, man. It's like majorly fuckin' important," the first message said. The second and third were more of the same.

I called him back, and he answered on the second ring.

"Flesh, where the fuck you been?"

"I been busy, kid. What's up?"

"I gotta talk to you."

"So talk."

"No, not on the phone. Gotta see you."

"I'm not in the mood to go anywhere. Can you come over to my place?"

"That ain't a good idea. Can you meet me at the Marina?"

"Yeah, give me an hour or so."

"Make it fast, man," he said as he hung up the phone.

I took a quick shower and brushed my teeth to get the taste of the tequila out of my mouth. It took energy to even stand, but I managed to do it.

WHEN I arrived at the marina, I noticed a flurry of activity, including several cop cars and an ambulance. I parked as close as I could and walked up to the caution tape. I was surprised to see Lex.

I called out to her, and she ran up to me.

"What're you doing here, Cris?"

"I'm meeting someone. What happened here?"

"O'Reilly and Curtis were patrolling the area. Curtis went to use the bathroom and O'Reilly saw a snatch and grab. Told the perp to stop, he didn't and pulled a gun. O'Reilly had to shoot him."

"Is he dead?"

"No," Lex answered, "But it doesn't look good. Who were you meeting?"

"Why?"

"Because I think I know who it was."

"Who?"

"Gabriel Vargas."

"How the fuck did you know...?" Then it hit me. She knew who I was going to meet because she knew the perp O'Reilly shot.

"Yeah, he's the kid O'Reilly shot."

"There's no way the kid would've pulled a gun on a cop. He just called me and asked me to meet him here."

"Well, I'm not going to question the word of an officer," she said.

"Yeah," I whispered.

I got into my jeep and followed the ambulance to the hospital. When I got there, I heard O'Reilly talking to the chief on the phone. He went over everything that happened, and I couldn't find any holes in his story, but I still couldn't believe that Gabe would pull a gun.

I was in the hallway when the doctors rushed Gabe into surgery. His eyes were open and he saw me. He reached out to me, and I grabbed his hand, moving along with them.

"Flesh." He could barely speak. "Be careful. Don't trust...." His voice trailed off, and the doctors went through a set of doors I wasn't allowed past.

I sat down in the waiting room, asking the nurse to let me know when Gabe was out of surgery. A short time later, I overheard Gabe's name and looked up to see a young Hispanic woman with a young boy talking to the receptionist. The receptionist pointed me out, and the young woman walked up to me.

"How you know Gabe?" she asked me.

"We have mutual acquaintances," I answered.

"You a cop, huh?" The boy was standing quietly and patiently next to her, and I could see Gabe in the little boy's face.

"Yeah, I'm a cop."

"You the cop that shot 'im?"

"No."

She stood there still looking at me, but I couldn't keep my eyes off the little boy.

"You that cop Gabe been calling? What's your name? Skin?"

"Flesh," I corrected.

"Yeah, that's it."

"He said he been helping you on a case? That the truth?"

"Do you want to sit down, Miss…?"

"You can call me Violet." She took the seat across from me. Violet was short and petite, with dark black hair that stopped past her shoulders.

"So was he telling me the truth?"

"Yeah, Gabe has been helping me on a case."

"What kind of case?"

"I can't disclose that information."

"You can't disclose shit, man. Gabe, he got a good heart, and he got brains, but doesn't always know how to use them, you know what I'm saying?"

"Sure."

"He wants to take care of me 'n Victor, but he don't know the right way to do it."

"He's trying his best," I said.

"You think this case he been helpin' you with part of why he got hisself shot?"

"I don't know, Violet."

"If it turns out it does, you gonna have me to watch out for, cop. You hear me?"

"Yeah, I hear you."

We sat there alone for several minutes.

"How're you going to pay for the surgery?" I asked her.

She looked at me. "Fuck if I know."

I handed her my card and told her to call me if she needed anything. Then I walked up to the receptionist.

"I want to pay for all his medical bills," I said, and I gave her all my information as well as my cell number with strict instructions to call as soon as Gabe was out of surgery and awake.

AT FIRST I began to drive aimlessly around Reno, not sure where I should go or what I should be doing. It dawned on me that I needed to talk to Colby. There was no answer at either his cell number or his office number. I was getting ready to drive to his place when I remembered he had told me he was attending a charity event for defending children or something like that. I couldn't remember the name of the charity, but did remember it was at the convention center, so I headed that way.

I walked into the convention center and was about to walk into the party when a large burly man and a man dressed in a tux stopped me.

"I'm sorry sir," tuxedo guy said, "this party is by invitation only. And there is a dress code." He looked me up and down. "And you certainly are not dressed in the proper attire."

All the men at the party were dressed in tuxedos; all the women wore black or white dresses. It looked like a sea of bobbing penguins.

"I'm a cop. There's someone here I need to see," I said.

"Very well. May I see your badge?"

I reached into my pocket before realizing I didn't have my badge. Of course I didn't. I had to turn it in.

"I must've forgotten it. You'll have to trust me."

Tux dude snorted. "I think not." He turned to the gorilla. "Jeeves, escort this guy out." Jeeves? Who the fuck names their kid Jeeves?

Jeeves easily escorted me out, and I sat in my car, unsure what to do next. I tried to dial Colby's cell again, but still no answer. I tried a few more times, and it started going right to voice mail—he had shut it off. Damn it!

While sitting in my car, I noticed a side door to the building open. One of the food servers stepped outside with a bag of trash and threw it in the Dumpster. I ran to the side door and slipped in without being noticed.

I inconspicuously made my way through the kitchen and peeked out the doors. I saw Colby standing only ten feet away from me, talking to a gorgeous Asian woman with long dark hair. She was wearing a tight white dress that accentuated her many curves.

Using different people to hide me, I made my way to Colby and tapped him on the shoulder.

"Cristian, what the hell are you doing here?"

"I need to talk to you. I've been trying to call you."

"I know," he said. "I wasn't answering because I'm busy."

"This is important," I insisted.

"I'm sure it can wait."

The Asian woman spoke up.

"Colby, why don't you introduce me to this interesting young man?"

"I'm sorry. Annabeth, this is my client, Detective Cristian Flesh."

"Oh, Detective Flesh, Colby has told me a lot about you." She shook my hand, and I couldn't help but notice how soft her skin was. If

I weren't queer, she would definitely be my type.

"And what has he told you about me?" I asked.

"That isn't important," Colby said. "Excuse us, Annabeth." He pulled me off to the side.

"What do you need, Cristian?"

"Who is she?"

"What do you want, Cristian?"

I repeated my question. "Who is she?"

"Annabeth is my…." He paused. "She's my girlfriend."

Those words felt like a punch in the gut followed by a kick to the balls.

"Your girlfriend?"

"Yes, she's my girlfriend."

I started to leave.

"Cristian, wait," he said. "What did you need?"

"Forget it. Just fucking forget it."

Tuxedo dude had a fit when he saw me and sent Jeeves after me.

"Forget it," I told Jeeves with my hand up. "I'm leaving."

Colby followed me, but I couldn't hear a thing he was saying, my ears were too full of other static. He tried to stop me at my car, but I swatted his hand away and left.

In the car I got a call from the hospital telling me Gabe was out of surgery but still unconscious. I was there less than five minutes later.

VIOLET stood up and walked to me when she saw me.

"The nurse told me you gonna pay for all this medical shit?"

"Yeah," I answered.

"Why?"

"Why not?"

"My man got something on you, something you don't want to come out?"

I shook my head no.

"Then why?"

"I like Gabe," I answered honestly. "I think he's a good kid who could have a bright future. I just want to help him, and you, out. I have the money and not much else I want to do with it."

She looked at me like I was speaking a foreign language. Like she had never heard of anyone doing such a nice thing without some ulterior motive. Without warning, she wrapped her arms around me and hugged me tight. I stood there motionless for a moment before I returned the embrace.

"Thank you. Thank you so much," she said. When she pulled away, she was wiping tears from her face.

The little boy, Victor, came up to his mom. "Mama, who's this man?" He stared up at me.

"This is Mr. Flesh," she said. "He's a nice man, a very nice man."

Apparently, his mother's endorsement of me was all he needed. He looked up at me and smiled, sticking his arms out.

"Up," he said.

I looked at Violet.

"He wants you to pick him up. Go ahead; it's okay."

I bent over and hefted the little boy into my arms. That close I could really see Gabe in the boy's face. Victor reached out and rubbed my bald head.

"Smooth," he said, and he giggled. Actually it came out "smoove." I couldn't help but smile back.

"Missta Fresh, smoove."

"Flesh, Victor, not Fresh."

"That's what I said, Momma, Fresh." We all smiled again. Victor had the bright, hopeful eyes of a little boy. I tried to remember a time when I felt positive about the future, but I don't think there ever was a time like that for me.

The happy mood was spoiled when I spotted a familiar face across the waiting room—O'Reilly. Curtis was sitting a few feet away from O'Reilly. He had the same apologetic look on his face he had at the precinct the other day.

I set Victor down. "Stay here, I'll be back."

I walked over to O'Reilly. His chest was puffed up, and I could tell he was in a pissy mood.

"What the fuck, Flesh?"

"What?"

"You know damn well what. Why are you paying the medical bills for some spic kid?"

"Watch your mouth, Red, before you find my fist in it."

He backed off from his puffed-up stance.

"I never thought you'd take the side of a perp over a fellow cop."

"I ain't taking sides, Red. I know the kid, that's all."

"You know him? How?"

"None of your fucking business."

O'Reilly stood there for a moment as we had a stare-down. I won, and he broke contact first. He let out a little laugh.

"He's a fag, huh?" I didn't say anything. Which apparently confirmed his suspicion. "That's it, ain't it? The kid's a queer, and he fucked you, huh? That's why you're taking care of him. Taking the side of a perp over that of a fellow cop isn't cool, at all."

"Well, Red. It's simple. He's my friend. You're not." I left him standing there, fuming, and heard him walk out.

"Who was that?" Violet asked when I got back to her and Victor.

"Nobody important," I said.

"That's him, ain't it? The cop who shot Gabe?"

I nodded. "Don't worry about him. I'll deal with him."

The surgeon who operated on Gabe came out a few minutes later. "I got the bullet out with no complications. Gabriel has an excellent chance at a full recovery. It's likely he'll be unconscious for the next twelve to eighteen hours," the surgeon said.

"Why don't you go home, Violet? Get some sleep."

"I don't got no car. We took the bus to get here and the bus ain't running this late. I wanna be here when Gabe wakes up, not clear on the other side of town."

I talked the nurse into letting Violet and Victor sleep on a cot in Gabe's room. I gave Violet my card and told her to call me if anything changed.

She hugged me good-bye. "Thanks again."

WHEN I got home, I saw Colby sitting in his car in the parking lot. I ignored him as he started to chase after me. He was just behind me as I unlocked my door.

"We need to talk," he said.

"About what?" I asked, playing dumb.

He followed me inside.

"I think you know."

I sat down in my recliner, and he sat on the couch. I grabbed the remote and turned on the TV.

"Cristian, turn off the TV, please." When I didn't do it, he repeated himself. "Please, turn it off."

I clicked off the TV and met his gaze. We stared at each other for a moment before he broke the silence.

"What was tonight about? What was last night about?"

"Something happened tonight. I don't know if it's connected to my case or not."

"What happened?"

"There's this kid."

"A kid?"

"His name is Gabriel Vargas. Originally, I thought Pryor had hired him to kill Sanchez. But that wasn't the case."

"This Vargas kid knows Pryor?" Colby asked.

"Yeah." He looked me in the eyes and was going to ask how Gabe knew Pryor, but my face must've given him the answer.

"He was involved with Pryor too?"

I nodded.

"Did you and he… spend time with Pryor together?"

"Not together, no. I slept with Gabe right after I met him a few days ago. I got my hands on the numbers Pryor had been calling while he was in the hospital. We traced it to Gabe. He said Pryor talked about paying him to kill Sanchez but didn't go through with it. Gabe has a rock-solid alibi for the night of the murder."

"You think Pryor has been… involved with a lot of men like he was with you?"

"I know he has. That's how all this started."

"What do you mean?"

I realized Colby didn't know the whole back story.

"Pryor and Ric Sanchez were lovers when they were in high school. Ric got into trouble and went to prison for murder, and Pryor turned his back on him. He got married, had kids, and became wealthy while the man he once claimed to love rotted in prison."

"It's not always easy for a gay man to accept his homosexuality, let alone come out of the closet."

"Fuck that," I said. "Life is never easy. Making the right choice isn't easy. I decided I wasn't going to hide my sexuality and those that can't accept me can go fuck themselves."

"Not everybody is as brave as you, Cristian."

I turned the TV back on, and we were both silent as we watched *Steel Magnolias*. A total chick flick but one of my favorites.

"Cristian, I need to know." Colby finally spoke. "What the hell was that at the bar?"

"Never mind. It doesn't matter." I didn't look him in the eyes.

"It does matter, if we're going to continue working together."

"Fine," I almost yelled. "I couldn't figure out if you were queer or not. I wanted to know."

"Why does that matter?"

"Just curious, I guess."

"No, there's more to it, Cristian. You went to a lot of work to get me there. Why is that?"

I didn't say anything, but I could tell he wasn't going to give up. I stood up and walked a few steps away.

"Fuck! Okay. Fine. I wanted to know if you were gay because I think you're hot, and I was hoping I turned you on as much as you turn me on."

I glanced at Colby and could see a little smile.

"I don't sleep with my clients," Colby said. Damn it. That still wasn't a denial of being gay. Most straight guys would throw a fit about someone thinking they were queer, but maybe he was just confident with himself.

"I have a meeting early tomorrow morning," Colby said as he stood. "Let's meet at Starbucks at noon. We'll talk about the case more then."

I shrugged my shoulders. I wanted to blurt out, "Are you gay or not?" but I figured his girlfriend was the best answer to that question. I decided it was time to put all fantasies about Colby Maddox away. He was my lawyer and nothing more.

"Good night, Bello," he said.

"Bello? What does that mean?"

"Nothing, just something my Italian nanny used to call me." With that he was gone, and I was alone—again.

It took me a long time to go to sleep that night. I wasn't drinking, and I didn't have the TV on, but I couldn't get my mind to slow down, let alone stop.

CHAPTER ELEVEN

I DON'T know what time I finally fell asleep, but I swear I hadn't been asleep more than ten minutes when there was someone banging on my door. Still half-asleep, I trudged to the door and opened it, not bothering to look through the peep hole.

"Big guy, what are you doing here? I thought we were meeting at lunch time. What time is it?"

Colby smiled as he looked me up and down. "Rough night?"

I realized I was only wearing a pair of boxers, and I had morning wood. "Oh, sorry," I said as I turned around, trying to will the blood to leave my cock and go somewhere, anywhere, else.

"Don't apologize to me. Looks like you don't have anything to be sorry about."

The comment threw me off, and I glanced back. Colby had a sly grin on his face, but I decided not to say anything.

He sat down on the couch. "We need to talk," he said.

"Again? Are we going to rehash everything we talked about last night?"

"No, we need to discuss your case."

I sat down in my recliner and pulled a blanket over my legs so my still raging hard-on wasn't as evident.

"Okay, shoot."

"Do you trust me, Cristian?"

"Do I trust you?"

"Yes, do you trust me? Do you trust that I know what I'm doing to help you?"

"Well, yeah," I answered. "I trust you."

"Then you need to let me make the decisions about how to defend you. Stop holding me back."

"What are you talking about?"

"I want to hold a press conference and tell everyone the truth."

"The truth about my relationship with Pryor?"

"Yes. And I know you're concerned about the details of your sex life coming out, but I don't think that'll be an issue."

"Okay," I said.

"Now don't turn me down right away—wait. What did you say?"

"I said okay. Let's go for it."

"I thought I'd get more of an argument from you."

"What can I say, big guy. I'm trying new things." I smiled at him, and he smiled back. Damn that smile was cute!

"Now get cleaned up. We have a press conference in one hour."

"Yes, sir."

I walked into the bathroom, slipped off my boxers, turned the water to the temperature I like—scalding hot—and climbed in. A few minutes later, I heard the bathroom door open.

"Hey, Cristian," Colby called out. "I need to piss. Hope you don't mind."

"I don't mind at all. Want to get naked with me?" Well, that's what I wish I could say, but actually I didn't say anything.

I heard him start pissing, so I tried to peek out the curtain to get a glimpse of his cock.

He turned his head just as I pulled the curtain back. "Hey, no peeking," he said, laughing as I jumped backward. I heard the door shut, and I felt incredibly embarrassed.

After the shower, I found a set of clothes on my bed.

"That's what you need to wear," Colby called out from the living room. He had laid out a rather simple set of clothes, not the clothes I would have picked for a press conference. It was a pair of khaki Dockers and a long-sleeved black T-shirt. Very simple.

I still had a towel wrapped around my waist when Colby walked in. "Those'll make you look like everybody else. Just an average guy getting railroaded."

"Yeah, until I talk about my sexual activities with America's favorite pastor."

"Nobody's forgotten Jimmy Swaggart and Jim Bakker. They'll be quick to crucify him and see you as a victim."

"I don't know."

"I do. Trust me. And, yes, you have to wear underwear. I know you like to show off your package, but this isn't the right time. Now get dressed."

I couldn't believe he had just made another comment about my cock. But I wasn't about to try to tell myself it meant anything.

COLBY and I stood on the courthouse steps in front of a small group of reporters. None of them looked very excited to be there, probably B-stringers sent out by their editors and producers as a favor to Colby. None of them were expecting any major news.

Colby started. "Thank you, everyone, for coming here. As most of you may know, my name is Colby Maddox, and I am here regarding the case against my client, Reno Detective Cristian Flesh. Detective Flesh is accused of murdering Ricardo Sanchez. This case isn't big news to most of you, except for the fact that an honored cop is the suspect. But this case has far-reaching consequences. This case involves a very prominent Reno citizen."

That last sentence perked up the ears of the bored reporters. They started taking notes a little more intently. Colby paused dramatically as all the reporters waited for the name of the citizen.

"The prominent Reno citizen I am referring to is Joseph Pryor."

Whatever boredom the reporters had hung on to was gone now. They were hooked, and Colby was in charge of it all. I was impressed by Colby and how he had commanded the attention of everyone present. A few of the reporters were on their cell phones while still writing in their note pads.

"Both the victim, Ricardo Sanchez, and Detective Flesh were involved with Joseph Pryor in the same way." He paused dramatically again. "They were both sexually involved with Joseph Pryor."

There were gasps from several of the reporters, and they began scribbling even more furiously. They started to shout out questions, but Colby ignored them.

"Ricardo Sanchez and Joseph Pryor were involved in a sexual affair as young men. Sanchez then served time in prison, and when he was released he tried to blackmail Pryor, demanding money for his silence. Mr. Sanchez wasn't the only man Joseph Pryor was sexually involved with over the years. Detective Flesh, an open homosexual, had sexual relations with Pryor a number of times over the years. When Detective Flesh and his partner, Alexandra Luther, were assigned to investigate Joseph Pryor's stabbing, Joseph Pryor admitted to Detective Flesh that Mr. Sanchez had been blackmailing him. However, when Pryor attempted to force Detective Flesh to pay Sanchez off and make him leave town, Detective Flesh went to his superior and asked to be taken off the case.

"Detective Flesh ended up meeting Sanchez at a local homosexual bar and returned to his motel where they had sex. At that time, Detective Flesh had no idea who Sanchez was, his connection to Pryor, or that he was the man who had tried to kill Pryor. They had sex and Detective Flesh left. Sanchez was still alive at that time.

"The next morning, Sanchez was dead. But not by Detective Flesh's hand."

"Isn't your client the one who found the body?" a reporter called out.

"That is true. My client returned to the motel to see Sanchez again, and that is when he found the body. He immediately called for backup and was always one hundred percent honest about sleeping with the victim.

"Allow me to repeat myself. My client was always one hundred percent honest. He never attempted to lie or hide anything."

"What do you think Joseph Pryor's response will be to these accusations of homosexual activities?" a reporter shouted out.

"I guarantee you I am telling the truth about the homosexual affairs. How Joseph Pryor deals with the truth is his business." More reporters shouted out questions, but Colby ignored them all. "That's it, folks. That's all we have to say." Colby grabbed my arm and escorted me through the throng of reporters to his car.

"Good job," he told me.

"Me? I didn't do a thing. But you were amazing." A smile was his response.

COLBY and I went to a nearby Starbucks to get caffeinated and talk about the case. We had only been there fifteen minutes when Pryor and Junior showed up. Junior was following his father like a dutiful puppy.

"What the hell do you think you're doing?" Pryor screamed at Colby. Colby was scanning some legal work and didn't immediately look up or respond to Pryor. When he finally did acknowledge Pryor's presence and question, he smiled at him.

"Mr. Pryor, how are you?"

That enraged Pryor even more. He slammed his hand on our table, causing our coffees to spill a bit. "Answer me, goddamn it."

"I'm sorry," Colby responded. "What was the question?"

Pryor's face was a dark shade of purple. His blood pressure had to be off the charts. I hoped he didn't stroke out right there in Starbucks.

"Why did you hold that press conference?"

"It was the best way to defend my client."

"Do you know what this is going to do to me? How am I going to handle this?"

"That is not my problem or my client's. That is totally and completely your problem."

I snorted a little laugh at how calm Colby was, and how furious Pryor was. Junior stepped up to me and grabbed my coat.

"You fucking faggot." Spit flew from his mouth. "You're going to pay for hurting my father."

I stood up and got into his face. Our noses were centimeters apart. "Touch me like that again and you'll be pissing blood for the rest of your life."

Pryor was on one side of me and Colby on the other.

"Don't talk to my son like that, boy," Pryor said.

I turned to Pryor. "I'm not your boy, Pryor. You don't get to boss me around anymore."

On the other side, Colby was touching my arm and talking in a low whisper to me. He was so close I could feel his breath on my neck.

"Cristian, it's okay. He's not worth it. Just leave him alone, and let's get out of here." I remembered rule number seven: You don't have to fight to be a man.

I looked from Pryor to Colby and realized, of course, that Colby was right. But I was still seeing red. I wanted nothing more than to tear Pryor apart. I made myself step back and turn around, heading for the door on the far side of the store. I had to get away from them before I did something I would regret. Behind me, I could hear Colby hurrying to gather our things and follow me. I stepped outside, turning to the brick wall and slamming my fist into it.

"Fuck!" I yelled. My fist was red and bloody.

"Cristian!" Colby exclaimed as he stepped outside and saw me holding my bleeding fist. "Why the hell did you do that?"

"I wanted to smash his face so bad, I thought pretending the wall was his face would feel good."

"Did it?"

"Did it what?"

"Did it feel good?"

I smiled. "No, it didn't feel good at all. Actually, it hurts like a sonuvabitch."

Colby chuckled. "I bet. Let's get to your place and clean that up."

AT MY place, Colby washed my hand and cleaned the cuts. His skin was soft, and he was gentle and caring.

"Thanks," I said.

"No problem. What are lawyers for?"

"You're more than just a lawyer, big guy. I consider you a friend too. And that's kind of a big deal for me."

"I consider you a friend too."

"Shouldn't you get back to work, big guy?"

"I don't have a meeting for another hour. Until then, I'm all yours." He stopped short and blushed as he turned away from me. "To work on the case, I mean," he amended quickly, and I had to laugh. "I had an idea earlier," he said, recovering from his embarrassment and turning back to me. "If Pryor tried to force you to bribe Sanchez into leaving town, is it possible he tried to hire someone else to do the job?"

"I'd be surprised if he didn't," I said.

"And maybe whoever he hired is the real killer."

"How would we go about trying to find who Pryor hired?"

"Is it possible he got O'Reilly or Curtis to do it?"

"I don't know. I mean, anything's possible. I've seen bad cops I would've sworn would never as much as jaywalk. But Curtis has been a cop his whole life. I don't know why he'd risk it."

"What about O'Reilly?"

I had to stop and think about that one. I knew that O'Reilly had secrets he would want to protect. I remembered that day in the station when Pryor had called O'Reilly Timothy in the same way he called me boy. I wondered if O'Reilly was one of Daddy Joe's boys. And if Pryor was willing to use his sexual liaisons to blackmail me, it was likely he would try to do the same to O'Reilly. "I could see O'Reilly taking a bribe. If he was being blackmailed, I can imagine him doing whatever it took to keep his secret hidden."

"Do you know of anything that might be used against him?" Colby wondered.

"Actually, I do," I said, chuckling. "O'Reilly's in the closet. Before he joined the force, he and I had sex."

"Jesus, Cristian. Have you slept with every man in Reno?" It could've been an insult, but he meant it as a joke.

"Not yet," I said, staring right into his eyes, and he rolled his eyes at me in amusement. "Anyway," I continued, "when O'Reilly joined the force he flipped out when he saw me. He was terrified I would tell everyone he was gay, even insisted he had been drunk when it happened. Since then, he's hated me."

"If O'Reilly's gay, is it possible he was one of Pryor's lovers?"

"Yeah, that's possible."

"I'll work on a way to confirm that," Colby said as he made notes in a large notepad. "I'm also working on trying to get a look at the evidence. For some reason, Curtis has been slow playing me on that. I'll get it, though."

"I think Pryor knew O'Reilly was gay. Maybe they've been having sex, or maybe Pryor found out some other way. And if Pryor knew, he would've used that info to force O'Reilly to visit Sanchez and give him the pay off money. I'd bet my life on it."

"What about Curtis? Do you think he was involved?"

"I don't know how he couldn't have been involved," I answered.

"If that's the case, do you think he'd talk?"

"I don't know. Maybe I'll talk to him."

"No way, Cristian. You stay out of it. I'll get my investigator on this."

"Okay, whatever."

After Colby left, and I was alone, a war broke out in my head. One part of me wanted to track down Curtis and try to get him to talk, the other part of me wanted to listen to Lex and Colby and stay out if it.

The smarter part of me that told me to listen to Lex and Colby prevailed, but only for a minute. I turned on the television and tried to focus on an old episode of *Matlock*. It didn't work.

I tried to keep my mind occupied, but the case was the only thing I could think about. I knew sticking my nose into it was not only breaking my promise to Lex, it was also a bad idea—a very bad idea. But that wasn't enough of a reason to not do it. It seemed as if I had two choices: I could either sit back, keep my promise to Lex, and let myself get hung for a crime I didn't commit, or I could break the promise and get to the truth of the matter, saving myself from life in prison. Maybe there were other choices, but I didn't see any at the time.

I picked up the phone and dialed the precinct. When the desk officer answered the phone, I asked for Curtis.

It took several minutes for him to answer. "Curtis."

I paused when I heard his voice, realizing I hadn't thought this thing out.

"Hello, anyone there?"

Finally, I spoke. "Hey, Curtis, this is Flesh."

"Flesh? Why the hell are you calling me?"

"Did Pryor pay you and O'Reilly to visit Sanchez?"

He paused. "What the hell are you talking about?"

"I'm pretty sure you know what I'm talking about, Curtis. I think when you and O'Reilly talked to Pryor about the stabbing he tried to get you to do what I wouldn't: visit Sanchez with money and pay him to leave town. Maybe he offered you both money." He stayed silent, which told me I was heading down the right path. "How much money did your soul cost, Curtis?"

"Leave me the hell alone, Flesh," he said, and he slammed the phone down.

I realized he hadn't denied anything. I knew I was right, but I didn't know how to prove it. I called Lex, quickly filling her in on what I learned, including my phone call to Curtis.

"You did what? You talked to Curtis? You promised me you would stay out of the case."

"I'm not really working on anything, Lex. I just did a little digging."

"Knock it off, Cris. Don't rationalize what you did. Just knock it off. No more digging. No more phone calls. Okay?"

"Okay, Lex. I won't mess around anymore."

I called Colby and told him about my call to Curtis. He had pretty much the same reaction as Lex did. Again I had to promise I was done interfering.

I HAD just fallen asleep, around eleven, when there was knocking on my door. A loud, persistent pounding, to be precise. I opened the door and was stunned to see Curtis standing there. He was leaning over and reeked of booze.

"Flesh!" His breath almost knocked me over. "How ya doin, young man?"

"Curtis, what're you doing here?"

He stumbled in and sat down on the couch. "Ya got anything to drink? I'm a bit thirsty."

"I think you've had enough to drink. Is there a reason why you're here?"

"Nuthin to drink," he slurred. "That's a crying shame." He started staring off into space.

"Curtis." I snapped my fingers. "Why are you here?"

"Why am I here? That's a good question. Why am I here? But really why is anyone here? Why are you here?"

"This is my place. That's why I'm here. Why are you here?"

"This all went too far. It wasn't supposed to go this far."

"What wasn't?"

"This whole thing." He waved his hands in the air. "I needed some money, needed it bad. I like the one-armed bandit. I didn't like the idea, but O'Reilly convinced me it wasn't a big deal."

"Are you talking about Pryor? He offered you money to scare Sanchez?"

"Yeah, we was just supposed to give the guy some money and scare him a little. O'Reilly hit him once, and I thought that was enough. But then Sanchez said something that really pissed O'Reilly off."

"What did he say?"

"Something about being a Daddy's boy. I didn't know what it meant, but O'Reilly went off and started pounding the guy. I had to pull him off of Sanchez."

"Was Sanchez alive when you left?"

"Yeah, he was breathing. But O'Reilly said something about going back. I told him not to, but he wasn't listening."

"Do you think O'Reilly killed Sanchez?"

"Can I get a drink of water? I'm really thirsty."

I walked into the kitchen, grabbed a water bottle out of the fridge, and walked back into the living room. Curtis was asleep on the couch, snoring and drooling. I figured I'd let Curtis sleep it off, and we'd talk more in the morning.

I crawled into bed and was out.

Chapter Twelve

WHEN I woke up in the morning, Curtis was gone.

"Damn it."

I called Colby, then Lex, telling them both about my visit.

"I'll see if I can find Curtis," Lex said. "Hopefully he's still in a talkative mood."

When Lex called back thirty minutes later, she didn't have good news.

"Curtis is gone."

"Gone? He's dead?"

"No, he's alive. I just don't know where he is. His wife and kids checked him into a rehab clinic late last night. They won't tell me where he is. I'm sorry, Cris."

"Damn it. He was our only lead."

"I'll keep working on it from my end. I've been stuck with a rookie as a partner. His name's Bailey. He means well, but he's always in my way, and I have to spell everything out for him. No common sense at all. I have to do this on the sly so he doesn't know. Trouble is, he's always looking over my shoulder."

"Thanks, Lex. Let me know."

"Will do, Cris. Don't give up."

I had just hung up with Lex when my cell rang again.

"Yeah?"

"Mr. Flesh? This is Violet. Gabe's awake, and he's says he gotta talk to you right away."

"I'm on my way." I closed the phone and called Colby. "Violet just called. Gabe's awake and asking for me."

"I'll meet you there."

COLBY and I arrived at Renown and walked in together. Gabe was looking weak and tired when I saw him, but his eyes were open. He smiled as much as he could when he saw me. I felt Colby looking at me and checking out my response to seeing Gabe.

"Flesh." His voice was weak and low.

"How you doing, kid?" I was at his bedside and holding back an urge to hug him.

"I been better, man." He smiled, and I laughed. Colby remained at the back of the room.

"Listen, man. I got some shit to tell ya," Gabe whispered.

"Take your time."

"You know I didn't try to shoot that cop, right?"

"Yeah, I know." He smiled at my reply, obviously relieved that I hadn't believed the lies.

"I think they want me shut up. Cuz of the stuff I was gonna tell ya." He grasped his stomach as a bolt of pain shot through him.

"Maybe you need to get some sleep," I told him. He shook his head.

"No, you gotta hear this." He waited a few seconds before continuing. "Before I got shot, I was asking around. I decided to talk to that hooker chick who says she saw you at the Aloha."

"Kismet?"

"Yeah, her. I had a hard time finding her, but I did it. She was living in a decent apartment, wearing some nice clothes. Not top-of-the-line shit or nothing like that, but nicer stuff than I would've expected a hooker to have. You know what I mean?" I nodded. "She was talking to me until I started asking about the murder. Then she shut up and refused to say a word. She acted like she was scared. Kept talking about someone finding her."

"Who was she talking about?" Colby asked.

Gabe sized Colby up for a minute before answering. "I don't know. She wouldn't tell me. When I went back the next day to talk to her again, she had moved out. I got no idea where she is now."

"We need to find her," I said to Colby.

"There's more," Gabe said. "A few people told me this guy named Moxley knew something about O'Reilly. Moxley works with just about anything in this city. He knows a lot of people. So I found him, and he agreed to talk, for a price. He said about four months ago, the cops were called when Moxley hit his girlfriend. Curtis was talking to the girl when Moxley talked to O'Reilly. Moxley said he offered O'Reilly a grand to make sure he didn't get arrested. Moxley's already been arrested a couple times, and he didn't want it to happen again. O'Reilly took the money. The girl had wanted to press charges after talking to Curtis, but O'Reilly insisted on talking to her. He convinced her not to press charges. Curtis was upset, but O'Reilly convinced him to drop it."

"Does Moxley know what O'Reilly said to the girl?" I asked.

"Yeah, she told him later. She said O'Reilly knew she was trying to get custody of her daughter back from child services. He told her if she pressed charges, he would make sure she would never get her child back. He said he could easily have her set up on drug charges."

"Damn, I didn't figure O'Reilly was that low," I said.

"It seems that Curtis wasn't on the take, at least at that point," Colby said.

"What're you talking about?" Gabe asked.

"I'll fill you in later, kid."

"What happened at the Marina?" Colby asked.

"I was waiting for Flesh and saw O'Reilly driving slowly, so I ran into the alley, thinking I could get away. There's a building on one side, and the door was locked. On the other side, there's a high fence, too high for me to climb. O'Reilly pulled in—I guess he seen me go in. There wasn't no place to hide. He told me I shoulda kept my nose out of everything. He pulled a gun and shot me before I could do anything."

"He claims you pulled a gun on him."

"I always carry. But I didn't pull it on him. I swear, Flesh. You gotta believe me."

"I believe you, kid." My statement relaxed Gabe a great deal, like my trust meant everything to him.

"He probably pulled your gun out and put it in your hand," Colby said.

"Yeah," I said. "And he probably would've killed you if the other people hadn't showed up when they heard the gunshots."

"How do you think O'Reilly knew you were asking about him?" Colby asked.

"Moxley," Gabe answered. "Guy would stab his own mama if the price was right."

"What's he look like?"

"He's a white guy, probably six foot or so. Ugly motherfucker with acne scars and ugly buck teeth. He also got a lame-ass hairdo. He's going bald on the top of his head, but has grown his hair in the back down to his ass. His hair is gray, almost silver."

I could see Gabe was starting to tire out and fighting to keep his eyes open.

"Get some sleep, kid," I told him.

Violet hugged me as Colby and I stepped out.

"What was that about?" Colby asked. I shrugged my shoulders like I didn't know.

When we stepped out of the hospital, I pulled out my cell. "Lex, Gabe needs protection. Can you arrange it?"

"How am I supposed to do that? Arrange protection for a suspect?"

"I don't care, Lex. Tell the chief he's got some good info for us.

Just do it, please."

"Okay, Cris. I'll do what I can."

"And make sure O'Reilly isn't allowed near him." I flipped the cell closed.

"We need to find this Moxley dude," I told Colby.

"We don't need to do anything, Bello. I'll call Phil and have him find Moxley. You need to do what you've been doing and chill out. You are not to be out looking into this yourself, you got it?" I didn't answer, so Colby grabbed my arm and spun me around so I could look him in the eyes. "Do you got it, Cristian? You have to stay out of this."

I loved the feel of his hands on mine. His eyes were beautiful, and I wanted to look into them as long as I could, but I broke away. His eyes told me a lot—they told me he was concerned for me. I wasn't used to having anyone care for me; Lex was the only person who really cared about me. It was hard to accept it, and it was harder to admit I cared for someone else. I cared about Lex, and I cared about Colby. It meant a lot that this guy, a relative stranger, was so concerned for me and my safety. I wished I could let him really comfort me. I wished I could let down the walls around me for just a moment and let someone hold me and make me feel better. But there was no way I could let that happen.

"Yeah, I got it."

"I have a lot of work to do. I'm going to take you home, and I want you to stay there. I'll get with you in the morning."

"Whatever you say, big guy."

Colby dropped me off at home. I walked into my apartment and started changing my clothes—I wasn't about to stay out of it. I had a few contacts that could lead me to this Moxley guy.

CHAPTER THIRTEEN

IT WAS in the early morning hours of Monday when I showed up at Colby's house and knocked on the door. He lived in an upscale subdivision of Reno called Damonte Ranch. The house looked somewhat modest from the outside, nothing extravagant or showy. I had kind of expected a more grandiose house, knowing that Colby came from a wealthy family. However, I also knew Colby wasn't out to show off to anybody, so the modest house made sense.

It took Colby several minutes to answer the door.

"Who the fuck—?" He stopped when he saw me at the door. He was wearing only a pair of black silk boxers and a terrycloth bathrobe. He looked at me with his jaw opened. "Cristian, what the hell happened to you?" I was bloody and bruised and my clothes were torn. I looked like I had been run over by a truck. "Get in here," he said.

I stepped in, and he closed the door behind me. I had to clutch my side as I walked in. The inside of the house was spotless, and the décor was outstanding. The finest art and the finest furniture. I had been inside the homes of some very wealthy men and usually disliked the décor. But Colby's place was warm and welcoming. It was not just a house—it was a home. I became self-conscious about the mess I could be making. I tried to make sure I didn't get blood on anything.

"Sit down," he gestured toward a white leather couch.

"I'm okay. I don't want to make a mess on your couch."

"Don't worry about it. I can clean it. Sit down."

"No, really."

"Really, Cristian, sit down. Now!" I acquiesced, but sat on the edge of the seat so I didn't make more of a mess.

"You look like shit," he told me.

"You should see the other guy."

"You beat him up?"

"Nope, not a scratch on him." I smiled. Colby didn't appreciate my humor.

"You're going to get out of those clothes, and then you will tell me what happened."

"Trying to get me naked, huh, big guy?" Colby looked at me and didn't smile. "I didn't interrupt anything, did I?"

"What do you mean, interrupt?"

"The hottie. Your girlfriend. She ain't here, is she?"

"No, she's not here." Colby walked into his bedroom and returned a few minutes later with a pair of gray sweatpants and a plain white T-shirt. He threw them at me. "Take a shower, then put those on. I'll get those dirty clothes of yours washing. Don't worry. I know how to get blood out of clothes."

I wondered how he knew how to get bloodstains out, but didn't ask. I grabbed the clothes and stepped into the bathroom. The bathroom was as big as my bedroom. I stripped my dirty clothes off and opened the shower door. I saw the water knob, but didn't see a spout. Unsure what to do, I turned the knob, and water began spraying out from all over the shower.

"Damn!"

I stepped into the shower and let the hot water rush over my body. I heard the bathroom door open.

"I'm just grabbing your clothes," Colby called out.

"This is one fucking incredible shower."

"Yeah, it is. I had it built according to my own specifications. There's a panel on the wall to control the water pressure from different areas."

I looked around and found the panel. I had missed it because it was sunken in. There was a bunch of buttons so I just started pushing them to see what happened.

The water directly over my head increased in water pressure. Another button made the water to my left spray harder. I played around with the controls until I had all the sprayers going all out.

Then I noticed a button marked with a B and pressed it. A spray of water shot out from the middle of the shower floor.

"A freaking bidet."

I squatted over the spray and let the warm water rush over my asshole. I cleaned myself out like I was expecting to get fucked, though I knew that wasn't going to happen soon.

The soap smelled like lavender and the shampoo like orange blossoms. I took his razor and shaved my face. When I was finally done, I climbed out, dried off, and slid Colby's clothes on.

Colby was sitting on the white leather couch, and the sound of classical music was drifting through the room.

"I got you a cup of coffee," he said. I picked up the steaming mug and took a sip. I leaned against a tall, antique-looking chair.

"What happened?"

"I was outnumbered. Three or four guys, I couldn't really tell."

"Where were you?"

"A dive bar downtown."

"Why were you there?"

"This is probably gonna piss you off, big guy." Colby didn't say anything, just continued to stare at me. "After you dropped me off, I made a few phone calls. An old snitch of mine knows this Moxley guy and told me where he liked to hang out. So I went down to this bar and spotted Moxley. Gabe was right; the guy's fucking ugly as they come. I just watched him for awhile before I approached and started talking."

"What did you talk about?"

"At first nothing. Then I mentioned Pryor and asked Moxley if he knew the guy. I guess that made him suspicious, but I didn't catch it at the time. Moxley told me to meet him in the bathroom so we could talk privately. He told me to go find a stall, and he'd follow me in a couple minutes."

Colby was just shaking his head.

"Yeah," I admitted. "I was sure it was a lead, and I wasn't listening to my gut. So I went into the bathroom, found a stall, and sat down. There was one guy there, and I heard him leave. Then I heard someone else come in and thought it was Moxley, right? Then the door to the stall was kicked in and this fucking giant was standing over me. I tried to tackle him, but he didn't budge. He picked me up like I weighed no more than a little girl and slammed me into the wall first, then the toilet. He dragged me out of the stall and there were a couple other giants and they took turns stomping on me. After a while, Moxley came in, leaned down and whispered in my ear. He told me to forget I ever heard his name, or the next time his boys'll finish the job. One of the giants picked me up and tossed me into the alley like yesterday's trash. I passed out for a while, and when I woke up I came right here."

Colby was looking at me with a look I hadn't seen before. I couldn't tell if he was angry, sad, upset, or something else altogether. When he finally spoke, his voice was barely more than a whisper. "I thought I told you to stay out of it, and let me handle it."

"Yeah, you did, big guy. But that ain't me. My life is on the line here, and I couldn't sit back and do nothing."

I didn't even see Colby move, and then he was right in my face.

"You need to fucking listen to me, Cristian." He was yelling now, and that pissed me off.

"I don't gotta listen to anybody, especially you." I pushed him away from me, but he was right back in my face a second later.

He screamed at me, and I screamed back. I was seeing red. Our puffed-up chests were bumping into each other as the spit flew from our mouths.

"I'm doing my best to save you, and if you keep butting in, you're going to screw everything up. I'm trying to help you, you ignorant ass."

"I can't sit back and put my life in someone else's hands."

"Maybe you should put yourself in someone else's hands for once. You haven't been doing so well taking care of yourself."

"I was doing just fine before all this shit happened. And even without you, I could've taken care of everything."

"I can take care of this; I can take care of you. You have to let me do my job."

"Is that all this is, a job? I'm just another client?"

"Of course you're not just a client. You know there's more to it than that. We're friends, Cristian."

"I'm done with this. I'm going home," I turned to leave, but Colby grabbed my arms and pushed me up against the wall. I tried to break his grip but couldn't. He was stronger than me; I should've realized that.

I finally managed to push Colby away from me.

"Get your fucking hands off me." I made a fist and threw it at Colby, but he dodged the punch, ducked, barreled into me, and flipped me to the ground.

I was not only surprised by the wrestling move, I also lost my breath for a second. In that second, Colby was on top of me, pinning my legs down with his legs and holding my hands down with his.

He was leaning over me, telling me to stop. I stopped struggling for a minute, and in that moment I realized my cock was hard. I was fucking pissed to the max, and I was popping a woody. I couldn't help it. I could feel Colby all over me, especially his breath blowing on my face.

Because I was wearing sweatpants, Colby had to know I was getting hard.

"Is this what you like? You like the rough stuff, huh?" Colby asked me. I realized he was hard too. He was rubbing his crotch against mine. It felt big, real big. I started to push back against him until the other head, the one with the brain, kicked in.

I pushed him off of me, but we stayed on the floor. I was still on my back, and he was leaning on his elbows. We were both breathing heavy.

He reached over and started to rub my cock. I brushed his hand away.

"I'm not some experiment for a straight guy."

"Relax," he said. "I'm gay."

I looked at him like he was crazy. "What about the hottie?"

Colby laughed. "Annabeth's a beard. It's a mutual agreement. She's a lesbian and has a girlfriend named Hillary."

"Is she in the closet?"

"Yes. She's a doctor—an OB/GYN. Apparently women want to see female gynecologists, but not if they're gay."

I started laughing.

"What's so funny?"

"I thought my gaydar was totally busted. I was getting these vibes from you, but everything you did and said contradicted those. Why didn't you say anything?"

"I'm not out, and very few of my friends know the truth. Lex and Kenny don't know. When I took your case I thought you might be some cheap boy toy of Pryor's.

"I was attracted to you from the beginning—don't get me wrong there. But I was fighting those desires. I wasn't about to let myself get drawn to you if you were going to cause me problems afterward."

"So why are you coming clean now?"

"I know you're an honest man caught in a bad situation. I was hoping to get you cleared of the charges before telling you I was gay and seeing where that would lead.

"But damn it, I can't wait anymore. I want to feel your body, man. It's all I've thought about lately."

"Me too, big guy."

Colby scooted closer to me, reached over, and began rubbing my cock through the sweats. For a moment I felt like playing hard to get, but that didn't last long. I'm a whore, after all. Plus the fact that Colby's smoking hot, and I'd been thinking about him for a while now. I'd be a fool to pass the opportunity up.

We took it slow; he wanted to explore my body, and I wanted to explore his. Colby pulled my sweats down far enough to free my cock. Colby grabbed it—his skin was warm and soft—and started slowly stroking it.

A low moan escaped from my lips, and he smiled at my response to his touch.

My eyes were closed, and I felt his lips touching the head of my cock. I wanted to plunge into his wet mouth, but he held me back. His lips parted, and his tongue was all over my prick.

When he finally took all of me in his mouth, he did it easily and expertly. Deep-throating was obviously something he had learned how to do. He sucked for several minutes, almost bringing me to the edge and then pulling back.

When he pulled totally off my shaft, I moaned, wanting it to continue, while still wanting what was going to come next.

He finished taking off the sweats as I peeled off the T-shirt. He took off the bathrobe as I helped him take off his boxers, thrilled to finally be able to see what I'd been dreaming about.

He was indeed a big guy. Bigger than me by a few inches and even thicker. Probably the thickest I'd ever seen. I had to stretch my mouth wide to take him in. His hands went to the back of my shaved head as he slid into my mouth, pulled out, and then went back in.

I was leaking serious amounts of precome onto his white carpet, playing with myself only a little so I didn't explode before the time was right. I tongued his balls and breathed in his manly scent.

Colby lay down on the floor, and we slid into a side-by-side sixty-nine position. His hands were all over my legs, first rubbing them, then pulling them apart so he could get access to my privates.

His tongue and mouth were all over my cock, balls, and taint, that special spot between the balls and the ass.

The feeling of him touching me was wonderful, and I had to concentrate to keep exploring him.

He pushed me onto my back, flipped around and sucked on my nipples, gently biting them alternately from left to right. His tongue trailed down my stomach and to my cock where he started sucking me again.

I pulled him off of me and pushed him onto his back. As I was exploring his body with my tongue, his hands were on my head, my back, and my arms. His taste and smell were exquisite. I could've licked him forever.

Colby pushed me on my back again, spread my legs and climbed between them. No confusion about who wanted what.

He leaned over me, rubbing his cock on my balls. He tried to kiss me, but I turned my head to the side. He smiled at me, kind of sad like, but it didn't stop him. He kissed my neck and sucked on my earlobe. He grabbed both our cocks and stroked them together. His cock felt warm against mine, and I pressed my body against his, loving the feel of his balls rubbing mine.

"Don't move." He stood and went into the bedroom. He returned with a condom and a bottle of lube. He slid the condom on and resumed his position between my legs.

He prepared to enter me. Like I said, his cock was big, and it wasn't easy to take him in, but I managed. As he burrowed into me, he stared into my eyes and held my gaze for so long I had to look away. His stare was so intense it seemed to reach right to my heart. No one had ever been that close to my heart. I had never wanted anyone that close. And I didn't want him that close, either. This was just a fuck, after all, nothing more.

The feeling of him inside of me was incredible. I don't think I could have stretched anymore than I did. He was buried in me, then almost all the way out, then deep in again.

I was pushing against him as best I could, not touching myself because I was afraid it would all be over if I did.

Colby didn't say a word as we fucked, just some grunts and

moans. He was caring and gentle and truly unlike any man I'd been with before. Even without words, I knew he cared how it felt for me and was taking his own enjoyment from my pleasure.

Colby started increasing his rhythm and then slammed into me with all his strength. I felt his cock exploding, pumping his juice into the condom. Without even touching myself, I started shooting come all over my stomach. Load after load pumped from me, and I could feel him doing the same.

When we were both spent, Colby collapsed on top of me, my come rubbing between us. He stayed there, still in me, for a minute, before he softened and slid out. He rolled off and lay next to me, one hand touching mine.

I did something I rarely, if ever, do—I didn't get dressed right away. We both lay on the floor for a while breathing heavy and hands still touching. He let go of my hand and stroked my arm up and down.

We were both covered in sweat and saliva and come, but it didn't bother me, and I don't think it bothered him, either. His skin felt great against mine. I wanted to return the caresses, but couldn't do it.

"I should've known you were gay when I used your shower," I said.

"Why?"

"Cuz no straight guy would ever have a freakin' bidet in a shower."

Colby laughed. "I'm filthy. Need to clean up. Want to join me?"

"No thanks." Rule number four. The idea of sharing a shower with Colby was enticing, but I stuck to the rule. I don't know how, but I crossed a line somewhere with him, and I needed to pull back.

I saw that sad, hurt look in his eyes again.

"You don't have to leave," he said as he stepped into the bathroom, but I could tell he knew I'd be gone when he got out of the shower.

I dressed quickly, ignoring the urges telling me to stay, to join him in the hot water. I left before those urges took over.

When I got home, I stripped and climbed into my own shower, continuing to wonder why I hadn't joined Colby. One part of me said that it would've been not just right, but downright awesome. Another part of me said I didn't want or need anything from Colby other than the monster between his legs.

I stood in the hot water 'til it got lukewarm, then stepped out and pulled on a pair of boxers. I turned on the TV and sat down in my recliner to watch *Commando* with Governator Ah-Nuld. I don't remember watching even a minute of the movie.

CHAPTER FOURTEEN

I WAS still in the recliner when I woke up to someone knocking on my apartment door. I knew who it was before I opened it—Colby. I opened the door and walked back to the chair. I glanced at the clock on the wall—it was a little past noon on Monday. I had gotten only a couple hours of sleep.

"What're you doing here, big guy?"

"Good morning to you, too, Cristian." He handed me a Starbucks cup. Espresso Macchiato. Damn, he remembered what I liked.

I mumbled a thanks for the coffee and started staring at the boob tube, though I had no idea what was on.

He sat down next to me, real close to me. "You didn't have to leave."

"Yeah, I did."

"Well, I wanted you to stay. We could've done some more fucking."

"I don't do sleepovers." Rule number three.

"You don't? Ever?"

"Never."

"Why?"

"Just one of my rules."

"You have a lot of these rules, Bello?"

I nodded my head, trying to ignore the heat radiating off his body and focus on whatever stupid show was flickering on the screen.

"Is no kissing one of those rules?"

I looked at him. "Yeah, I guess so."

"Well, I think you're missing out on something there. For me, kissing can be wildly erotic."

"Not if the guy is clueless about what to do with his tongue, and you end up with his slobber all over your face."

"So you have done it? Kissed a guy, I mean."

"Of course I have. That's a stupid fucking question to ask." I could tell my rudeness was annoying him.

"How long has it been since you kissed a man?"

"Years, big guy. Many years. You got any other stupid questions to ask me?"

I saw the annoyance flare in his face again. "I'm just trying to learn something about you, Cristian. Is that such a bad thing?"

"I just don't see the point. You gonna ask me to go steady, big guy?"

"Jesus. Why are you always such a dick?"

"It comes naturally." I smiled at him. We sat silent for a minute before he spoke again.

"I don't expect us to jump into any kind of committed relationship. But I do think we have some chemistry, and I would like to see where that might take us."

"I don't do committed relationships." I met his eyes, then quickly looked away. No committed relationships was rule number thirteen.

"Another one of those rules of yours?"

"Yup."

"Of course. Always keeping people at a distance, huh?"

"What the hell are you talking about?" I stood up and walked into the kitchen, leaning over the island. Colby stood up and walked to the other side of the island to face me.

"These rules. No kissing, no sleepovers, no committed relationships, even calling people by funny nicknames. It's all done for the same reason."

I was getting pissed now. "So tell me, Dr. Freud, why do I do all those things?"

"Like I said, to keep people at a distance. You don't want anyone to get too close to you. Are you afraid of getting hurt, Cristian? Is that what it is?"

"You don't know shit about me or my life."

"Maybe not, but it's not because I don't want to. But I bet no one knows anything about you or your life. You never let anyone get close enough to find out. What happened to you to make you like this?"

I slammed my fist down on the counter. "Fuck you, asshole. You ain't my shrink. You're not anything to me. Nothing but a good lay."

Colby walked around the island and got in my face. "Fuck you, Cristian. You don't have to be such a prick just because I may care about you even the slightest bit."

"I didn't ask you to care about me, and I certainly don't want you to. You're free to get the hell out of my life."

Colby grabbed my face and pulled me into a kiss. His tongue snaked into my mouth, and it took me a moment to react.

"Get the fuck off me. Get the fuck out of here!" I pushed him away from me.

He pressed up against me. "I'm not going anywhere, Cristian. Not now."

We were both breathing heavy, and I inhaled the scent of his warm breath. I could still taste his tongue in my mouth, and damn it, I wanted it again.

I raised my arms to push him away again, but he grabbed my arms and held them there. I tried to pull away but his strength had me at a disadvantage again.

I realized I was hard, and so was Colby. Neither one of us spoke. We just stood there staring into each other's eyes.

"Fuck you," I said, finally breaking the silence. "You're wasting your time with me. I'm not worth the energy. All I want from you is your cock."

Colby spun me around and bent me over the counter.

"No, fuck you. If all you want is my cock, then that's what you're going to get. I'm going to fuck you… hard."

He was holding me down with one hand as he pressed his bulging crotch against my ass. I struggled to break free, though both of us knew that I really didn't want to go anywhere. Of course, the added benefit of my struggling was that I was rubbing my ass against him.

Colby was moaning as he ground against me, with one hand traveling up and down my back, occasionally reaching over to tweak a nipple. Using his free hand, he pulled my boxers down and reached between my ass cheeks, rubbing my hole with his thumb before slipping it in.

I moaned, while still trying to maintain the façade of the struggle. I was facedown on the counter, and my eyes were closed. I heard Colby spit and then some wet fingers began probing my hole. One finger, then two. More spit, two fingers, three fingers. He was driving me wild.

Turning my head sideways, I watched as Colby used his free hand to undo his belt, pull down his zipper and get first his pants, then his underwear, past his hips.

I swear his cock was even bigger than it had been before. It was throbbing, and I could see glistening precome on the head.

"You goddamn asshole," I said. "Let me go."

"Shut the hell up, Cristian. You said all you want is my cock, so that's what you're gonna get. You want it rough; you got it."

He spit into his hand and started stroking himself, and applied more spit to my hole. Grabbing his prick, Colby lined it up to my hole and started to push in.

"Jesus!" I moaned as my ass tried to open to let the monster in. The lack of lube added to the difficulty of me taking him, but neither one of us was going to let that stop us.

Colby pushed into me harder, and suddenly his head popped in. I grabbed the ends of the counter and gritted my teeth, trying to get past the pain. Thankfully, he didn't move and in moments the pain subsided… somewhat.

He slid in a bit further, and I could feel his cock rubbing my prostate. He did short strokes, gently rubbing my sweet spot, and the pain was totally forgotten.

I moaned and pushed back against him, letting him know I was ready for him to go on. He slowly, deliberately, pushed all of the way inside of me until I could feel his balls pressing against my ass.

Buried in me, Colby released me, then leaned over me. His breath felt magnificent against the back of my neck. One hand rubbed my head.

"This is good, isn't it?" he asked. I grunted my agreement; I could barely form a coherent thought, let alone string some words together.

"There's more to life than this," he whispered. "As good as this is. There is a lot more than this."

Then he started giving more. Colby slid all the way out and then quickly slammed into me. Then he did it again. I was pounding against the counter as he rammed into me.

We were both sweating like crazy. He was grunting, and I was whimpering. Whimpering in pleasure, I was being taken like I had never been taken before. It was hard and rough, and I swear my entire body was on fire. My cock was leaking precome like a faucet, but I couldn't reach it to stroke it.

He started grunting louder and then slammed into me one last time. I could feel his come spray inside of me, and it was possibly one of the best sensations I had ever felt. No, it was single-handedly the best sensation I had ever felt.

Colby leaned against me, his shirt and tie rubbing against my sweaty back. He slowly started to soften and then plopped out. He stood up, and I started to do the same, but my legs had turned to Jell-O and I began to fall to the ground.

Colby caught me in his strong arms and helped me to stand up.

"Whoa," I said. "Thanks."

"Lean against the counter for a second." Colby pulled up his pants and then wrapped his arm around me again. "Couch."

"I can do it myself." But when I started to walk, I realized I was wrong. His arms were still around me, and he helped me to the couch.

We sat down on the couch, close to each other, but said nothing.

"I'm sorry," Colby said.

"Sorry? For what?"

"I was kind of rough. I hope I didn't hurt you. Make you bleed or anything like that."

I snickered. No one had ever said anything like that to me before. I had taken a lot of rough stuff before, during sex and at other times, but no one had ever apologized for what they had done.

"You didn't hurt me, big guy. I wanted it all too."

"I know we both wanted it. I sure as hell wanted it. But I don't know if I would've been able to stop if you hadn't wanted it."

I looked him in the eyes. "I think, no. I know you would've stopped if that had been the case. You don't have it in you to be truly evil."

"Thanks."

We didn't say anything for a few minutes. "I guess I should go," he said.

Surprising both of us, I put my hand on his. "No, I don't want you to go. Unless you have to."

"No, I don't have to go."

"Good." I smiled. I lay down on the couch and put my head on Colby's legs. "I didn't sleep good last night. I just need a little nap. Later, we can do it again. I haven't come yet."

"Sure thing, Bello."

One of his hands grasped one of mine, our fingers entwined. His other hand began rubbing my head. "I wish you had hair. I love to play with a guy's hair."

I smiled, closed my eyes, and was out.

When I woke up it was more than an hour later, and Colby was asleep. His head was lolled backward, his mouth was open, and a little drool was trailing down his chin. I smiled at how peaceful he looked.

I sat up and looked at Colby sleeping for several minutes. I asked myself what I was doing with this guy. I definitely didn't deserve him, and he could do better than me, for sure.

Colby woke with a start and looked at me with a surprised expression on his face.

"What're you doing?" he asked.

"Watching you." I smiled, and he wiped the drool from his chin and grinned. "Why are you here, big guy?"

"I'm here because I like you, Cristian."

"Why? I don't have anything to offer you."

He got a sad look on his face, reached his hand out, and stroked my chin.

"You're wrong. You have a lot to offer."

"You hungry?" I asked, wanting to change the subject as soon as possible.

"No," he said. "I ate before I got here. You?"

"Not really. Not for food at least."

Colby smiled. "That's right; you haven't come yet."

I leaned forward and pressed my lips to Colby's. It was a soft and gentle kiss and lasted only a few seconds.

"What about the rules?"

"I'm reevaluating the rules. Not too fast, though. You're a good kisser, so we can start there."

When I kissed him again, it was with more pressure and more passion. Our tongues pressed against each other and took turns sliding in and out of our mouths. I sucked gently on his tongue, and he bit my bottom lip.

We slid to the floor, still kissing, with Colby on top. Continuing to kiss, I started taking Colby's clothes off: first his tie, then his jacket. I was having trouble with the buttons of his silk shirt, so Colby tore the shirt in half and threw it to the side. I laughed at him and stared at his gorgeous muscular chest.

I took a nipple in my mouth and bit it gently, then sucked it. He bit my nipples, sucked on my neck, and trailed his tongue over my chest.

He stood to get his pants off. I slipped my boxers off again, freeing my erection. He pulled off his clothes and the sight of his cock was magnificent. I got to my knees and slowly took him into my mouth. I took as much as I could before sliding it back out and paying attention to his balls. His manly, sweaty scent was incredibly erotic as I licked and sucked him.

I sucked him in again as he caressed my head, urging me on.

"You're going to make me come, Bello," he said as he pulled me off of him.

I smiled as I lay down on my back and spread my legs. Colby lay down on me, pressing his face to mine as our cocks pressed up against each other. There were so many sensations all over my body I couldn't tell anything apart. My mouth was his and his cock was mine.

"Lube," I moaned as I felt Colby rubbing his cock against my hole. "We need lube this time."

He smiled, and we both stood up. He followed me into the bedroom, where I flopped onto my bed, reaching into a nightstand drawer to get the lube.

Colby climbed on the bed behind me and spread my cheeks. I moaned as I felt his tongue swipe against my hole. He pressed his face harder into my cheeks, his tongue flicking and probing my ass.

"You don't have to do that," I told him.

"I know I don't have to. I want to."

I got up on my knees, giving Colby easier access to my ass. He bit gently at my ass while thoroughly licking me, before sliding one finger into me.

This was more than preparation for sex; it was sweet and gentle fun. He softly finger-fucked me, finding my prostate and rubbing it.

"Damn, that feels good," I said.

Colby grabbed my hips and flipped me over and inhaled my cock in a single move. I gasped as he deep-throated me before pulling off of me. He pulled me to the edge of the bed and stood between my legs.

When I handed him the lube, he flipped the cap open and coated first my ass then his cock with it. "I got condoms if you want 'em."

"It's a bit late for that," he said, laughing. "I'm clean, but I'll put on a condom if you want me to."

"It's okay. I believe you. I'm clean too."

He pressed his lubed-up cock against my hole and pressed in as I pushed toward him. He slipped in easier than last time, and I immediately hit that point of extreme ecstasy. I breathed in heavily.

"Am I hurting you?" He was genuinely concerned.

"No. It feels... awesome."

Colby leaned over, trapping my cock against our stomachs, and kissed me again. While still kissing me, he began to piston himself in and out of me. His tongue in me, his cock in me, I rubbed my cock against his stomach, stimulating it.

"Oh, damn. You feel so good. Fuck me, fuck me hard. Pound it into me."

Colby pressed a finger to my lips. "Shh, Cristian. No rough stuff this time. No hard pounding. This is making love, and it's just as enjoyable. Trust me."

I said nothing, just leaned my head back and closed my eyes, allowing the sea of sensations to flow over me. Colby slid in and out of me, gently making me feel so incredible I didn't know anything could be like this.

"Feels so good," I said. "Freaking unbelievable."

I started stroking my cock but he moved my hand away. "Let me do it," he said.

He started stroking me, matching the rhythm of his cock sliding into me. His skin was soft and warm, so different than the feel of my own hand. He knew how to stroke me, like he had been with me forever.

Strong upward strokes, putting pressure on the ridge of my head, and slow, soft downward strokes, using my precome as lube. The rhythms started to increase.

"I want us to come together. Let me know when you're ready to shoot."

It only took a few minutes, and I was there.

"I'm. Gonna. Come." It took all my willpower to get those words out.

"Yeah, Bello. Let it go." Colby urged me on, and I felt the orgasm building and building. Suddenly, my prick let go, and I sprayed several loads onto my stomach. At the same time as I was exploding, I could feel Colby coming inside of me again.

He leaned forward and kissed me again before rolling off of me and lying next to me. He put one hand on my come-soaked stomach, rubbing it in.

"That was pretty good, Cristian."

"Oh yeah."

"We both need to shower. Shall we conserve water?"

I looked at him, shaking my head no. "No. Not yet, anyway. Breaking one rule is all I can handle for now."

Colby laughed and walked to the bathroom. I lay there, smelling the scent of sex and wondering what the hell I was doing. There was no way this would end well.

When Colby was out of the shower, I climbed in. His scent was still on the bar of soap and I loved the idea of rubbing it all over my nude body.

When I got out, Colby was half dressed. "I need to borrow a shirt." I laughed as I remembered him tearing his shirt in half in the heat of passion.

I went to my closet and threw a T-shirt to him. The shirt fit me perfectly, but it was stretched to the maximum on Colby because of his mass.

I got into the freezer and pulled out a frozen pizza. I threw it into the oven and leaned against the island. Colby had taken a seat on the other side. He reached out and grasped my hand.

"What are we doing, big guy?"

"Do we have to label it?"

"I just want to be on the same page. I can't promise commitment or monogamy. The head on my dick leads me more than the head on my shoulders. I don't want to hurt you."

"I don't expect a commitment or a promise of anything. I just want to be able to spend time with you, without pressuring you for more than you can give. So let's take this one day at a time. Deal?"

"Deal," I agreed.

COLBY left for work, and I headed to Renown to see Gabe. I was glad to see there was a cop posted at the door. It was a young rookie cop I had met once or twice—Simpson. A cute guy with dark eyes, but he was married, and I was sure we didn't play on the same team.

He recognized me and greeted me with a firm handshake. Even though he knew me, he checked my ID against a list of few people who were allowed to see Gabe.

Gabe was awake and alone. He beamed when he saw me, and I couldn't help but do the same.

"It's good to see you're doing better, kid," I said.

"It's good to be feeling better, man."

I grabbed the chair and scooted near his bed. "How's Violet and Victor?"

"Victor's doing great. He's handling all this real well."

"And Violet?"

Gabe paused. "We weren't exactly doing great before this happened. I mean, we been together for awhile, but mostly it's been for my boy. I played around on her, with the hustling and with other chicks. I'm pretty sure she's done her fair share of fooling too.

"Do you love her?"

"I don't know, man. I ain't never really had anyone love me, so I ain't sure how it feels."

"You're a good kid. You'll figure it out. And even if you and Violet don't stay together, you can still be a good father."

"Hell yeah. I ain't gonna take off like my daddy did. I ain't seen him since I was three years old. Don't really care if I ever do. I'm gonna be the best damn dad I can be. This thing here just helped to realize I was making some wrong choices, some really bad choices. I'm gonna get my life turned around."

"Good for you, kid. I know you can do it."

"It's because of you, Flesh."

"Me? You wouldn't be in the hospital if it weren't for me."

"Maybe. But you were cool with me when you didn't have to be."

We sat silent for a moment. I didn't want Gabe to emulate me, but I didn't know how to say that to him without hurting his feelings

Gabe reached out and grabbed my hand and squeezed it gently. A few seconds later, he spoke.

"Man, I am so fucking horny." We both chuckled. He pulled back the sheet to reveal a large erection.

"What did the doctor say about sexual activity?" I asked.

Gabe sighed and pulled the blanket back over himself. "He said I should wait. If I strain too hard I could hurt myself."

"Rain check on the fun, then, kid." He smiled at me.

I HAD just stepped out of the hospital when Colby called.

"Cristian. Phil Hunter, my investigator, just got some good info. Can you meet us at your place?"

"I'm on my way there now, big guy."

"Give us fifteen minutes."

Colby arrived first. We had enough time for a quick kiss before Phil showed up.

Colby introduced us. "Cristian, this is Phil Hunter."

We shook hands, and I could see Phil was sizing me up. I probably didn't fit his idea of a queer. I'm sure he didn't know Colby was gay and wondered how surprised he would be if he knew.

Phil sat in my recliner while Colby and I sat on the couch.

"Tell us what you found out, Phil," Colby said.

"I've been following O'Reilly for a couple days now. It wasn't hard at all. He don't do a whole lot. He goes to Suzie's a lot. Goes into one of the back rooms and is there for awhile. Not sure what he's doing back there, jacking off to porn flicks, I guess."

I smiled because I knew exactly what he was doing. Suzie's is the Walmart of adult toy stores. It has every kind of sex toy, movie, or book you could ever want. There's a hallway with video booths on both sides. The back two booths on the left hand side are the most used. Those rooms share a glory hole. O'Reilly was there to either get his dick sucked or to suck someone else's. It's the place for closeted men to go for some quick, anonymous action.

"He doesn't have many friends, doesn't go see anyone, and no one comes to visit him. But for the past couple days he's been visiting Pryor's church. And it was at weird times, early morning or late at night, when there was no one else. He always wore a hat pulled down over his eyes.

"I thought the whole thing seemed weird, so I snuck in the church one day and hid after everyone else but Pryor left. Sure enough, O'Reilly showed up and went into Pryor's office. They left the door open. I guess they figured no one was there to catch them. Probably not the best idea because they were making so much noise they wouldn't have heard anybody coming."

"What were they doing?" Colby asked.

Phil hesitated like he was embarrassed to say what they were doing. Of course, I knew what the answer was, but I wanted to be sure.

"They were doing… queer shit. You know, sucking each other's cocks. Butt fucking."

"You watched?"

"Yeah, not 'cause I liked it or anything. I mean, I got nothing against fags, but it's just not my thing. I watched to make sure it was Pryor and O'Reilly."

"Was it?" I wondered.

"Yeah, it was them." He handed us a manila envelope. We opened it and found several pictures showing Pryor and O'Reilly engaged in various sexual activities.

"Thanks, Phil," Colby said as we all stood. "I'll get in touch about our next step."

"You got it, Mr. Maddox." He shook both our hands before he left.

"This is awesome," I said.

"You know it's nothing we can use in court, right?"

"Yeah, I know. But at least we know we're on the right track."

"I have an hour before I have to go to a meeting. Can you think of anything we can do for an hour?"

"Hell yeah." I smiled, flipped around so I was sitting on his lap, and kissed him hard. His hand went to the back of my head, massaging my scalp as he pulled me closer toward him. We kissed hard. I don't think I would've ever stopped if I hadn't had to take a breath.

We stared into each other's eyes as I ran my fingers through his hair. His hand slipped under my shirt, caressing my back. He pulled me toward him, and we kissed again. He gave me pecks across my cheek and to my throat, giving me shivers as he bit and sucked at different spots on my neck. He pulled my shirt off and threw it over the back of the couch. He pushed me back a bit so he could pinch my nipples, making them hard. I shivered again as he leaned forward to gently suck on my left nipple. I moaned as he gently blew on my nipple before biting it softly.

The heat between us was amazing. I reached toward the bulge in his pants, but he grabbed first one hand, then the other, and forced them behind my back. With just one of his large hands, he grabbed both of mine and continued torturing me with the suck, blow, bite technique on my nipples. He manipulated my body expertly, and I couldn't do anything but sit there and revel in the tingling sensations.

"Take your clothes off," he said. I climbed off of his lap and quickly stripped. He did the same, sat down, and pulled me onto his lap again. With one hand he grabbed both shafts and began to stroke them together. The other hand grabbed the back of my neck and pulled me into a vigorous kiss. He increased the strokes, and I couldn't hold back. I moaned into his mouth as I felt myself erupt. He started to pull back as he did the same, but I grabbed the sides of his head with both my hands and kept the kiss going. I kept kissing him even as I felt his body relax.

Colby wrapped his arms around me well past when we had both gone soft. I buried my face in his neck, and he rubbed my back.

"I need to clean up," I said, and I climbed off his lap. I walked into the bathroom and used a hand towel and warm water to wash up. Colby, still naked, stepped in as I stepped out. I grabbed my pants and had just zipped up when there was a knock on the door. "We got company," I called out to Colby, hoping he heard me over the running water. I peered through the peep hole and saw Lex.

"Lex," I said as I opened the door. "What're you doing here?"

"I came by to see how you're doing, Cris."

Colby walked out of the bathroom still naked as the day he was born. I guessed he hadn't heard me.

"So what are we going to do for dinner tonight?" He stopped when he saw Lex and quickly covered himself with his hands.

"Oh. Hello, Lex."

Lex smiled the biggest smile I had ever seen. "Hello, Colby. It's so nice to see you." She placed a special emphasis on the word "see" as she glanced at his crotch.

She turned to face me, still smiling from ear to ear. "You're coming over for dinner at my place tonight."

"I don't know if I can make it."

Lex waved her hand. "I wasn't asking you. I'm telling you. Be there at seven." She turned and opened the door. "Colby, you're coming too." She walked out, closing the door behind her.

"I guess we have plans for dinner tonight, huh?" Colby laughed.

"You don't have to go," I said.

"No, I don't think Lex would be happy if I didn't show up. I guess I'm coming out to her and Kenny. You don't think she'll tell anyone else?"

"No. She's excellent at keeping secrets. I would've ended up telling her sooner or later anyway."

While Colby was still taking in what had just happened, I tackled him to the floor. I had the advantage for only a minute, and then he flipped me and was on top of me, holding my hands down and kissing me.

COLBY and I were at Lex's place at 7 p.m. sharp. She opened the door and greeted us both with bear hugs. Colby was visibly nervous, something I hadn't seen on him before.

Kenny greeted us with firm handshakes. "Glad you guys could come."

I looked at Lex. "I don't think I had much of a choice." We all laughed.

"Kids are in the living room," Lex said. "Dinner's almost ready."

"What's for dinner?" I asked.

"Spaghetti."

"Awesome. My favorite."

"I know," she said as she walked into the kitchen.

The kids—Ariel, twelve, and Henry, nine—were playing a video game, but they dropped their controllers when they saw me.

"Uncle Cristian!" they said in unison, and both ran to me, showering me with hugs and kisses.

"Hey, kids. What's happening?"

They both began talking to me at the same time. Ariel talked about a boy she had a crush on, and Henry talked about a cartoon show. Kenny and Colby were talking, and I tried to listen to what they were saying while also talking to the kids.

"How's the job going, Colby?" Kenny asked.

"Good."

"Glad to hear it."

They sat quiet for a moment, obviously trying to ignore the big, gay elephant in the room.

"So... you're gay," Kenny said.

"Yep, I'm gay." Colby smiled.

"How long?"

"How long have I been gay? My whole life."

"I mean how long have you known you were gay?"

"Since I was a teenager."

"So even in college?"

"Yeah, Kenny. I knew I was gay in college when we were roommates."

"But you went out with all those women. You had sex with them in our room."

"I was trying my damnedest not to be gay. I slept with women trying to prove to myself, and everyone else, that I was straight. But even then I was sleeping with guys. All the women in the world couldn't have taken away my desire for guys."

"But you dated some hot women."

Colby smiled. "I know."

"I never would've guessed," Kenny said.

"To be honest, man, you were pretty busy having fun and getting laid yourself. You didn't really pay a lot of attention to what I was doing."

"I can't deny that," Kenny admitted.

"Is it a problem, Kenny?"

Kenny looked at Colby. "A problem. Because you're gay? Of course not. I got no problem with anybody being gay. I just never would've guessed. We spent all that time together back then, and I never even suspected. But I never would've guessed Cristian was gay unless he was out."

They were quiet for a moment before Kenny spoke. "Hey, Colby, I got a question."

"Yes?"

"All that time in college, did you ever think about trying to hook up with me?"

I had to do my best not to burst out laughing, and I could see Colby was doing the same. It took a moment for Colby to be able to speak.

"No, Kenny I never thought about hitting on you."

"Why not? What was wrong with me? Wasn't I good-looking?" Kenny was obviously offended. This time neither Colby nor I could hold in the laughter. Kenny stared at us, clueless.

"Kenny, I knew you were totally and completely straight. I don't go for straight guys. But if you had been gay, I would've been all over you."

"Okay," Kenny said, his self-esteem successfully restored.

"So we're good?" Colby asked.

"Of course."

Just then Lex walked in and smiled at all of us.

We all stood up.

"Kenny was pretty shocked when I told him about you, Colby. But I had my suspicions."

"You did?" Colby asked, astonished.

"Yeah, I thought your relationship with Annabeth never seemed real."

We all laughed.

"Dinner's ready," she said. "Let's eat."

The spaghetti was top rate, as usual.

Over dinner, Lex told me a little about what was happening at the precinct and about Bailey, her temporary partner.

"I can't wait until you get back to work, Cris."

"If I get to come back," I corrected.

"You will come back, Cristian," Colby said.

Later, Kenny and Colby were talking in the living room while Lex and I talked alone in the kitchen.

"So what's up with you and Colby?"

I looked at her and grinned. "He's a great lawyer. I'm sure he's gonna help me get off."

"I think he already did that—help get you off, I mean." She roared with laughter, and I couldn't help but join in.

"Seriously, Cris. What's happening with you two?"

"He says we got chemistry. So we're exploring that. No commitments, no promises of fidelity, nothing more than great sex."

"He's a great guy. He could be very good for you."

I looked away. "I don't think I can handle anything that good."

"Cris, you deserve the best."

"No, I don't. I don't deserve anything close to the best. Colby deserves the best, and that ain't me. He can do way better than me."

She had a sad look on her face, and I decided I didn't want to discuss the subject anymore, so I changed the subject to the kids. She knew what I was doing and let me do it.

Colby drove me home around ten.

"Want to come in?" I asked.

"I wish I could, Cristian. But I have a 6 a.m. meeting."

"That's cool." It wasn't cool, but what else could I say?

Before I got out of the car, Colby pulled me into a deep kiss.

"Good night, Bello."

"See ya, big guy."

Chapter Fifteen

WHEN I woke up Tuesday morning, I desperately wanted to call Colby and had to force myself to not do it. Instead, I headed to Renown to see Gabe again. Simpson was standing guard again, and again he checked the updated list to make sure I was still on the list to see Gabe. When I walked in, I could see Gabe wasn't feeling well.

"You in pain, kid?"

"No, not physically, anyway. Violet and I had a big fight last night. I'm pretty sure we're over."

I pulled the chair up next to his bed.

"Sorry, kid. What happened?"

The kid paused for a moment. "I told her I loved her, but that I was in love with someone else."

That certainly surprised me. Gabe hadn't mentioned another girl.

"Who is she?"

"Not a girl."

"Not a girl? A guy?"

"Yeah."

"What's his name?"

He looked at me like I was being stupid.

"You don't know?"

"Of course I don't know. How'd I know?"

"Cuz it's you. I'm in love with you, Flesh."

"Me?"

"Yeah, you. You been nicer to me than anyone in my entire life. Letting me sleep at your place and not expecting anything from it. Doing what you did to that guy. Paying for my medical bills."

"Kid, you got your whole life ahead of you. I ain't no one to fall in love with. You don't know anything about me. Fuck, you don't know anything about yourself."

"I know enough about you and enough about myself to know that I want to be with you. Fucking you was awesome."

"Yeah, the sex was hot, kid. But hot sex doesn't equal love. You still like pussy, so how can you think about tying yourself down with any guy, especially me? And if you are gay, that's cool, but there are so many guys out there to meet and fuck."

"I don't need other guys to fuck, or we can go fuck them together."

"Kid... Gabe, you don't know what you want or need. But trust me, you don't want me."

He reached out and grabbed my hand. "I do want you, Flesh. I want you so much it hurts."

I pulled my hand away and could tell he was hurt. I realized that there was no easy way to let the kid down. I was going to have to hurt him, and I hated that idea. "Look, kid," I said as I stood up. "I like you. You were a good fuck, but that's it. I'm not out for any kind of commitment or even an open relationship. If you want a hook-up give me a call anytime, but that's it."

Gabe's face dropped, and I felt horrible, but I knew I was doing the right thing.

"But I'm in love with you."

"And I'm not in love with you, kid. Sorry, but I'm not."

"Get the fuck out of here, Flesh."

I just stood there and watched the kid's heart break. He looked up at me and screamed, "I said get the fuck out of here. I don't want to see you, ever."

"Sorry, kid," I said as I walked out.

Simpson said bye to me, but I didn't acknowledge him.

I CALLED Colby.

"Hey, Cristian," he answered.

"Hey, big guy, you busy right now? I could use some company."

"I can spare an hour, want to meet at Starbucks?"

"See ya there," I replied.

I got there first, but Colby arrived just a few minutes later. I already had his coffee waiting for him.

"What's up?" he asked.

"I didn't have a good morning."

"What happened?" Colby reached across the table and grabbed my hand for a few seconds.

"I went to see Gabe. He told me he's in love with me."

"Uh oh."

"Yeah, it wasn't good. I tried to let him down gently, but he wasn't listening."

"So what did you do?"

"I did what I had to do. I broke his heart. I told him I didn't love him and only wanted him for a good fuck. The kid was devastated, big guy. Totally heartbroken."

"You did what you had to do, Cristian. Gabe is young. He'll get over it."

"Yeah, I know. But that doesn't make me feel any better right now."

"This is a side of you I've never seen."

"What are you talking about?"

"You're showing some feelings."

I tried to hide a smile and ended up blushing.

"I care about the kid. I was hoping we would've been able to stay friends. But it doesn't look like that's going to happen. If I get out of this murder charge, it'll be because of him."

"Maybe he'll forgive you, and you can be friends."

"I doubt that's gonna happen."

"Hello there." I heard a female voice behind me. I turned and recognized Annabeth. With her was a short white woman with blonde hair that reached to her shoulders.

Colby and I both stood. He hugged Annabeth and gave her a peck on the cheek.

"Hello, Hillary," he said. I realized she was Annabeth's girlfriend. The two of us were the secret lovers.

"Hello, Annabeth," I said. I shook hands with Hillary. "You must be Hillary, I'm Cristian."

"I know who you are," she said as she shook my hand. "It's good to finally meet you."

Annabeth and Colby sat close to each other, slipping right into their dating personas.

"You'll get used to it," Hillary said in a low voice.

"Get used to what?"

"Seeing the two of them together. It used to bother me, but it doesn't anymore."

"He can do whatever, or whoever, he wants. It's not like this is some committed relationship or anything."

"Whatever you say," she said with a smirk. She had a look on her face like she knew something I didn't.

Annabeth and Hillary left, and Colby said it was time for him to head back to work. We said good-bye, and I went into the bathroom to take a piss. I was standing at the urinal, just finishing up, when Colby came in. He took a quick peek around to make sure we were alone then grabbed me and pulled me into a deep kiss, reaching down to give my cock a squeeze.

"I'll see you tonight, Bello," he said as he walked out of the bathroom, leaving me breathless.

I FIGURED the day couldn't get any worse, but rather than tempt fate I decided to hang at home and chill in my recliner. I was watching an episode of *Reno 911!*, laughing my ass off, when Lex called on my cell.

"What's up?" I said.

"You home, Cris?"

"Yeah."

"Turn the channel to any news station. You won't believe what's happening."

I hit a few buttons on the remote and landed on a local station. I saw Pryor standing at the pulpit in his church, and the man was crying. Not just a few tears running down his face, but full on blubbering.

"I'll call you back, Lex." I shut the phone and turned up the volume on the TV.

Pryor was speaking in a hushed tone as he looked skyward.

"I have sinned against you, my Lord; I am a liar and a sodomite."

"Holy shit, he's pulling a Jimmy Swaggart." I watched the confession in awe.

"I have broken my marriage vows, lied to my beloved wife and sons, lied to the congregation, lied to myself and most importantly I have lied to my Lord. As a young man I engaged in homosexual activities, a fact for which I am not proud. I accepted the Lord Jesus Christ as my Savior when I became an adult and swore to never return to those evil ways. But I fell, my beloved people. I fell into the mud, and I wallowed in it. I wallowed in the evils of homosexuality, consorting with liars, thieves and whores."

I snorted. "I'm not a thief or a liar, so I guess that makes me a whore."

Pryor continued as he wiped the tears from his eyes. "I was tempted and succumbed to that temptation. The sins of the flesh were hard to avoid, and I was seduced by the wicked men who condone and support homosexuality. I tried to cover my lies with more lies until I decided I could lie no more. And today I admit to everyone, my family, my congregation, my loved ones and my Lord that I am a sinner. I have confessed to my wife and sons, and by God's grace, they have forgiven me."

Right on cue, Pryor's wife and two sons walked to his side, and they all embraced each other. After the short embrace, Junior held Pryor's right hand, while Madeline held his left. The second son stood next to his mother.

"And now I ask my congregation to forgive me. Without you, I am nothing. You, my beloved people of this fine city, have listened to and supported me for years."

People from the audience started to shout out, "We forgive you, Pastor" and "We love you." I wondered if it was all staged and there were teleprompters telling the audience what to do and say.

"Thank you, my people, thank you," Pryor called out as he reached his hands out to the people. "And now I must ask forgiveness of the Father, the Son, and the Holy Ghost. Forgive me, Father," he cried as he fell to his knees, his hands raised in the air. "Forgive me, Jesus. I ask that your precious blood wash and cleanse me."

People started chanting hallelujah, praise God, and other things. With his hands raised in the air, Pryor started shaking and moaning. He repeated, "Thank you, my Lord" over and over again.

Then suddenly everyone was quiet, again making me think there were Teleprompters for the audience. Pryor stood with the help of his son and wife. He was shaking and crying.

"I have felt the beauty of God's forgiveness wash over me. Jesus's blood has cleansed me of my sins."

"Oh my fucking God," I said.

"But the Lord has told me there is a price I must pay for my sins. I must step down as the leader of this congregation and Pryor Ministries."

People in the audience stood to their feet yelling, "No," "Don't go," and "Don't leave us, Pastor." Pryor quieted everybody with a wave of his hand.

"It's okay, my children. I am willing to do what the Lord requests of me, and you will have a new shepherd to lead the flock. God spoke to me just now telling me that my beloved son, Joseph Junior, will step up."

Everyone, even Junior, Mrs. Pryor and the other son, acted in total surprise. Like they hadn't discussed this ahead of time.

"Is anybody buying this load of horse shit?" I wondered.

Junior got the mic and spoke.

"This is such a surprise. I never expected this. I'm, I'm... speechless."

The audience laughed, and Pryor stepped up to his son and said "Speak from your heart, Son."

"Thank you, Father," he said to Pryor, and then he looked upward. "And thank you, Father. I humbly accept what the Lord has instructed. I will take over as pastor of this congregation and the leader of Pryor Ministries."

Pryor stepped forward, grabbed his son's hand, and lifted it into the air, like Junior had just won a boxing match.

I had had enough and flipped off the TV.

"Bullshit." Having heard Junior's anger at his father in the hospital, I was sure Junior had forced his father to step down.

My phone rang again. I was expecting Lex, but it was Colby.

"Did you just see that?" he asked.

"Fucking amazing, wasn't it. Pryor's acting like he decided totally on his own to come forward, when we both know it was your press conference that gave him no choice."

"He's a piece of work," Colby uttered.

"I don't see how anybody could possibly believe a word he said."

"A secretary here in the office cried the whole time. She said Pryor is an awesome man of God."

"Fucking unbelievable."

"I'll bring Chinese for dinner, okay?" Colby said.

"Whatever you want, big guy."

"I want you, Bello."

"Me and sesame chicken." I laughed. "Good combination."

BY THE time Colby got there with the Chinese food, I was starved. We scarfed down the food while watching *Gone with the Wind*.

When the food was gone, Colby turned to me.

"We need to talk about your case."

I had kind of put my case out of my mind. It was enough dealing with Colby and whatever it was that we were doing, as well as Gabe. I had almost forgotten there was a murder charge over my head. "Good news, I hope," I said.

"I'm afraid not. Phil can't find anything about Moxley. He just can't get close enough to him to find anything out. I still haven't got my hands on all the evidence. I keep getting excuses about the journal. I filed a motion today for Cahill to provide the journal ASAP. My medical techs have poured over all the forensic information and can't find anything concrete to clear you. There's nothing to say that you didn't kill Sanchez."

"There's nothing saying I did, either, not even a motive," I said loudly.

"I agree, it's a purely circumstantial case, but guilty verdicts have happened with less than what they have against you."

"Thanks for the cheery news, big guy." I stood up and walked around the couch. "Damn it!"

Colby stood, walked to me and stood behind me. He grabbed my shoulders. "We'll figure this out, Cristian. I promise you won't hang for this."

I broke away from his grip. "You can't make that promise. You could be the best lawyer in the world and still lose this case."

I leaned up against the window, looking out over the city. Colby walked up behind me again and wrapped his arms around me. He didn't say a word, just leaned his head against my shoulder. Damn, it felt good, and that pissed me off.

"Get the hell off me. I don't need you to comfort me like I'm a goddamn baby." I pulled away from him, and I could see the hurt in his eyes.

"You can be such a hard-headed asswipe, do you know that, Cristian?"

I wanted to laugh at the comment, but I was trying too hard to be pissed.

"Go to hell!" I said as I pushed him away. He grabbed my arm and pulled me against him, wrapping his arms around me in a tight bear hug.

I tried my best to break out of his grip, but he had my arms so tight against me that I couldn't get a hand free. I did manage to move the two of us around.

"Calm down, Cristian!"

"Fuck you!"

We ended up near the couch, and I threw my weight so we went over the couch and landed on the floor with me on top. The fall broke Colby's grip and knocked the air out of him. I used the opportunity to grab onto his hands, holding them down with all my weight.

Colby smiled. "You got me down for once. Good job. But can you keep me down?" He started to wiggle and break my grip, and I could think of only one thing that might stop him.

I leaned down, put my lips to his, and kissed him as hard as I could. I was right; he stopped squirming and gave in to my kiss. His mouth opened and I slid my tongue in, licking the roof of his mouth. I also started rubbing our cocks together. We were both rock hard.

"Looks like you're staying down," I said. "Except for this." I rubbed against his dick. He smiled a wide smile.

"You got me, Bello." I could tell he loved it. I pulled both his hands over his head and used one hand to keep them there. Using my free hand, I unbuttoned his shirt, exposing his gorgeous, brawny chest. I bent down and bit his left nipple until he squirmed. Then I gently sucked it.

I turned to his other nipple, repeating the motion, bite, then suck. I licked down his stomach as far as I could go, then reached down, unzipped him and fished his cock out of his boxer briefs.

I used the precome as lube and softly stroked him. I pulled out my own stiff prick, wrapped my hand around them both as best I could and started stroking.

"Oh, damn, Cristian. That's incredible."

I leaned down and kissed him again, releasing my grip on his hands at the same time. He grabbed my face in his hands and kissed me harder, then turned my face to the side to bite my neck and suck on my earlobe.

I continued stroking our cocks together as his hands roamed all over my body, sliding under my T-shirt to playfully tweak my nipples. He grabbed my pants and pulled them down so he could reach my ass. He played with my ass cheeks, and then started rubbing my opening with his finger.

I leaned forward to grant him better access. He slipped a couple fingers into my mouth, and I sucked on them, getting them nice and wet. Then he slid first one finger, then two into my ass. The sudden entrance took my breath away, and I let his digits sink into me.

He started probing my ass, finding my prostate and rubbing it.

"Oh yeah," I moaned.

In one quick move, Colby pulled his fingers out of me, grabbed my hips and scooted me forward and placed his cock in my ass cheeks.

"I've got to fuck you, Cristian. Sit on my cock and ride me."

I quickly stood up and pulled away from him, stuffing my already wilting cock back into my pants. The sudden movement took Colby by surprise, and he lay there for a second before speaking.

"What the hell was that about?"

"I don't do that position."

"You don't do that position?" Colby stood and zipped up. He walked up to me and wrapped his arms around me. I started to pull away but let him hold me.

"Why?" he asked.

"It's just one of—"

"One of your rules," Colby interrupted, and I could feel him smiling.

"Yeah," I said. Rule number five.

"And you're not going to tell me why you have that rule are you?"

I shook my head.

"Okay," he whispered in my ear. "It's okay. We have plenty of other ways to make love."

He reached into my pants and brought my cock to life again. I leaned back as he stroked me while biting my neck at the same time. He pulled me over to the couch, yanked down my pants and started fingering my hole again. I reached into the couch cushions, where there was a bottle of lube, and handed it back to him. He squirted some lube on his fingers and rubbed it into me, then squirted some on his dick. I bent over and felt the head of his cock start to slide in. As soon as the head was in, I pushed backward, taking every last inch.

"Now fuck me, big guy."

"You got it."

He was rough in the way that I like it, but I could still feel the gentleness that was part of him. He slammed it into me, and it took only a few minutes for me to shoot all over the back of my couch.

Seconds later, Colby unloaded into me. He pulled out, turned me around, and kissed me deep.

"You're an awesome fuck, Bello."

"Thanks, you ain't so bad yourself."

"Shower with me?" he asked.

I shook my head no.

"Not breaking any rules tonight, are we?"

I laughed. "Sorry."

"I guess a sleepover is out of the question, then."

"Afraid so," I replied. Colby just shook his head and walked into the shower, ditching his clothes as he went.

We watched a little more TV after we showered. It was just before midnight when we both reluctantly said good-bye. I knew I was getting close to breaking another of my rules, and I hated that. I decided I needed to do something to make sure that didn't happen. I decided I needed to get fucked by someone else. That would mean I wasn't exclusively sleeping with Colby. I told myself a couple fucks or blow jobs from strangers would put my head back on straight.

I threw on some clothes and headed to Steve's. Steve, the owner, was working.

"How you doing, Flesh?"

"Not bad. Just looking for some fun."

"Got a good crowd tonight," Steve said. "Good mix of ages, races… and sizes." He shot me a smile.

"Good to hear." I grabbed my key and towel and headed for my room. I was quickly naked and walking around. Steve was right: there were lots of open doors, a few trolls, but a good mix of ages.

"Flesh," I heard a thick Italian accent call out to me—Gino.

I stepped backward a few steps and saw Gino lying on his back, stroking a nice thick, uncut piece of meat.

"Hey, Gino. Using one of your free nights?"

"Yeah. Good crew here tonight. I already blew two guys and fucked another. I'm horny as hell. Your ass is looking pretty good."

"Thanks, I might take you up on that. I want to get a good look around first."

"Yeah, always gotta check out what's available, huh?"

"You know it. Okay, Gino. I'm sure I'll see you later." I walked out, then thought of something and stepped back into his room.

"Hey, Gino, I got a question."

"What's that?"

"What does Bello mean?"

"Why're you asking that?"

"It's something a friend of mine keeps calling me. He won't tell me what it means but says he learned it from his Italian nanny."

Gino smiled. "This guy who calls you Bello, he a hottie?"

"Yeah. He's good-looking."

"Good."

"Why?"

"Bello means beautiful. This hottie is calling you a beautiful boy."

That really surprised me. I was thinking it meant something like stud or sexy. Beautiful, that was different, odd. I considered myself good-looking, maybe even handsome, but not beautiful. Definitely not beautiful.

I walked around in a daze for awhile, not really paying attention to any of the guys. Several of them were checking me out, touching my chest or pinching my ass. I was oblivious to them all. When I did finally wake up from the haze, I remembered I was there to get sucked and fucked.

My moods and desires change from day to day. Tonight, I was looking for an older guy. His body didn't matter, well, it didn't matter that much. He couldn't have a humongous gut and needed at least an average-size cock.

I spotted what I wanted about ten minutes later. He was just a bit shorter than me, with a full head of gray hair and bright green eyes. It looked like he was in his mid-forties. I was walking into the video room as he was walking out. Our eyes met, and he looked me up and down, and I did the same to him. He smiled and nodded his head, indicating he wanted me to follow him. I trailed a few feet behind him, and he looked back several times, making sure I was coming.

When he got to his room, he was fumbling with the key, so I stepped behind him, pressed my body to his, and reached around under his towel to massage a growing shaft.

"I'm Evan," he said.

"I'm horny."

He chuckled. Then he finally got the door open, and we tumbled in. I quickly shut the door behind me, spun him around, got to my knees and started sucking his cock. It went from semi-erect to fully erect very quickly. His cock was long and had a slight upward bend at the tip. He moaned as I sucked him.

I stood, and he got to his knees, pulling my towel off and marveling at my size. He stroked it for awhile, kissing my balls, and then finally taking me into his mouth.

He was a good cocksucker. Very good, in fact. But I kept comparing how he did it to how Colby did it. Colby had different moves, different techniques that made the whole experience totally unique. I tried to push the images of Colby out of my head and concentrate on the hot guy blowing me. But every time I looked at Evan, it was Colby I saw. But it didn't stop with me putting Colby in Evan's place. I started thinking about all the time I had spent with Colby and all the things—sexual and otherwise—that we had done together. Before I realized it I had gone soft.

"You okay, kid?"

"Yeah. Why?"

"It seems like you're not really into this." I looked at my soft cock.

"I'm into it. Just got some shit going on in my head."

"You sure? We can stop if you want?"

"No, let's do this." I decided to forget about the oral sex and get to the anal. "Fuck me, Evan." I lay down on my back and spread my legs.

"Sure," he said. He grabbed a condom and opened it. The sound of the foil tearing struck me as odd. Using a condom had always seemed an essential part of sex, but now that I had been doing it without one, I realized sex was better without one. Actually, I knew it wasn't using a condom, or not using one, that made sex special, it was who you were doing it with that made it special.

I realized coming to Steve's was a mistake as Evan placed his prick up against my hole.

"Wait, I'm sorry. I can't do this," I said as I put my hand on his stomach. I was worried he was going to be pissed. "I'm sorry, Evan. It's not about you. You're a good-looking man."

He grinned at me as he climbed out from between my legs and pulled the condom off. "Go be with the guy you're thinking about."

"How did you know I've been thinking about someone else?"

"Kid, you think I've never been in love before?"

"No, it's not that. I mean, well, there is a guy, but I'm not in love with him. We aren't in love. I like him a lot, but it's not love. Good sex, that's all."

He looked at me and smiled. "Get the fuck out of here."

I grabbed my towel and left the room. I went to my room, got dressed, and prepared to leave.

"Flesh, where're you going?" Gino called out.

"Not feeling well," I said.

"Say hi to the hottie for me."

Steve was equally shocked to see me leaving so soon. He even offered me a refund, but I turned him down.

"I got what I needed," I told him, and I left.

I drove around for awhile, first heading to my place, then toward Colby's, back to mine, and finally back to Colby's. I parked outside his house and sat there for twenty minutes when I was startled by my phone ringing. It was Colby.

"Umm... hello," I answered.

"How long are you going to sit there in your car?"

I looked to Colby's place and saw him at the window.

"Umm...." I didn't know what to say.

"Get in here," he said, and he hung up.

I stepped out of my car and slowly walked to the front door. Colby opened the door when I stepped on the front porch. I stepped in, and he welcomed me with a warm embrace.

"I think I'm ready to break one more rule," I said.

"Which one? Shower? You want to be on top?"

"Sleeping over," I whispered.

Colby smiled. "Good." He took my hand, and we walked to his bedroom. He took off the bathrobe he was wearing and watched me as I stripped down to my boxers. Colby climbed into his big bed, but I stood there for a minute.

"Cristian, get into bed," he whispered as he pulled the covers back.

I climbed into bed, facing Colby with space still between us. Colby covered half the distance, and I slowly covered the rest. He gently kissed me.

"I'm glad you're here," he murmured in my ear. I wanted to say I was glad, too, but didn't.

He lay down on his back, and I pulled myself close to him, nestling myself into his neck and putting an arm on his chest. I played with his nipples.

"Do you really think I'm beautiful?"

Colby chuckled. "Yes, I do. *Molto bello*. Very beautiful."

"You're crazy, big guy. Absolutely fucking nuts."

He didn't say a word, just rubbed my back and kissed my head. I closed my eyes, and it took no time at all to fall asleep.

Chapter Sixteen

I WOKE up turned on my left side with Colby spooned up against me. He snored quietly, and I loved the feel of his warm breath against the back of my neck. I pressed back against him, feeling every inch of his body against mine.

I remained awake but didn't move for almost an hour. He eventually started stirring. After a big yawn, he said, "Good morning, Bello."

"Morning, big guy."

"This is nice." He hugged me, pulling me closer to his warm body.

"Yeah," I replied. "It's kinda weird."

"Weird? Why is that?"

"I've never really done this before. You know, the morning-after thing. I don't really know what I'm supposed to do."

"First of all, there aren't rules. You just do what you want. Second, you've never slept all night with a guy?"

I paused before answering. "Well, I have done it. But it was a long time ago. I was pretty young, and it was more of a business thing than a romantic thing."

Colby leaned up on his elbow so he could look me in the eyes, but I avoided his gaze. "Business? What do you mean by that?" I closed my eyes and didn't answer. I wasn't sure if I wanted to say more or not. That would mean breaking another rule. Rule number six: I don't talk about my past. "Do you mean hustling? Prostitution?"

"I'm sorry. I shouldn't have brought it up. I don't like to talk about my past," I said quietly.

"Another one of your rules?" he asked.

I nodded my head yes. Colby continued looking at me for a moment before lying back down and snuggling up against me again. "I'll be here whenever you want to tell me," he whispered in my ear. "But it doesn't matter what you've done in your past; it won't affect how I feel about you."

I wish I could say that my past didn't affect how I felt about myself, but I couldn't.

Colby and I lay there for several more minutes before I flipped around so we were face-to-face. I leaned forward and kissed him gently on the lips. He gave me the sweetest smile I had ever seen in my entire life, and it turned me on like crazy.

I reached down and grabbed Colby's hard cock and started stroking it.

"Don't start something you don't intend to finish," he told me. I smiled at him and increased the stroking. "What do you want?" he asked me.

"Just this, just you."

"You sure?"

"Absolutely."

We lay there face-to-face as I stroked him, occasionally gently pressing our lips together. It didn't take long for him to shoot onto my hand and stomach. I reached off the side of the bed and wiped my hands off with a towel. His hands traveled over my back and sides, and I ran my hands through his hair for a while.

I decided to break the sweet moment and remind us both that we were in the middle of a bad situation. "How I am gonna get out of this murder charge, big guy?"

He sighed and looked at me for a moment. "We have to find the person who did kill Sanchez, or at least find someone that could've done it to create reasonable doubt. Can you think of anyone that might want to send you away. Any enemies?"

I snorted. "I'm a cop. A damn good cop. I've sent away dozens of people that have vowed to get me back. But I don't get the feeling this is just a case of payback. This feels real personal."

"Are you thinking Pryor is involved in this?"

"I don't know for sure. It's possible Pryor hired O'Reilly and Curtis to scare Sanchez, then O'Reilly went back and killed Sanchez. But I don't think O'Reilly's smart enough to have framed me."

We lay there silent again for a several minutes. He reached out and stroked my head.

"Is that a rule?"

"What?"

"You never top. Is that a preference or a rule?"

"Rule number one, big guy."

"Man, I wish you had hair."

I laughed. "Yeah, you've told me that."

"So you've done it?"

"Done what? Had hair?"

"No," he laughed. "Have you ever topped?"

"Yeah, I have, a long time ago. Goes along with the whole morning-after thing."

"And that brings us back to the rule about not talking about your past."

"Yep."

"Damn, you've got a lot of rules. You need to write them all down someday for me so I can review them every once in a while."

"Smart ass." I laughed as I jabbed him in the ribs. He chuckled again, so I grabbed his ribs and tickled. He burst out laughing like a little girl, and I couldn't help myself—I tickled him mercilessly.

He and I thrashed around on the bed and ended up with him on top of me, holding me down again. We kissed hard and touched each other everywhere, but it wasn't about sex; it was about fun.

COLBY and I ate breakfast—Shredded Wheat—and he got ready for work.

"You can hang out here if you want," Colby told me.

"Thanks, but I think I'll head home."

I had only been home a few minutes when there was a knock on the door. I was hoping it was Colby but it was Lex, which was almost as good.

"Hey, Lex," I said as I opened the door, and she walked in.

"You're in a good mood, Cris."

"Yeah, I'm feeling pretty good."

"Any reason why?"

"Like what?"

"I don't know," she laughed. "Maybe a certain, sexy lawyer?"

"Colby?" I tried hard to act surprised at the idea.

"You can't fool me, Cris. I know you way too well. So you and Colby are together?"

"We're not engaged or anything like that, Lex. Like I told you before, it's just sex, great sex."

"Okay, whatever you say, Cris."

"Are you here just to give me shit, Lex?"

"No, I almost forgot. I wanted to tell you Gabe was released from the hospital this morning."

"What about the charges?"

"Dropped. He was totally cleared."

"That's freaking great!"

"There's more, Cris."

"Uh oh."

"No, it's good news. O'Reilly is under investigation for officer misconduct. He's in trouble for shooting Gabe."

"How did this happen? I know they wouldn't just take the kid's word on what happened."

"Right. There was a witness. A young mother was nearby when she heard a commotion. She peeked through a chain-link fence and saw the whole thing. O'Reilly had a gun pulled on Gabe. Gabe didn't have his gun pulled. She says O'Reilly told Gabe that he should have kept his mouth shut, then shot him. She saw him pull a gun from Gabe's pants and put it in his hand."

"Why didn't she come forward sooner?"

"She says she was afraid O'Reilly might have come after her, but decided she had to come forward with the truth."

"I'm glad this is going to work out for the kid."

"It'll work out for you, too, Cris."

I sighed. "I'm not holding out hope."

"If anybody can do it, it's Colby."

"I agree with you on that one, Lex."

Lex and I talked for a few more minutes before she took off for work.

Less than five minutes later there was another knock on my door. I spied through the peephole and saw Gabe.

"Hey, kid," I said as he came in.

"Hi, Flesh. How ya doing?"

"Me? You're the one that just got out of the hospital. Get in here and sit down."

Gabe slowly walked in and sat down on the couch. I sat in the recliner.

"You feeling okay, kid?"

"Yeah, better than okay, actually. You hear the charges against me were dropped?"

"Yeah, Lex was just here and told me everything. I'm real glad for you, kid."

"You believed me the whole time, Flesh. That means a lot to me, it really does. I never had trust like that before."

"It's nothing. I follow my instincts, and my instincts told me you were a good kid."

We sat there quietly for a few minutes.

"Look, Flesh, about the other day—"

"Don't worry about it, kid."

"No, I need to say it. I'm sorry I got so pissed at you. I was upset, but I didn't have the right to say what I did."

"You always have every right to say what you want. You don't ever need to censor yourself, kid."

"That doesn't give me the right to be a dick. Especially to you, Flesh. You've done so much for me, and I treated you like shit. That's not cool."

"It's okay, kid. I don't stay angry."

"You know those drugs, those painkillers had me all screwed up. I wasn't really in my right mind. They had me all... loopy, ya know what I mean?"

"It's cool."

"What I'm trying to say is that I'm not really in love with you. I mean, I like you and all that, and I think the sex between us was pretty awesome. But it's not love."

"You and Violet work things out?"

"No, not yet. I told her that I been cheating on her with another chick and had fallen for her. I told Violet I ended things with the other girl. We're gonna see what happens between us. I do need to sort out my feelings... if I want to be with girls or guys."

"It doesn't have to be one or the other, you know? There are lots of bisexual guys. They say it's the best of both worlds."

"Yeah, yeah. I know, but I have to figure it out no matter what."

"How you gonna do that?" I asked.

Gabe smirked. "I figure the best way is to have sex as much as possible, with both girls and guys."

"That's a damn good idea, kid," I said, laughing.

"I just really wanted to say I'm sorry, and I hope we can still be friends. And if we can fuck sometime, that would be cool too."

"I'd like to be friends, kid. And we'll figure out the sex thing too."

"Cool." Gabe stood up. "Thanks for listening."

"No problem."

We said good-bye, and I had barely shut the door when there was a knock again.

This time it was who I wanted it to be—Colby.

"Hey." I smiled as I pulled him into my apartment and into a kiss. Damn, it felt so good to kiss him. He pulled me close to his body and returned the kiss.

"I saw Gabe come in and decided to wait for him to leave." Colby walked to the couch and sat down.

"Yeah, he got some good news."

"I heard about the charges being dropped and about O'Reilly being under investigation. That's good news."

"Hell yeah, it is. I was sure the kid was gonna get a raw deal."

"Did he talk about anything else?" I knew what Colby was really asking.

"Yeah, he said he realizes he isn't in love with me. Said the drugs made him loopy, and he was confused."

"And you believe him?"

"Sure, why wouldn't I?"

"Maybe he's just saying what he thinks you want to hear."

"What do you mean?"

"Well, he wants to stay in your life and maybe claiming he isn't in love with you is the way he plans on doing it."

"You're being paranoid. The kid was confused. He's trying to figure out if he's gay, straight, or whatever. That's a confusing time, I'm sure you remember."

"Of course I remember what it's like. I also remember falling in love for the first time. When it was over, it hurt like hell. I was still in love with him for a long time afterward. I told him I wasn't in love with him. I even told myself, but it wasn't true."

"It doesn't matter," I replied. "Even if he is in love with me, I'm not in love with him."

"I just want you to be careful, that's all."

"Always."

We were kissing when my front door suddenly opened—it was Gabe.

"Oh, hey there." He smiled. "I'm sorry. I didn't mean to interrupt you. Wow, this is a scene I never thought I'd see."

Neither me nor Colby knew what to say. We stood there, speechless.

"Flesh, I was just gonna tell you that anytime you want to hook up, just give me a call. Of course, lawyer dude is more than welcome to join us. A threesome would be hot. Call me... anytime."

He pulled the door shut, and Colby and I stood there silent for another minute.

"You think he's going to tell anyone about us, about me?" Colby wondered.

"He's good at keeping secrets. We don't have to worry about him."

"I hope so."

"I need some coffee," I said.

"Starbucks?"

"Sounds great."

WE HAD our coffees and were talking quietly when O'Reilly and a sharp, well-dressed man walked through the door. I was about to get Colby to make a quiet exit, but O'Reilly spotted me. He and the man, who I assumed to be his lawyer, walked toward us. The lawyer was trying to stop O'Reilly, but he wasn't listening.

"You stupid motherfucker," O'Reilly said as he got right into my face. I leaned back and held my temper. I didn't need a public scene.

"What's your problem, Red?"

"What's my problem? My fucking problem is that your gangbanger spic friend is claiming I shot him on purpose."

"Yeah, him and another witness."

"Fuck him, and fuck the witness. It's all lies. I'm being set up." He was getting in my face again, and my hands were clenched into fists.

Colby stood up and addressed the lawyer. "Get your client under control, Hibbs."

Hibbs looked at Colby and shrugged.

"I've been suspended from duty, Flesh. I'm probably gonna lose my job."

"You'll be lucky if you don't lose your freedom, Red. But I'm sure you'll love prison. Lots of guys will like that cute ass of yours."

"Fuck you." Red was right in my face. Colby put his hand on my shoulder, but I was in total control and wasn't going to let this lowlife make me lose it.

"Let's get out of here, Cristian," Colby said softly in my ear. I nodded but didn't say a word.

"I'll get you, Flesh," O'Reilly yelled at me. "You will regret fucking with me. I promise you."

Colby drove me back to his place. "Stay here until I get home tonight, okay?"

"Don't worry, I won't leave."

I LOUNGED on Colby's couch for the rest of the day. I had dozed off when Colby got back with dinner—deli meats and cheeses with French rolls. We chowed down in the living room while watching *Citizen*

Kane. By the time the movie was over, Colby was resting his head on my lap, and I was playing with his hair.

"That's it? The whole movie is about a sled?" I snapped.

"Well, it's more than that. The sled represents his childhood, what he lost when he left his parents."

"When I die the last words on my lips will be 'Fuck me'."

"Somehow, that doesn't surprise me," he said. He stood up and grinned down at me. "You ready for bed?"

"I'm not tired," I said.

"Neither am I," he said with a wink, and he started walking into the bedroom. I chased after him, and we fell in a pile on the huge, soft bed and began tearing each other's clothes off.

After sharing incredible orgasms, Colby and I lay down with me in his arms.

"You going to stay?" he asked me.

"I don't know." I wanted to stay, but one sleepover had been scary enough. I wasn't sure if I should do it again.

"Well, I'd love it if you stayed, Bello. But I won't pressure you. You make the decision."

"Let's just stay in bed for now," I replied. "If I need to leave, I'll let you know."

"Good," he said as he pulled me close. Minutes later, he was lightly snoring, and a few minutes later I was joining him.

Chapter Seventeen

My RINGING cell phone woke me. It took a minute to find my cell, and by that time the caller had hung up. The call log said I had three missed calls and three voice mails. All three missed calls were from the same phone number—one I didn't recognize. The first message was Violet. She sounded desperate.

"Mr. Flesh. Please call me right away."

The second message was from Violet. She said the same thing as the first message but was even more desperate.

Violet was crying almost uncontrollably in the third message.

Mr. Flesh… Cristian. Please call me right away. Please. It's very important. It's about Gabe. Please, I need help."

I slipped into the bathroom to return the phone call and not wake up Colby.

"Violet," I said when she answered. "It's Detective Flesh."

"Oh, my God. Flesh, it's Gabe. He's in trouble."

"What happened?"

"He's missing. He's gone."

"You mean he took off?"

"No, someone took him."

"How do you know that?"

"There's a note."

"What does it say?"

She read it to me over the phone. "'I got your man. Only Flesh can save him. Tell him to come to the construction site east of town—alone.'"

"Is that all it says?"

"Yeah, that's it. What does it mean? Do you know who took him?"

"Yeah, Violet, I know who took him. I'll get Gabe back. I promise."

"Please, Detective, I'm begging you. I love him so much. I can't lose him."

"I'll bring Gabe home." I hung up the phone and stepped out of the bathroom and started gathering up my clothes. I dressed in the dark and watched Colby for a few minutes before leaving, grabbing his car keys on the way out. I thought about waking Colby and asking for his help. But I knew he would try to talk me out of it. I didn't want him there, risking his life. Risking my life was one thing; risking *his* was totally different. Few people would miss me if I was gone. Colby's death would affect a lot more people.

I didn't like going to the scene without a weapon, but I didn't have a choice. I headed to the construction site O'Reilly had specified.

Six months ago, construction of a multi-level office building had been started, then abandoned when the economy took a shit. The site was still there, halfway finished: a skeletal edifice with floors and stairs but no walls.

When I arrived at the site, I couldn't see O'Reilly anywhere. I jumped when my cell rang—it was him.

"Second floor. Use the stairs."

I took the stairs slowly. When I emerged onto the second floor, O'Reilly was there holding a gun on Gabe. Gabe was tied to a vertical beam support. His hands were bound behind the beam, his feet tied directly to the girder. His head hung low; I knew he was unconscious.

"Did you hurt him?" I asked.

He laughed. "So concerned about your precious spic lover. You faggots make me sick."

"Don't forget you're a faggot too."

"Shut the fuck up!" Red screamed at me. "I was drunk, and you confused me."

"Did Pryor do the same thing?"

He looked at me, shocked I knew about that.

"You been with Pryor just recently. I got pictures of him fucking the hell out of you."

O'Reilly glared at me. Our attention turned to Gabe as he groaned and opened his eyes. He lifted his head with considerable effort and focused on me.

"Flesh, what're you doin' here?"

"I came to get you out of here, kid."

"You shouldn't have. I ain't worth it. You're worth a thousand of me."

It broke my heart to hear him say that. "That's not true, kid."

"Aah, you fags are so freakin' sweet," O'Reilly spat.

"What do you want, Red?"

"I want you, Flesh."

"I'll be your captive as long as you let the kid go."

"I don't want him. I want you. I'm gonna make you pay for messing with me."

"I don't care what you do to me. Let him go, and I'm yours."

"No way, Flesh. I don't let him go until you're tied up like the pig you are."

"How do I know you'll let him go once I'm tied up?"

"I guess you'll have to take my word for it. You don't have much choice in the matter, do you?"

He was right, I didn't have a choice. I nodded that I would do what he wanted. He came toward me and told me to turn around. He tied my hands behind my back, and had me back up to a beam in front of Gabe's. He wrapped rope around my chest, stomach and feet, tightening it so I was pressed hard against the beam.

Once I was secure, O'Reilly looked at me and laughed.

"Let the kid go, Red. Be a man of your word."

"You're a goddamn idiot if you thought there was ever a chance I would let him go. He's as dead as you are."

"Let him go," I screamed. "He's got nothing to do with this."

"He's got everything to do with this. I'm gonna make you watch as I beat him to death."

"No, Red. Don't... please."

"Don't beg, Flesh. It's not very sexy."

I was forced to watch as Red grabbed a crowbar, pulled back like he was taking a swing with a bat, and clobbered Gabe's right leg. The kid screamed out in pain, and I begged Red to stop, but he didn't listen. O'Reilly swung again and again, hitting Gabe in the legs, the arms, the chest, even the head. Gabe was unconscious, and I could see blood pooling at his feet.

I struggled to get free. It seemed useless, but I didn't, I couldn't, give up. Suddenly the ropes that secured my feet and stomach to the beam loosened and fell to the ground.

My hands were still tied, but I managed to get my hands in front of me and charged O'Reilly.

He saw me coming and swung the crowbar at me, knocking me across the head and slamming me to the floor. O'Reilly jumped on me and was about to hit me with the crowbar when I made my hands into a fist and hit him across the face, knocking him to the ground.

"Motherfucker," he moaned.

I got to my feet and kicked the crowbar out of his hands. He grabbed my foot and threw me to the ground. Jumping on top of me, he got his hands around my throat and squeezed. I felt the breath leave my body. I saw stars and knew I was going to lose consciousness.

There was a flash of movement from the stairs, and suddenly O'Reilly was off of me. I tried to focus and could only see a dark, broad figure sitting on O'Reilly, repeatedly punching him.

I finally focused enough to see it was Colby furiously beating O'Reilly. I jumped to my feet and ran to Colby, grabbing his shoulder.

"Stop, you're gonna kill him."

"That's what he deserves, Cristian. That's what he was going to do to you and Gabe."

"It is what he deserves, but don't do that to yourself. He's out. Just tie him up."

I could see Colby relax as he stood up. He reached into his pocket and pulled out a pocketknife, cutting the ropes from my wrists.

I threw my arms around him, and he held me in a tight embrace.

"What're you doing here?" I asked him.

"You took the 'vette," he answered. "It has GPS, remember? And it's connected to my cell phone. I borrowed a neighbor's car and used the GPS to track you here." I laughed because I hadn't even thought about the GPS.

"The cops should be here soon," Colby said. "I called them as soon as I saw what was going on."

I ran to Gabe and cut him down. He was unconscious and bleeding badly. Colby tied O'Reilly's hands behind his back.

"C'mon, Gabe. It's not your time to die." I heard sirens and looked up. Colby was standing a few feet from the edge, but a movement off to the side caught my attention. It was O'Reilly. He was awake and racing toward Colby.

"Look out!" I screamed. Colby turned and saw O'Reilly running toward him. He tried to step out of the path, but O'Reilly plowed right into him. I was frozen in one spot as I saw both men fall over the edge and heard them scream simultaneously on their way down. I could picture the two bodies splattered on the ground below. I felt myself shaking.

"Cristian?" It was Colby, shaking me. My mind caught up with the actual events. Colby had managed to avoid O'Reilly. O'Reilly went over the edge alone.

I grabbed Colby, and we fell to the ground with him on top. I grabbed his face and kissed him hard.

"This really isn't the right time for sex, Cristian."

I laughed. "I thought I was gonna lose you."

He smiled. "It's good to hear that you care."

"Yeah, I care."

"That's good enough for now." He was right. Just saying I cared was a huge leap for me, and I wasn't sure if I could ever do more than that.

By the time the cops and ambulance arrived, Colby and I were upright. They took care of Gabe first, rushing him back to the hospital he had just been released from.

Lex arrived a few minutes later than everyone else. She hugged me tightly.

"I'm so glad you're okay."

"Thanks to the big guy here," I said.

"You saved me too," Colby said. "I wasn't paying attention. If you hadn't let me know O'Reilly was up, I would've ended up splattered like he did."

"Lex, what about O'Reilly? Is he dead?"

"Yeah, Cris. He's dead. He broke his neck when he landed. I knew he was a little off, but I never suspected it would be this much."

I filled Lex in on the things Gabe had told me and Colby about O'Reilly taking bribes. "I wonder what else he's been up to," I said.

Chapter Eighteen

GABE went into surgery in the early morning hours of Friday. I stayed at the hospital despite Colby's pleas to go home and sleep. Violet showed up right after I did, and she ran into my arms, crying. I held her tight and calmed her down. We sat down on the floor with her in my arms and fell asleep. I woke before she did but remained there until she started to move. Shortly after she woke, the surgeon came out. We got to our feet and ran to him.

"Gabriel is going to be fine," the doc said. "The internal injuries were all relatively minor, and we were able to repair them surgically. But he does have a broken arm and a concussion. There's also a great deal of soft tissue damage, which only time can heal. It's likely he'll stay unconscious for several days, but there's no reason a strong young man like Gabriel shouldn't make a full recovery."

"Thanks, Doc," I said.

"He's gonna be okay, Flesh." Violet cried as she hugged me again.

An hour or so later, Violet and I were allowed to see Gabe. He looked like shit, bruises everywhere. I sat there with Violet for another hour or so before I headed home and crashed for several hours. Colby woke me up by climbing into my bed. I was out again minutes later.

I SLEPT until eight a.m. Sunday morning. Colby wasn't in bed; he was in the kitchen making bacon.

"Good morning, Sleeping Beauty," he teased me.

I shuffled over to him and gave him a kiss on the cheek. A small smile crept across his face when I did that. That type of thing wasn't something I ever thought I'd want, or like, to do, but it felt surprisingly natural. It felt good to be able to give someone else a little pleasure with such a simple thing. And if I was being honest, the feel of his skin on my lips made me feel good as well.

After breakfast, I went to see Gabe again. I had been sitting alone with him for an hour when Violet and Victor showed up.

"Mistah Fresh, Mistah Fresh." Victor ran laughing to me and gave me a big hug on the leg.

"Hey, little man."

"Up, Mistah Fresh." He put his arms in the air.

I leaned over and picked him up. He wrapped his arms around my neck and squeezed, giving me a wet, sloppy kiss on the cheek. He rubbed my head, which I hadn't shaved for a couple days.

"It not smoove, Mistah Fresh. How come?"

"Been busy," I said.

Violet smiled as she watched us. "Leave Mr. Flesh alone, Victor."

"No, it's okay. He's fine."

Violet pulled up a chair next to me, and I sat down with Victor still in my arms.

"Mr. Flesh, I want you to know I love Gabe. I love him so much. I'm gonna make things work with him, no matter what it takes."

"He loves you, too, Violet. Just remember that no matter what happens."

I stayed at Renown with Gabe most of the day.

I HEADED to Colby's place after leaving Renown. He greeted me at the door with a big smile.

We spent the afternoon watching movies. I was perfectly content to spend all day inside with Colby, but he had other plans.

"We're going out," he said. We had been sitting next to each other on the couch, and he stood up.

"Where?"

"The Chocolate Bar."

"I don't know, big guy."

"I do know. We're going. Go, get ready." When I didn't get up right away, he grabbed my hand and made me stand up. He pushed me toward the bathroom and swatted my ass. "Get in the shower."

When I got out of the shower, Colby stepped into the bathroom, already naked. I moved up to him and wrapped my fingers around his shaft. "Sure you don't want to stay home and do something else?"

He gave me a gentle kiss on the lips. "Later, Bello." He stepped into the shower. "I laid out clothes for you on my bed."

I walked into the bedroom. On the bed was a set of new clothes. He had to have bought them specifically for me since he and I didn't wear anywhere near the same sizes. A quick look at the brand name—Christian Dior—told me what I suspected. These were very expensive clothes.

There was a pair of slacks and a shirt, both in the same shade of dark gray. There was also a pair of silk boxers. I slipped on the boxers, marveling at how nice the soft fabric felt on my skin. The slacks were a perfect fit on my waist. They weren't skin tight, but they accentuated my legs and butt. The shirt didn't have buttons so I pulled it over my head. It had long sleeves and had a V neck that came halfway down my chest. It was one of those shirts you weren't supposed to tuck in, so I let it hang down to the top of my ass.

When I was dressed I looked at myself in the mirror. I had to admit two things. The first was that Colby had impeccable taste. The second was that I looked damn fine. I had once been given clothes this nice, more expensive, even. Well, not so much given, but allowed the unlimited use of. I remembered closets full of the best pants, shirts, shoes, and suits. At the time, I thought I was in heaven. I hadn't realized there was a cost associated with the gifts.

I had come to hate the fancy clothes and expensive gifts when I realized what it all meant. The heaven became like a hell, and I despised myself for allowing it to happen and the men who made it happen. For so long, nice clothes meant another party, hours spent on the floor submitting to every whim of the so-called refined men of society.

But this, these clothes from Colby, meant something totally different. These weren't meant to be anything but a nice gesture with no ulterior motives.

"Look at you," Colby said when he walked into the bedroom with a towel around his waist. "Looking nice, hot stuff."

I smiled at him. "These are nice, big guy. Kind of expensive, though. You shouldn't be throwing away so much money on me."

"It's not throwing it away. I wanted you to have something nice."

"Are you saying I don't have nice clothes?" I joked.

"Cristian, you look good in whatever you wear. You look good in nothing at all. I just wanted to buy you something different than the jeans and khakis you have."

I stepped up behind him, wrapped my arms around him, and kissed the back of his neck.

"Thank you." I blew in his ear.

"You're welcome."

THE Chocolate Bar was packed when we got there. It was one of the places where the rich people of the community went. I had never been there because I would've been out of place in my normal jeans-and-T-shirt attire. It specialized in various chocolate drinks and desserts, but also had a unique dinner menu. Kenny and Lex had come here for their anniversary last year, and Lex said the food was fabulous.

I was sure we wouldn't be able to get a table or that we would be waiting for an hour or so for an open one, but when the host saw Colby, he recognized him right away.

"Right this away, Mr. Maddox."

"They know you here?"

"Constance McPhee, one of the firm's partners, is very good friends with the owner. We bring clients here a lot, and there is always an open table for us."

"Is that what I am tonight—a client?" I teased.

"You know you're more than that."

The host seated us at a table in the back, one of the more secluded and private tables. We weren't surrounded by other people and didn't have to talk as loud to be heard over the conversations of others.

"This is a night for decadence, Cristian. Let's go all out. Order what we want, no worries about calories or costs."

"I can do that."

We started with coffees. Colby had a white peppermint latte—white chocolate melted with minty cream—and I had a West African espresso—cream and dark chocolate.

As an appetizer, we ordered chocolate fondue, using pound cake, pineapple, and strawberries as dippers. Absolutely indulgent.

For the main course, I ordered the Mediterranean chicken with grilled polenta and an artichoke salad, and a Guinness to chase it down. Colby ordered the lamb chops with minted roasted peppers. He ordered a draft beer—Rogue Chocolate Stout.

Colby and I talked quietly, occasionally reaching out to touch one another's hands when we were sure no one was looking.

"This is incredible," I said.

"I agree. The lamb chops are superb. Do you want a bite?"

"Sure. You want to try my chicken?"

"Of course."

We both stabbed bites of our food with our forks and fed it to each other. We had just set our forks down when an older woman with short graying hair came up to our table.

"Hello, Colby."

Colby swallowed down his bite of chicken and quickly stood up. "Constance, how nice to see you." He kissed her on the cheek.

She looked from me to him and then to me again.

"Hello," she said as she stuck out her hand. "I'm Constance McPhee."

"I'm sorry," Colby said quickly. "Constance this is my client, Cristian Flesh."

I stood and shook her hand. "Nice to meet you, Mrs. McPhee."

She laughed. "Please, I haven't been a Mrs. for years. Call me Constance." She turned to Colby. "Enjoying the meal?"

"Definitely," he answered. I couldn't put my finger on it, but there was something about Colby that had changed when his boss showed up. A change in the tone of his voice, even in how he held himself. The aura he was putting off was purely professional.

"Well, I'll let you get back to your... dinner," she said. Colby kissed her on the cheek again. "Good-bye, Constance."

She didn't bother giving me a second glance as she turned and stepped away. Colby and I sat down. He resumed eating, while I stared at my plate for a minute. The sweet closeness between us had been broken and had been replaced by a thick tension.

We finished the meal in silence. "You want dessert?" he asked me. I had been planning on ordering dessert, but now I was in a hurry to leave as soon as possible.

"No, I'm good." He didn't argue with me, just got the check and paid for it. He remained silent on the way home.

Back at his place, Colby flopped down on the couch and turned on the TV. I remained standing and looked at him, expecting him to say something. Finally, he glanced up at me. "What?"

"What the hell was that back at the restaurant?"

"What are you talking about?"

"Are you serious? You don't know what I'm talking about?"

"No, I don't."

"One minute we're enjoying dinner and enjoying being together. Then the snobby bitch shows up, and you're totally different."

"She's not a snobby bitch."

"She acted like I wasn't even there!"

"You're overreacting."

"No, I am not. She looked at me like I was a piece of trash. And you acted like I wasn't even there."

His eyes met mine, and I could see sadness in them. My anger melted, and I sat down next to him.

"I'm sorry, Cristian. I freaked out when I saw Constance. You know I'm not out, especially at work. I was afraid she would see something between us. To me it feels like we radiate attraction between us, and I had to shut that off. I hated doing it. Really hated doing it."

"So that was the fake Colby," I said.

"Not the fake me, just the one I have to be in other people's eyes."

"I don't like that Colby very much. I don't like him at all."

"It's not always an easy choice to come out of the closet. There are hundreds of different considerations."

"Not in my mind. I see it as a choice between being who you are or hiding a part of you."

"I don't see it as so black and white. Was it easy for you to come out of the closet?"

"I didn't come out of the closet so much as I never went into the closet. When I started the academy I just decided not to hide it. I told a couple other cadets I was gay, and the word spread from there."

"And it was just that easy?"

"I never said it was easy. I had to fight a few battles to prove I wasn't a limp-wristed fairy. I eventually got the respect of most of my cadets. I worked as hard as they did, harder than some of them. I also never flaunted my homosexuality or threw it in their faces."

"What did you do for sex? Because I know you were having it as much as possible."

"Of course I was." I laughed. "I'd go to bars or other places. I never hit on other cadets, but quite a few gay or curious ones found their way to me."

"I wish I could be as strong as you." Colby lay his head in my lap, and I ran my fingers through his hair. Colby telling me he thought of me as stronger than him was odd. I had been seeing him as the strong one, so in control of his emotions and desires. I saw myself as the unstable one and him as the stable one. But maybe not everything was as clear cut as I thought.

"Why do you stay in the closet?"

"My career is probably the biggest reason. The firm still has lots of conservative clients. These people would freak out if there was a queer working on their cases. They would either fire the firm, or the firm would fire me."

"So?"

"My career is important to me."

"Start your own firm. You got the money to do it."

"I need a better reputation first. It's not the right time."

"I don't agree, big guy. But it's your choice."

"Thanks," he said.

I CALLED Lex Monday morning.

"What's going on, Lex?"

"Everything Gabe told you about O'Reilly has been confirmed. Apparently, he had also been extorting small businesses for protection money."

"Where'd you learn this?"

"Curtis is back in town. He's talking a little bit at a time. He already told us what he told you the night before he disappeared. Apparently he's had a guilty conscience for a while now. His drinking got out of control because of what was going on. He hadn't been actively participating in O'Reilly's extortion and bribery schemes. He was just looking the other way."

"But he did take money from Pryor?"

"Yeah, and that's when he started feeling guilty about what was happening. When O'Reilly wanted to kill Gabe, Curtis refused to have anything to do with it. I'm positive O'Reilly killed Sanchez. I'm sure you're gonna be cleared soon."

"What should I do?"

"Just stay quiet and wait for us to figure everything out."

"Yeah, I can do that."

And that's what I did. I hung out at my place or at Colby's and visited Gabe every day. Like the doctor said, Gabe remained unconscious, but I didn't have a doubt he would come out of it when he was ready.

Chapter Nineteen

THE biggest news came on the Thursday after O'Reilly's death. I had spent the night at Colby's after two nights alone at my place. I was at Colby's, sitting in the hot tub and just relaxing. I had a feeling things could only get better, and I was right.

Colby had been at work filing motions regarding my case, and I wasn't expecting him back until that evening. So when he showed up in the middle of the day, it was a surprise. He had a big smile on his face, and I knew he had news to tell me.

"What's up, big guy?"

"I've got some good news."

I waited for him to tell me, but he just sat on the edge of the hot tub smiling at me.

"You gonna tell me?"

"I finally got my hands on Sanchez's journal. When I read it, I noticed there were several pages missing. So I called Lex, told her, and she got a warrant to search O'Reilly's place. Guess what they found?"

"The missing journal pages?"

"Some of them at least. Sanchez was planning on blackmailing O'Reilly like he was going to do to you. He had proof that Pryor and O'Reilly were screwing around. My guess is O'Reilly went back, killed Sanchez, and saw the journal."

"Why didn't he take the whole thing?"

"He probably left the other pages so it would give you a motive to kill Sanchez."

"That's possible."

"Possible and highly probable, Cristian."

"Yeah, but...."

"But what?"

"The rest of the cover-up and frame job was major. I just don't think O'Reilly had the brains to pull it off."

"We don't have to worry about that."

"Why?"

"There was enough evidence to point to O'Reilly as being the killer. I went to the judge today with a motion to dismiss the case against you. It was granted, Cristian."

"No fucking way!" I slapped the water.

"The charges against you were dropped today, Cristian. You are a free man."

"No fucking way!" I stood up. Of course, I was sitting in the hot tub naked, and Colby's eyes automatically went to my cock, which was springing to life.

"Damn, Bello. I'm glad to see that the good news hasn't affected your sex drive."

I glanced down at my hardening cock.

"There isn't much that does diminish my sex drive. I freely admit I'm a whore. I think sex is like money—you can never have too much."

"Well, I might put that to the test someday and see exactly how much sex you can handle." Colby laughed. I grabbed him and pulled him into a kiss, pressing my soaking body against his.

He pushed me away.

"Asshole," he said, laughing, "I have to get back to work. I just wanted to break the news in person."

"I don't care." I grabbed his arms and pulled him into the water. He tried to stop himself from going in, but the edge of the tub was wet and slippery, and he fell into the water with me. Laughing and smiling, Colby climbed the rest of the way in, pressing me up against the side and kissing me with his powerful tongue forcing itself past my lips. I gave in and let him take control.

"Stand up," Colby ordered me.

I stood, and he swallowed me completely. I gasped at the sensation of his warm tongue on me. I leaned back against the hot tub, putting my hands on the edge to steady myself while also pushing my hips out.

One hand traveled up my chest to my mouth. I sucked on a couple fingers, then the hand went down between my cheeks and slipped in. Another gasp escaped my lips. It felt like he was deeper in me than anyone else had ever been. He had gone further than I'd known possible. With me in his mouth and his fingers buried in me, it was like we were one whole being instead of two distinct and separate people. The joining of our bodies felt like more than just a sexual act. It was a sharing of bodies, of emotions. It was sensual and sweet, lustful and loving.

I tried to hold back, wanting to prolong the absolutely exquisite sensations, but it was like trying to stop a tidal wave, and I just let out a loud groan. He increased the pressure as the tidal wave crashed over me. When the wave subsided, I pulled him up to me and kissed him hard, tasting myself on his tongue and lips.

I reached down and started to undo his pants.

"No, I've got to go."

"I just want to return the favor." I kept trying to undo his pants. Colby grabbed my hand and moved it away.

"It's not about keeping score or returning favors. I'm happy getting you off, whether I come or not."

"It's what I'm best at. One of the only things I'm really good for."

Colby looked me in the eyes, and I could see that sad look in his eyes again. I looked away, but he lifted my chin and made me meet his eyes.

"That's not true. That's not even close to the truth. Yes, you are an excellent lover, but there is a lot more to you than that. I can see it, and someday you will see it too."

I climbed out of the hot tub. "You better get dressed and get back to work."

Colby followed me into the bedroom as he started to take off his soaking clothes.

"Why would you say something like that, Cristian?"

"Something like what?"

"Don't play stupid. You basically said that sex was the only thing you were good for."

"So?"

"Why would you say that?"

"It's just something someone said to me."

Even though my back was to Colby, I could feel his eyes on me.

"Who? Who said that to you? Because they're wrong."

"It doesn't matter. Forget it."

He stepped up to me and pressed his naked body against mine.

"Who said it? You can tell me."

"Sorry. It's part of my past. Don't forget the rules."

He laughed softly as he pressed his lips to my neck.

"Okay, Bello. I'll drop it."

He kissed my neck and chewed on my ear lobes for a few minutes before he pulled away. We got dressed in silence and said good-bye with a quick embrace.

"Will you be here when I get home?" he asked me.

"Don't know," I answered honestly.

"Okay." I tried not to see the sad and hurt look on his face as he left.

AN HOUR or so later I heard my cell phone ringing in the other room. By the time I got to it, it had gone to voice mail. The voice mail was from Chief Brunson. "Flesh, get to the station immediately."

I didn't return the call, just drove there as fast as I could. There were actually two possibilities of what was going to happen. It was possible that I was going to get my badge back, and I would be a cop again. The second possibility was that I would be fired. Even though the murder charge had been dropped, there was still a chance I wouldn't be reinstated.

I didn't like the idea of being some mall rent-a-cop. For once, I tried to be optimistic.

It was an odd and surreal moment when I stepped into the station. It had only been a few weeks since I had been there, but it felt like years. As I walked in, the other cops acknowledged me with a curt nod, but no one came up to talk to me or to congratulate me on the charges being dropped. In fact, many of them were trying not to meet me in the eyes. Not a good thing.

Chief Brunson's secretary waved me into the office. Lex was in there with Brunson.

"Hi, Cris," Lex said quietly. I started to get that sinking feeling in my gut.

"Flesh," the chief acknowledged.

"Chief Brunson."

"I understand the murder charge against you was dropped."

"Yes, sir."

"Well, that is good news for you. But you understand there could be other issues. You did attempt to interfere in the investigation. "

"Yes, sir."

"We have no choice but to deal with those issues, you understand."

"Yes, sir, I understand."

"Follow me, Flesh. Let's go talk in the conference room."

Fuck. I was sure Internal Affairs was going to have a panel in the conference room. IA didn't believe in innocent until proven guilty, they assumed you were guilty, and it took a lot to prove innocence.

Chief Brunson walked into the conference room a few steps ahead of me, and Lex was a few steps behind me. As I stepped in, Brunson flipped on the lights.

"Surprise!" a chorus of voices yelled out, making me jump.

I looked up and saw a couple dozen cops and other police personnel. And they were all smiling. Even Brunson, and he never smiled.

"What's going on, Chief?"

"What's going on, Detective Flesh, is that you're getting your badge and gun back."

I looked at Lex, and she was smiling too.

"I don't understand," I stammered.

"We're just having a little fun, Cris." Lex wrapped her arms around me, and I hugged her back after a moment.

I turned back to Brunson as he extended his hand. I shook it, and when we released, he handed me my badge and gun.

"Welcome back to the force, Detective."

"Thank you, sir. But what about the other issues?"

"Forget about them," Brunson said, "you were set up by an officer. I think the department owes you more than just your job back. I made sure the IA investigation is totally closed."

"Thank you, sir. Thank you very much."

Then everyone started to surround me. Simpson was there slapping me on the back and shaking my hand. There were officers I recognized, officers I had known for years, and officers I barely knew. And they were all congratulating me and welcoming me back. Before I knew it, I was laughing and smiling, telling jokes and stories.

I was a cop again.

The party started petering out. Brunson told me that I was getting back pay for the time I was off and that I didn't have to report back to duty for a few more days. He urged me to enjoy the weekend and insisted I enjoy a three-day weekend and come back to work on Monday. Lex agreed, and I was basically forced to go along with the idea.

I went home to my empty, quiet apartment and sat there. There was a part of me that wanted to call Colby and tell him what had happened. But there was that other part that was feeling exposed and vulnerable. Colby was seeing a side of me that no one had ever seen before, and I was afraid one of us was going to get hurt.

I made the decision to spend some time alone and enjoy the solitude. Damn, that was no easy thing to do. I couldn't find anything interesting to watch and not even porn could get me excited.

"I need to get out of here," I told myself after less than hour of sitting there.

I packed a few clothes and called Lex.

"Hey, I'm going out of town for a few days."

"Great. Where're you and Colby going?"

"No Colby. Just me. I'm going camping up at Lake Tahoe. I need nature, but I'll be back Sunday."

"Camping? Like camping in a four-star hotel with room service?"

"No, Lex," I said, laughing, "camping with a tent and sleeping bag and all that."

"You don't own any of that stuff."

"I will in a minute. I'm heading to Cabela's right now."

"You sure about this? Why don't you take Colby?"

"No, I need to do this without Colby."

"Cris, don't chase this guy off."

"Lex, I'll call you when I get back. Good-bye."

I hung up before she could say anything else.

At Cabela's, I bought a sleeping bag, a tent, hiking boots, and other stuff. Leaving Cabela's, I headed to Tahoe.

Chapter Twenty

WITHOUT reservations it was difficult to find a camping spot, but I did find one on the North Shore, on the California side of Tahoe. A small spot called Sandy Beach Campground. It included a rest room and hot showers. I was roughing it, but couldn't deal with the idea of not taking a shower.

After setting up camp, I went on a hike. The views were gorgeous, and I encountered few other people. One of the people I did see was a sexy-looking young man with long dark hair and a tight body. He wasn't wearing a shirt and had a hot six-pack. My eyes met his as we walked by each other, and his gaze dropped to my package. I smiled at him, and he smiled back. A few steps after we passed each other, I glanced back and saw that he was walking backward, staring at me. He winked at me before turning around and walking off. I climbed to a beautiful view, sat down in the dirt and grass, and stared out for more than an hour.

I hiked back down, threw on a pair of swimming shorts, and walked a short hike to the swimming area of the camp site. The water was cool, but my body adjusted. I swam back and forth, diving under every so often, and taking in the warm sun. I spread out my towel on the sand and stretched out. A short time later, my sun disappeared. I looked up and saw it was actually being blocked—by sexy six-pack guy.

"Hi." He had a deep, attractive voice.

"Hey there." I covered my eyes to block the sun, so I could get a good look at him. He was wearing a pair of tight shorts that outlined a large package.

"Mind if I sit down?"

"I don't own the beach."

He sat down right in the sand and gazed out on the lake, laughing at the kids playing in the water.

"You're looking kind of hot there, man," he said to me. He emphasized the word hot, and I knew it had a double meaning.

"Wanna take a swim?" I asked. He jumped to his feet and ran into the water, and I followed him. We jumped in with a splash and were soon playing around and accidentally grabbing each other's ass and crotch. It was evident what we both wanted when he grabbed me from behind and pressed his hard-on against my butt. I pushed back, letting him know I wanted the same thing.

We climbed out of the water and dried off on the beach.

"Your place or mine," I whispered to him, and we both laughed.

"Well, I'm sharing my tent. You alone? Or we can find a secluded spot."

"My tent's cool." I imagined he had come here with some friends. I told him where my camping spot was, and he said he'd be there in thirty minutes. We walked part of the trail together before splitting up and going in different directions. I realized I needed to pee, so I headed toward the restrooms. Halfway there, I saw Six-Pack walking into a large camping area. I saw several guys his age sitting around, and a young woman and a small boy running to Six-Pack.

"Daddy!" the little boy, about three years old called out, and Six-Pack picked him up. The woman walked up to him and gave him a big kiss on the lips.

"Hi, honey," I heard her say, "how was your hike?"

"It was good, babe. I met a guy who needs help changing a tire on his trailer. I said I'd go over and help him out in a bit."

"You're such a sweet guy," the woman said, and she kissed the guy again. He patted her on the ass, and she giggled.

I was floored. I don't know why I was so surprised. Of course there were lots of closeted married men, and I had even been fucked by more than a few of them. But I hadn't gotten that feeling from this guy.

I continued walking to the restroom, purposely diverting my walk so I would pass Six-Pack's site.

He was surprised when he saw me walking by. I met him in the eyes and with just a glance he knew that I had watched the little scene with his woman. I walked to the restroom, stepped up the urinal, took out my cock and started peeing. A moment later, a man stepped up to the urinal next to mine. Without looking, I knew it was Six-Pack.

"We still on for later?"

I snorted. "Nah, I don't think so. I can fix my own flat tire."

"Oh, come on. It's not like we're gonna start a relationship or anything; just wanted to fuck, that's all."

"What would your wife say about that?" I looked at him. I'm not sure why I cared. I sure hadn't cared when I was sleeping with Pryor. But being with a man I cared about, being with Colby, made me think about things I'd never thought about before.

"You gotta know how it is. I knocked her up, didn't have much choice but to marry her. I love her. I like pussy, but sometimes I need to be with a guy."

I zipped up and washed my hands. He stepped next to me.

"So what's the deal? We gonna fuck or not?"

"I'll pass. I ain't passing judgment on you or anything like that. I just don't want to get fucked by a married man. Just not what I'm looking for. Sorry."

"You don't know what you're missing." He stepped out. I stayed there for a minute, looking at my reflection in the mirror. He was wrong. I did know what I was missing, and he was miles away in Reno.

I went into town and got a few beers. I returned to my tent and sat down outside and downed several bottles before crawling into my tent and crashing.

I WOKE up around six a.m. Friday and walked down to the beach. The scene was gorgeous, and I wished I wasn't alone. I sat there for a few hours watching the other campers slowly making their way to the beach.

It surprised me how much I missed Colby. I wanted to be with him. Not just for the great sex, but for the person he was. I missed watching movies with him. I missed sitting and talking to him. I missed eating pizza with him. I missed... well, I missed everything about him.

I'd been so stupid. For so long I'd been using the rules to protect me from getting hurt. They were a shield saving me from pain. But I was using those rules to put distance between me and everybody else. Colby had called me on that, and he was right. By avoiding the bad things in life, I was also avoiding the good things in life.

He had done so much for me. Not just helping me on the case, but helping me see something about myself and something about life. Colby had awakened something in me. Something that wanted everything I had been avoiding for so many years. I'm not a man who uses ten-dollar words when two-dollar words work. But to call what happened to me at that moment just a realization would be greatly understating it. It was an epiphany. No other word for it would suffice.

I had never wanted someone to care about. But I cared about Colby. I had never wanted a relationship. But I wanted one with Colby. I wanted him to be my boyfriend, though that word felt terribly juvenile, like I was going to ask him to go steady.

I didn't know what having a boyfriend entailed, and I certainly didn't know how to be one. But I was going to find out. I just hoped it was what he wanted.

I couldn't stop thinking about Colby. I had to see him. I headed back to my tent, fully intent on throwing everything into my car and going home. I didn't know what I was going to say to him, but I figured I'd know by the time I saw him. I was wrong.

I was wrong because I saw him as soon as I was back at my tent. At first I saw someone sitting in my lawn chair outside my tent. I was ready to get pissed and yell at them for invading my space.

I stopped in my tracks when I realized it was Colby sitting there. He didn't see me, but he was looking around. I resisted the urge to start running, but as I got closer Colby saw me, stood up, and started walking my way.

He was smiling, and I couldn't help but grin as well. I told myself to play it cool, to not let him know how thrilled I was to see him.

I stopped when I was a few feet from Colby, but he stepped up close to me, grabbed me, pulled me close to him, and kissed me gently on the lips. I didn't resist at all. I couldn't. I just melted in his arms.

"Why did you leave without saying anything to me?"

"I thought I wanted to be alone. I thought I needed some time away from you, from everyone and everything."

"But?"

"I just realized I didn't want, or need, to be away from anything or anyone, especially you." A wide grin spread across his face. "I don't know what I can give you, big guy. I want to be with you, but commitments scare me, I don't know if I can promise a commitment."

"We'll figure it out, together. I want to be with you too. That's why I'm here."

"How'd you know I was here?"

"I forced Lex to tell me where you went."

I laughed. "You're a goddamn liar. Lex called you and told you where I was and sent you to get me."

He chuckled, but didn't deny it. "Yes, she called me yesterday."

"And it took you all night to decide to come after me?"

"Yeah, took about the same time as you to figure out it was up to me. I was sure you wouldn't be the one to give in first."

We laughed and hugged.

"I didn't bring anything," Colby told me, "no change of clothes, no sleeping bag, nothing like that."

"I got a sleeping bag we can share."

"And clothes?"

"Who needs clothes?"

"I don't mind the idea of us walking around naked all weekend long, but the other campers might not like that. Maybe we'll do that sometime at home."

"We can figure all that out later, big guy. C'mon, let's go take a nap in my tent."

"I'm not tired," he said.

"Me either," I said, laughing.

We managed to make it all the way into the tent before we were tearing our clothes off. I hadn't thought about having sex this weekend, so I hadn't brought lube. I did have a bottle of baby lotion. I handed Colby the lotion as I lay on my back and spread my legs. He positioned himself between my legs, lubed us both up, and began to push in. With one hand on my dick and the other hand on his, he slid deep into me and slowly pulled his length in and out.

This time we both wanted to savor the moment. We weren't in a hurry. He was slow and deliberate, bringing himself close to the edge and then backing off. He did the same thing with me, driving me crazy. He leaned down to kiss me, wrapped his arm around my neck, and kissed me hard as he started pounding me harder and harder. We moaned into each other's mouths. He slammed into me one last time, and I could feel him shooting inside of me. I stroked myself and shot onto my stomach.

We lay there not moving for several minutes, still kissing and touching as he slowly softened.

"That was great," I said.

"I agree."

Colby lay down next to me and wrapped his arm around me. I laid my head on his chest, and soon we were both asleep.

I WOKE an hour or so later, but Colby was still snoring. I quietly dressed and slipped out of the tent. I had been sitting outside the tent about twenty minutes when Six-Pack walked up.

"Hey." He nodded at me. I nodded back.

"I'm sorry about before," he said.

"Forget about it." I didn't meet him in the eye.

"I'm sure it was a shock and all to learn I was married. I'm just looking for a little fun, and I think you are too. Any chance of reconsidering?"

"I was looking for a little fun."

"Huh?"

"I was looking for some fun, past tense. I got something better than some quickie in my tent."

"And what do you have that's better?"

The tent flap came open, and Colby stepped out. He was wearing only his pants, and both Six-Pack and I stared at his gorgeous chest.

"That would be me, I guess," Colby said, laughing.

"Yeah, I was talkin' about you, big guy. You're so much better than anything I could have had with anyone else."

Colby smiled. "Good to hear."

"Damn." Six-Pack grinned as he eye-fucked Colby. "You guys are a couple of studs, ain't you? Any chance of the three of us getting together?"

Colby looked at the guy like he was sprouting horns from his head.

"No thanks." He said it in such a way that Six-Pack knew there wasn't any point in arguing. He shrugged and walked off.

"Who was that?"

"Just somebody I met on the beach." I had to look away. I couldn't look in his eyes. "I was planning to fool around with him, until I realized he was married."

"And?" Colby asked. I was relieved to hear that there was no judgment in his voice.

I met his gaze again and said sincerely, "He would've been a mistake. Just thinking about a casual hook-up made me realize how much I wanted to be with you."

He smiled a huge grin and kissed me gently on the lips. "Let's go into town and get me some clothes," he said.

We drove into town, and Colby picked up some hiking shoes, a couple pairs of shorts, jeans and shirts, and some swimming trunks. Back at the tent, Colby changed into a pair of shorts and a plain white T-shirt. I couldn't believe how sexy he looked in such a plain outfit. An outline on his crotch told me he wasn't wearing underwear, and I laughed.

We set out on a hike carrying some lunch meats and water bottles. I led him up the trail I had taken the day before and stopped at the same great viewing spot I was at the day before. We sat, ate lunch, and held each other.

"I'm thrilled the charges against you are gone, Cristian. But I've been thinking about what you said before."

"What're you talking about?"

"When you said O'Reilly wasn't smart enough to have framed you. I know O'Reilly was mentally unbalanced, and I know he hated you, but the idea of him setting up the whole murder and framing you just doesn't seem right."

"I know what you mean. But the evidence points to him."

"I know all that. I'm just saying that it all doesn't seem to fit right. It's kind of like a huge puzzle where you've got all the pieces right and the last two pieces you have to force in."

"Do you remember what you said the day the charges against me were dropped?"

"No."

"You said we didn't have to worry about it. You were right. I'm free. We're here together. Let's not make trouble when we don't need to. Let it go."

"Okay, okay. I hear you."

We didn't talk about the case for the rest of the day. We just enjoyed being together. That evening, after a dinner of roasted hot dogs, Colby and I made love in the tent. I had never realized what a difference there was between making love and fucking. The same physical act, but as distinct as night and day. The emotions involved were what made the difference. It was hard for me to accept the feelings I had for him and even harder to accept the feelings he seemed to have for me. It didn't make sense that such an attractive man, a truly good person, would fall for me.

After making love, Colby lay in my arms as I ran my hands over his thick chest. I loved the feel of him pressed against me. I put my hand on his chest and felt his heart beating. I traced his muscles with my finger and trailed it up to his hair. I ran my fingers through his hair, leaned in and smelled it.

"I think we need to spell out a few things," I said.

"More rules?"

"Yeah, smart ass. I think we need a few rules, just so we both know."

"Okay, Bello. What are these rules?"

"I can't promise monogamy. I can tell you that right now."

"I appreciate the honesty, but what does that mean? Are you going to be out fucking other guys all the time?"

"No, but if the opportunity arises I want to be able to take it."

"Fair enough. But I want you to tell me about it afterward."

"The details gonna turn you on?" I joked.

He sat up so we were eye to eye and looked at me—dead serious. "No, I don't want details. I just want to know it happened. I need you to be honest with me about it. And I can't promise I won't be jealous or bothered by it, but I'll get over it."

"I hear ya."

"I know you've broken rules with me. Is that going to be an open door for you to break the rules with other guys?

I had to think about that for a second before I answered. "No, I won't break any of my rules with any other guys. No kissing, no showering, no sleepovers."

"No feelings with these other guys?"

"Definitely no feelings for anyone else."

Colby grinned. "I'm glad to hear that."

"And there will be times when I need my space. You can't take it personally if I decide to spend a few days without seeing you."

"Okay."

"And the playing around thing applies to you too," I told him. "If you meet a guy you want to suck or fuck, you're free to go for it."

"Thanks, but I won't need to. I know you'll be plenty for me." I looked at him and knew he meant it. "I've got strong feelings for you, Bello. I just want you to know that."

"Thanks," I said as I leaned down to kiss him. I had strong feelings for him, too, and I wished I was able to tell him so. I hoped he knew it.

The weekend at Tahoe was incredible. Colby and I laughed and played and made love and fucked and hiked. When Sunday came, I didn't want to go home. I wanted to stay in Tahoe forever, just me and Colby.

We pulled camp slowly, and when it was done, we had to say good-bye. We both had our own cars, so we had to drive separately. The drive was a short one, but it was going to be too long for me. I drove home and unpacked my car and called Lex to tell her I was home. She wanted me to tell her everything about my weekend with Colby, but I wasn't in the mood. I told her I would see her at work and hung up.

I had just spent an entire weekend with Colby, and I wondered why I was already missing him so much.

My cell rang, and I thought it was Lex at first, but I lit up when I saw it was Colby.

"Hello," I answered.

"I miss you already."

"Me too."

"I can't tell you how glad I am to hear that."

"Why?"

"Open your front door."

I went to my door, opened it, and saw Colby standing there.

"What are you doing here?" I asked, still speaking into the phone.

"I got home, threw my clothes on the floor, and realized I wanted to see you, so I drove right over here. But then I sat in my car because I remembered what you said about sometimes needing your space, and I didn't want to intrude, so I was sitting there not sure what to do."

I realized we were both still talking into the phone. I hung up my phone. Colby looked at his phone and did the same, smiling.

"You're babbling," I told him.

He smiled. "I know. I tend to do that when I'm nervous."

"This is a side of you I haven't seen."

"So I called you, hoping that you wanted to see me too."

"And what would you have done if I said I didn't want to see you?"

"I would've turned around and gone home and thought about you all night."

"What do you want for dinner?"

He looked at me and gave me an evil grin. "You."

I laughed. "You gotta catch me first."

He chased me around the couch and nearly had me a couple times, but I got away. He cornered me in the kitchen, but I scrambled over the counter and got away. At one point Colby managed to grab my shirt, but I pulled out of it.

"I got you half-naked at least!" he yelled as we ran around my apartment. I finally let him catch me in the bedroom. We landed on the bed but continued to wrestle, and we fell off the side of the bed. He landed on top of me so hard I lost my breath for a minute. He immediately freaked out.

"Cristian, are you okay? Ohmigod, I'm so sorry."

When I could finally breathe, I laughed. "I think I need mouth to mouth." He grinned and leaned down and kissed me.

When he pulled back up I said two simple words—"Fuck me."

After amazingly mind-blowing sex, he lay with his head on my leg as I ran my fingers through his soft hair. "Wanna stay the night, big guy?"

"I don't know. I need my space, you know?"

It took me a second to realize he was teasing me. I jumped up, straddled him, and started tickling him mercilessly. He begged me to stop, but I refused until he agreed to spend the night, which he did. We took turns showering, then slipped into bed. I fell asleep with Colby in my arms.

CHAPTER TWENTY-ONE

GOING to work on Monday was equal parts weird, fantastic, and surreal. I said hello to everybody, and I swear they were all looking at me like I had grown a second head. I couldn't figure out what they were staring at.

Lex was sitting at her desk, and I sat down in my desk across from her.

"Good morning, Lex. How's it going?"

She gave me the same look that everyone else had been giving me.

"What? Do I have a booger on my face or something? Everyone keeps looking at me funny today."

"I like the new look, Cris," she said, smiling.

"What new look?" I looked at my clothes, the same ones I had already worn dozens of times.

"You're wearing something new."

"What are you talking about, Lex?"

"You're wearing a smile. A huge, gorgeous smile. That's unusual for you."

I laughed at her. I couldn't deny it. That was why everybody was staring at me.

Before we had a chance to talk any more, Brunson called us into his office, and just like that, she and I were working on a new murder case.

ON WEDNESDAY, I heard really great news—Pryor had been arrested. He was facing a list of charges, bribery and blackmail being the most serious. They weren't major charges.

Curtis had agreed to testify against Pryor. In return, he was allowed to retire from the force without losing his pension.

Pryor didn't even try to fight the charges. He took a deal, pled guilty, and was sentenced to one year in prison.

THURSDAY morning, I was eating breakfast with Colby at his place when my cell rang.

"It's Violet," I told Colby. "Hey, Vi, what's up?"

"Flesh, Gabe's awake and asking for you."

"We'll be right there."

When we got there, Gabe was sitting up with his arms wrapped around his legs. He was shaking and looked scared, petrified, actually. He seemed to relax a bit when he saw me.

"Flesh, man. I don't know what's going on." He was trying hard not to break into tears.

"You're okay, Gabe. Everything's okay."

"I can't remember much of anything, except for… that cop, that red-headed cop who shot me. He had me tied up, and he was… he was… was beating me with a crowbar."

I walked up to Gabe and put my hand on his leg.

"He's gone, kid. He won't hurt you again."

He looked at me with so much hurt and pain in his eyes that I almost started crying myself. "He's… he's gone?"

"Yeah." I sat on the edge of the bed and put my arm around his shoulder.

"You mean, like, he's in jail or…?"

"He's dead, kid. It's all over." He relaxed instantly and put his head on my shoulder and started weeping. I wrapped my arms around him and held him as he cried. Colby and Violet slipped out of the room as I continued to hold Gabe.

"I was so scared, Flesh," Gabe managed to say between sobs.

"Of course you were."

I held him while he cried, rubbing his back, making hushing sounds, and assuring him it was going to be okay. Eventually, he was able to stifle the tears, and his breathing returned to normal. He went stiff in my arms, pulled away from me, and hurriedly wiped the tears from his cheeks.

"I can't believe I'm crying like a baby."

"It was scary thing, kid. You got every right to feel overwhelmed, and no one, certainly not me, would judge you because you cried."

"Thanks for saving me, Flesh."

"The big guy was a big part of it. If it weren't for him I wouldn't have been able to save either one of us."

"I want to thank him. Will you get him and Violet?"

I stood and peered out the door. Colby and Violet were sitting in a pair of chairs a few feet away. I motioned for them to come in. Violet went to Gabe, and he hugged her. He looked at Colby.

"Flesh told me you helped us both out with O'Reilly."

"It isn't a big deal," Colby said quietly.

"It is for me," Gabe stated, "and I owe you a big thanks." Gabe stuck out his hand. Colby walked up to him and gripped his hand. They remained that way for longer than usual as they looked into each other's eyes.

"I need to get going, Cristian," Colby told me when he and Gabe finally let go.

"Okay." I turned back to Gabe. "I'll be back later this evening, okay, kid?"

"Cool."

Colby was quiet on the way back to the station.

"Something wrong, big guy?"

"Nope." He shook his head, but didn't meet my gaze.

"I'm gonna visit Gabe after work. Maybe I'll stop by your place afterward. That cool?"

"That's fine."

I SPENT the day taking care of paperwork and making phone calls. Lex and I slipped out a few minutes early, and I headed to see Gabe. The kid was alone when I got there.

"Where's Violet?"

"She hadda go to work."

I pulled a chair up close to his bed.

"How ya feeling?"

"Better than before. I'm really sorry about blubbering like a baby."

"Forget it, kid."

We were both silent for a few minutes.

"I told Violet the truth," he said, breaking the silence.

"The truth?" I wasn't sure what he was talking about.

"That I been sleepin' with guys."

"Wow. How'd she take it?"

"At first she was pretty upset, but I told her I liked girls too. And that I loved her and wanted to be with her. I guess since I like chicks and dicks, I'm bi. So that's what she and I talked about. I said I knew she had slept around on me a few times, and she admitted it."

"Honesty is good, kid. What does this mean for your guy's relationship?"

"We both love each other, and we want to be together to raise Vic. But I guess we're gonna have one of them relationships where we can fuck other people."

"An open relationship?"

"Yeah. One of them. And as long as there are no feelings involved, it's just sex. I don't know if it's gonna work, but we gonna try."

"Good for you, kid. That's pretty mature of you, telling her she can fuck other guys."

He laughed. "Yeah, I ain't real crazy about the idea of her being with other guys, but I can't expect her not to do it if I'm out screwing around with guys and girls. You and the lawyer got one of them open deals?"

"Yeah, kind of."

"Kind of?"

"We can fuck around as long as we tell each other about it afterward. Gotta be honest. And there are other rules, like always wearing protection, no kissing, shit like that."

"Because kissing is just for you two, right?"

"Yeah." He looked at me for a couple seconds, but I wasn't sure what he was thinking.

"Look, about what I said before, ya know about me being in love with you?"

"Forget about it," I told him.

"I mean I do like you a whole lot, but it ain't love. I do hope that maybe we can fool around again, since you and him got that deal."

"Yeah, that'd be fun."

I stayed by his side until he started to drift off to sleep, then I left the hospital and headed for Colby's.

"Hey, big guy. Let's go get something to eat," I said when he answered the door.

"I already ordered Indian food."

"Well, when it gets here, put it in the fridge. I want to go out tonight."

"I'm just not in the mood to go out tonight. Let's have a quiet night in."

"That's all we ever do. We never go out. I'm not asking you to go clubbing or anything. I just want to eat dinner at a restaurant instead of on a couch."

"Cristian, please. It's been a long day."

"Is this because you're tired, or is it something else?"

"What else would it be?"

"You're afraid of being seen with me in public, aren't you? You don't want anyone to see you with a queer like me. Because then they might think you're a fag too. That's it, isn't it?"

"Try to understand, Cristian."

"I understand perfectly. Before the case was over, we could be seen together, but now that the charges against me are gone, you don't have a reason to be seen with me. Can't have anyone thinking the wrong thing, can you?" The conversation was put to a halt when there was a knock on the door. Colby paid for the food and put the food on the counter.

"Let's eat," he said. "We'll finish our talk afterward."

We ate in silence, letting the sounds of the TV fill the air. I helped Colby put the leftovers away and cleaned up the few dishes we dirtied.

"I don't know what I'm supposed to say, Cristian. You know I care about you, and I want to be with you. But I am not ready to proclaim my homosexuality. I'm sorry if that hurts you because that's not my intention."

"Honestly, I don't get why you have to hide yourself."

"Homosexuality is just a small part of who I am."

"That's not true. You are gay. You are a gay lawyer. A gay black man. Not just a lawyer who happens to be gay or a black man who happens to be gay. The only way gay people will ever have to stop hiding or stop being ashamed is by people like us showing it can be done."

"I don't feel like arguing anymore. Let's go to bed."

"I think I should go home." I stood and grabbed my coat, but Colby touched my arm.

"You don't have to leave just because we had a fight."

I turned and faced him, and he took my hands in his. "We can sleep on it. Sleep next to each other. We'll figure it out in the morning. Come on, Bello. Let's go to bed."

I put my coat back down and followed him into the bedroom. We stripped to our boxers and climbed into bed. I curled up on my side. He gave me a quick hug and a kiss on the cheek before he lay on the far side of the bed.

I fell asleep surprisingly quickly.

WHEN I woke up, I was snuggled up against Colby with my head on his chest and his arm wrapped around me. I didn't want to move and ruin the moment. I loved the feel of my ear pressed against his chest, hearing his heart beat. I loved the feel of his breath on the top of my head.

I lay there for as long as I could, trying to ignore the call of nature. I got up as quiet as I could so I didn't wake Colby and walked quietly into the bathroom. I had just flushed when Colby stepped into the bathroom. I wasn't sure if he was going to continue the conversation and wasn't prepared for what he did. He reached out, grasped my face with both hands and pulled me into a gentle kiss.

"I am so sorry, Cristian," he whispered in my ear when he finally stopped kissing me. His arms were around my waist, pulling me close.

"I'm sorry too. I overreacted." It wasn't easy for me to apologize. I didn't like admitting I had done something wrong.

"I'm sorry if I did something that hurt you," he said.

I stepped back so we could look into each other's eyes, and he grabbed my hands.

"No, you didn't do anything," I said. "Not really. We're going to have to agree to disagree when it comes to that. You have your opinion, and I have mine. So let's get past it."

"Sounds good," he answered.

Chapter Twenty-Two

THREE weeks later, I came into work around noon on Monday after working late the night before. I was walking to my desk when I heard a familiar voice—a high squeaky voice with a Jersey accent. Kismet, the prostitute who had claimed she saw me at Sanchez's motel room right before he was murdered.

She was sitting at Simpson's desk.

"What do you got here?" I asked Simpson.

"We caught her giving a dude a blow job in a casino bathroom."

"He was horny," she said, laughing. "Couldn't make it back to his motel room. I offered to give this cop one, too, but he turned me down. He must be queer like you." She looked at me. "He didn't do it, ya know?" she said to me.

"What are you talking about?"

"That red-headed cop isn't the guy I saw at the motel."

"How do you know? It was dark."

"Not that dark. 'Sides, there was enough light to see he didn't have red hair. No hair, actually."

"This guy you saw was bald?"

"Yeah. That's what I said in court. Looked like you from behind, height, weight, clothes, and the shiny shaved noggin."

"You remember anything else about that night?"

"Nuthin'." I could tell she was lying.

"Simpson, I think she has information on a previous case. I need to talk to her in private."

"No problem, Flesh. I'll get my paperwork done and be here when you're done with her."

I took Kismet into an interrogation room.

"I got nuthin' to say to you," she said.

"I just have a few questions for you." She sat on one side of a desk, and I sat on the other. "A friend of mine talked to you a while back. A young Hispanic kid named Gabe."

"Tejon? Sure, I know who he is. Yeah, he visited me. So what?"

"Gabe said you were living in an apartment and wearing clothes that seemed too unusual for a… woman of your profession."

She laughed. "For a hooker, you mean? I ended up with some extra cash."

"Where did you get the money from?"

"I won a jackpot."

"You're lying."

"My grandma died and left me some money."

"You're lying again, Kismet. I will find out, one way or the other. You can tell me now and work out a deal, or I'll find out, and you get nothing."

"I talk and I'm dead," she whispered.

"Who would kill you?"

"I ain't saying."

"Fine. Let's start with the money. Tell me where you got the money."

She paused for a few minutes, and I was beginning to think I would have to up the stakes when she finally spoke.

"I had just finished with another john, and I noticed the door open."

"Room 212 at the Aloha?"

"Yeah, the one where the dead guy was."

"What did you do?"

"I poked my head in and saw the dead guy. I was just gonna leave whcn I saw a bunch of moncy under the bed. Lots of hundreds."

"How much money was there?" I asked.

"Seven G's."

"Seven thousand?"

"Yeah. I grabbed it all but didn't have nuthin' to put it in. My clothes didn't have no pockets, ya know?"

"So what did you use?"

"There was some kinda package under the bed too. So I grabbed that and stuffed the money into it."

"A package? What was in it?"

"That I ain't saying until I know what you gonna offer me."

"What do you want?"

"I want these charges dropped. I want protection."

"I'll see what I can do. Without the information, it'll be hard to get anyone to agree to do anything for you."

"That's the deal, take it or leave it."

"I'll see what I can do."

"Don't take too long."

I grabbed Lex and went into Brunson's office. I told them about what I had previously learned from Gabe and what Kismet had just told me.

"She hasn't given us anything, Flesh. I can't offer a deal unless I know what information she has. For all we know she's got jack shit and is trying to get something for nothing."

"Look at the evidence. First, whoever was at Sanchez's room after me, it couldn't have been O'Reilly. The guy Kismet saw had a shaved head. O'Reilly had a full head of red hair. Second, we know O'Reilly and Curtis left the bribe money with Sanchez. But it was gone when Kismet found the dead body. Someone was there and took the money, leaving some behind."

"That could've been O'Reilly," Lex said. "Maybe he decided to keep the money since Sanchez was dead."

"I don't think he would've double crossed Pryor like that," I said. "She took the package, the package I was talking about."

"So what? The package could have nothing to do with the case," Brunson replied.

"But it may have everything to do with the case," I pleaded.

"Unless she is willing to say what she knows or what's in the package, there is nothing I can do to help her, Flesh."

"Cris, let it go. It's over."

I stormed out of the office and headed to talk to Kismet again.

"There's nothing I can do unless you tell me what you know."

"Then we got nuthin' to talk about."

I knew there was no changing her mind. When I went back to talk to her again a couple hours later, she had been bailed out. I asked the clerk who had fronted the money.

"Tall, ugly guy with long, straggly hair down his back."

I knew from the description it was Moxley and wondered how deeply involved he was in everything.

SATURDAY night, Colby had to attend a big party for his law firm, which meant he had to put on the straight act and go with Annabeth. I decided to sleep at my place that night and was checking out some porn when there was knock on the door. I looked through the peep hole—it was Hillary.

"Hillary? What's up?"

"Can I come in?"

"Of course." She stepped in, and I shut the door. "Have a seat. Can I get you anything to drink?"

"You got any beer?"

I smiled. "Guinness."

"Perfect."

I grabbed two bottles, opened them, and handed one to her as I sat down on the recliner opposite her.

"I hate nights like this," she said, and I instantly knew what she meant—nights when Colby and Annabeth went out pretending they were straight and involved with each other.

"Yeah, me too. How do you deal with it?"

"Not always very well. I get jealous sometimes. As stupid as that sounds. I'm jealous because my lesbian girlfriend is out with your gay boyfriend."

"I know exactly how you feel. I'm jealous of Annabeth too. I wish I was the one out there with Colby. And I don't even like those big fancy parties, hanging out with the rich and famous."

She laughed. "Me, either."

"How long have you and Annabeth been together?"

"Three years. I want to spend my life with her. I love her to death. I wish I could tell everyone that we're together, but her job makes that impossible."

"It'd really be that much of a big deal to her patients?"

"Would you be comfortable with a gay doctor?"

I laughed. "I'd love it."

"Bad example," she said, laughing.

"I think Annabeth's reason for being in the closet is better than Colby's reason."

"That's how you see it. Colby sees it differently, and that's what matters. He can't make the decision to come out because it's what you want. He has to do it because he is ready to do it."

"I don't know how you deal with it," I said. "I don't know if I can."

"It comes down to how much you want to be with Colby, how much you love him."

"We're not in love," I snapped.

She looked at me with a small smile on her lips. It was the same look she had the first time we met. The look that said she knew something I didn't. "Well, whatever feelings you may or may not have for him. If you want to be with him, you have to accept his decision."

"And if I can't accept it?"

"Then move on."

I knew she was right. I had to make a choice, but I didn't know if I could do either one. Hillary called Annabeth and left a message on her cell telling her she was at my place. When the party was over, Annabeth and Colby showed up together. Annabeth and Hillary greeted each other with a sweet hug and kiss. I gave Colby a quick peck on the lips.

"Did you guys have a nice evening?" I asked.

"It was okay," Colby answered. "What about you guys?" I could tell Colby and Annabeth were curious about what had gone on between Hillary and me.

"We had a nice talk," Hillary answered.

"Yes, we did."

"Let's get home, baby," Annabeth said. "I need some loving."

"Eww, TMI," Colby joked.

"See you later, guys," Hillary said as she and Annabeth left.

As soon as the door was closed, Colby spun me around and pushed me up against the door. He pressed his crotch against my ass as he bit my neck. All my questions and concerns were forgotten as Colby's hands were all over me.

CHAPTER TWENTY-THREE

I TRIED my best not to focus on the issues I was having about Colby being in the closet. I didn't complain that every dinner we ate together was in my place or his. One time he even barbecued steaks for me. Why would I not be happy about that? But I wasn't happy, and I couldn't seem to push the issues out of my mind. I heard Hillary's advice in my head again and again: "Accept it or move on." I knew it was good advice. I just didn't know which choice was the right one.

One evening I went to his place expecting him to have ordered dinner again. However, when I stepped in, he was all dressed up.

"What's up, big guy?"

"We're going out. Get ready."

"Where are we going?"

"Vincenzo's in Carson City."

Vincenzo's was a small, elegant Italian place that had an excellent reputation. I showered and dressed, and we took off.

On the short drive there, I was enjoying the sweet moments between us. His hand rested on my knee, and my hand was on his neck, gently rubbing. More than once, I leaned over to kiss him.

I hadn't realized that the restaurant was isolated. There were only a few other businesses near there, and they were all closed for the day. When we stepped inside, I was more than a little surprised that there were so few people eating. Vincenzo's had been the talk of the town for several months.

"Why is there hardly anyone here?" I asked.

"They used to be closed on Monday's. Just changed the days off last week. Word probably hasn't gotten around."

"How did you know?"

"Constance."

I interrupted him. "Let me guess. Constance knows the owner."

"Yes."

"Do we have to worry about running into her tonight?"

"No, she's entertaining a client."

There was a large open area with tables, which only had a few occupied. There was also a separate room that was probably used for large parties. I was surprised when the host escorted us to the private room.

"Why are we in here?"

"I asked for a private table."

There was something odd with everything, but I couldn't quite figure out what it was that was bothering me.

Colby ordered a bottle of red wine and shrimp scampi as an appetizer. For the main course, I ordered Linguine Pescatore—shrimp, scallops and mussels tossed with linguine in a spicy marinara sauce. Colby had the veal, sautéed and topped with mushrooms, prosciutto, and a wine sauce.

I should have enjoyed the meal and the time with Colby. He was doing everything right—reaching across the table to touch my hand and giving me loving glances. But it seemed fake, an act to make me think he was giving me what I wanted.

"This is still hiding," I said.

He looked at me. "What do you mean?"

"This is still hiding," I repeated. "You knew there would hardly be anyone here. You requested the private room. There's no chance anyone you would know could run into us here. It's still hiding. You're just trying to make me think you're giving me what I want, but it's not."

"Cristian, I don't know what you want me to do."

"I want you to quit hiding me like the secret mistress. That's what I feel like. Some rich guy's slutty mistress. Good for fucking, but God forbid anyone knows about the relationship."

"Damn it. I'm doing my best. Why does this have to be such a big fight? You know I care about you. But I'm not ready to come out."

"This isn't the type of relationship I want with you."

"Well, it's the only kind we're going to have. Accept it or move on."

The fact that he said the same thing Hillary had wasn't lost on me.

We finished the dinner and left.

"I don't like feeling like you're ashamed of me," I said during the drive home.

"What the hell do you want me to do? Fuck you in the lobby of the firm? Take you around and introduce you as my life partner?"

"I wish you could be honest about who you are."

"I wish I could be honest too. I wish things were different. I'm not ashamed of being gay, but I have a career to consider."

We didn't speak again until we got home, and then it was just to say good night and climb into bed.

IN THE morning, I tried to put on a happy face and pretend everything was fine. Colby seemed happy that I wasn't interested in continuing the fight.

At work, Lex could tell something was wrong.

"What's the deal, Cris? Why are you moping?"

"Argued with Colby last night," I answered.

"About what?"

I didn't really want to talk about it, but I knew she wouldn't relent until I did.

"I'm having issues dealing with him being in the closet. I've spent my entire adult life not hiding who I am, and now I feel like I've been forced to hide because I'm seeing Colby."

"You knew he was in the closet when you started up with him."

"Yeah, but it was just sex originally. Now that I've got feelings for him, things are different. At least for me, they're different. I want everyone to know we're together. "

"But if you care about him, you shouldn't try to make him do something he isn't ready for. My advice—get over it."

"I know, Lex. I'm trying."

Changing the subject, she said, "The Policeman's Ball is next week, you guys going?"

"Of course."

The annual Policeman's Ball, a benefit to raise money for a local children's charity, was the one event I never missed. I was comfortable in a room full of cops. I didn't even mind wearing my dress blues.

ANNABETH and Hillary arrived at Colby's place before we all went to the ball. Of course, Colby and Annabeth had to go together. Hillary and I were each other's dates as well.

The ball was already going strong when we got there. Colby and Annabeth went in arm in arm. It surprised me how good the act was between them. If I didn't know better, I would've sworn they were madly in love.

"Cristian." I heard Lex calling me. She walked up with Kenny, who looked very uncomfortable in his suit.

"This party is fabulous," Lex said. She slurred her words because she was at the beginning stages of getting drunk. I heard Hillary and Lex talking and tried to pay attention, but I couldn't keep my eyes off of Colby and Annabeth.

"Stop obsessing," Hillary said as she poked me. "He only has eyes for you. Remember that?"

"Let's dance," I said as I pulled Hillary onto the dance floor. We got as close to Colby and Annabeth as we could.

"Want to switch partners, Annabeth," I said when we were all next to each other.

"I wish we could," Colby whispered.

When the song was over, Annabeth excused herself to use the bathroom. Hillary followed her in.

"Need to use the bathroom?" I asked Colby.

"No, I'm okay."

"You need to use the bathroom," I repeated. He got it that time. I walked to the bathroom, and he was a few steps behind me. Inside the bathroom, I looked around to make sure we were alone, then pulled him into a deep kiss.

"You make me so horny in your dress uniform," Colby said. "I can't wait to get you out of it."

I smiled. "This is difficult for me."

"What's difficult?"

"Seeing you and Annabeth together. I know it's an act, but it really bothers me."

"I'm sorry, Cristian. Just remember you and I are going home together."

"Yeah, I know."

We were interrupted when another guy came in, so we stepped out of the bathroom.

I made the rounds talking to fellow cops and other people I knew. No matter what was going on, I couldn't keep my eyes off Colby and Annabeth. I cringed when I saw them kiss.

A few hours later, my tensions hadn't eased the slightest bit. Lex had a great time, and by then she was more than a little drunk.

"Okay, Cris," she slurred. "Kenny and I are going home." She leaned into my ear and tried to whisper. "Kenny thinks he's gonna get lucky. Kinda goes with the drunk thing." I looked at Kenny and smiled.

They took off, and I noticed Constance talking to Colby and Annabeth.

"You guys have been dating for a while now," I heard Constance say. "Any chance you'll take the next step?"

Colby put his arm around Annabeth and pulled her close. "We've discussed marriage."

Constance was thrilled with the news. She pressed for more information, but they refused to say anymore about it. I knew the announcement was nothing more than a show for the public, but that didn't make it hurt any less.

I couldn't stay there any longer or I knew I was going to do something I would regret. I tried to find Colby and talk to him alone, but he was too busy to pay attention to me. I gave up, called a cab, and went home. When I got home I called Colby's cell and left a message. "I wasn't feeling very good so I left. Talk to you later."

I stripped and crawled into bed, falling asleep almost right away.

Three hours later, there was a knock on my door. I tried to ignore it, knowing it was Colby, but he wouldn't give up. I finally got up and answered the door.

"What's up, big guy?"

"Why didn't you go to my place?" He stepped inside and closed the door. I sat in my recliner and looked at him.

"I dunno. Just felt like coming home."

He sat on the couch and looked at me. "What's wrong?"

"Not feeling good."

"Don't try to lie to me. I know you too well."

"I don't think I can do this."

"Do what?"

"I can't be with you when you insist on hiding who and what you are."

"Are you still obsessing on that? Holy shit, Cristian. We've been down this road so many times now. There's nothing new to say."

"Yeah, I know. That's the problem. Seeing you and Annabeth together was hell."

"It's all an act; you know that."

I sat up so I could meet him in the eye. "You have pushed me to break my rules. I have opened up with you more than I ever thought possible. But what changing have you done? You want me to make all the changes, but you won't make any."

"Your rules were stupid rules to keep you from really experiencing life."

I looked at him in awe. "Stupid rules? For years those rules were all I had to protect me from the hell I was living. Those rules kept me alive. You getting me to break them wasn't a bad thing, but don't call them stupid."

"Even with all your strides, you still haven't really opened up to me. You won't talk about your past. You make comments about living in hell, but won't tell me what you're talking about."

"Those are painful memories I don't want to relive. Not now and maybe not ever. But that hasn't stopped me from opening myself to you. I'm still the man you care for, even if you don't know about every moment of my life. But this being-in-the-closet thing stops you from fully being the man I know you are. I see the real you when we're alone, when we're making love. But I hate the fake you that I have to put up with in public. I've never hidden anything about myself, and I don't want to start now."

"Listen, Cristian. I am done talking about this. I can't come out, not yet. Maybe someday, maybe not. I don't know. But you need to get over it, or this isn't going to work."

"I can't get over it," I said softly.

"What are you saying?"

"I can't get over it. I can't accept it. So we're just wasting our time."

"You're going to give up on us because of this issue? You are fucking unbelievable." He was to his feet and yelling. I remained sitting. I couldn't look him in the eye.

"Are you going to say anything?" he asked me.

"I don't think there's anything else to say."

"I guess that tells me everything I need to know. I'll be seeing you, Cristian." He turned and walked out the door, leaving it open. The open door seemed like an invitation for me to go after him. I wanted to do that. I wanted to run and stop him, but I couldn't do it. My legs didn't want to move. And even if I did go after him, I didn't know what I would say.

I don't know how long I stood there looking at the open door. Finally, I closed it, climbed into bed, and forced myself to sleep.

Chapter Twenty-Four

I DIDN'T see Colby at all for close to three weeks. Lex pushed and pushed to get me to make the first move, but I couldn't do it. I figured it was better that it ended now before he really got hurt.

One day, Colby came into the station. For a minute I thought he was there to see me. It turned out he was there to see a client who had been arrested on drug charges. We ran into each other in the restroom. Actually, I saw him go in, and I followed him. I took the urinal next to his, and for a moment we didn't talk, and the only noise was our piss hitting the ceramic wall of the urinal. I spoke when we had both zipped up.

"How ya doing, big guy?"

"Not bad," he said curtly. "And you?"

"Pretty good," I lied.

He washed his hands. "Good to see you, Cristian. I lied," he said, his voice just above a whisper. He stopped and turned to me. "I'm not doing pretty good. I'm pretty awful, actually. I miss you. I miss spending the nights with you. Is there any way we can try this again?"

I smiled. "I miss you too. But I don't think that's enough. I don't think it can ever work between us. I'm sorry. " I turned and left the bathroom, leaving him there.

I refused to talk to Lex about what happened, and she gave up asking. I worked late and didn't get home until almost eleven. When I got home, Gabe was sitting in front of my door.

"Hey, Flesh," he said. "I was about to give up on you."

I opened the door and he followed me in.

"How you doing?"

I didn't answer.

"That good, huh?"

I walked up to him, dropped to my knees, and pressed my face into his crotch. He was hard almost instantly. I undid his pants and fished out his meat. I started sucking, and he started groaning, grabbing the back of my head and shoving his shaft down my throat. After ten minutes of oral fun, I stood and walked into the bedroom. I needed to get fucked. I needed it to forget about Colby and his goddamn arrogance. I was naked by the time I got to the bedroom. Gabe was just taking off his shirt. I lay on my back on the bed and spread my legs. Gabe smiled.

"Oh yeah, I've missed this." When he was naked, he climbed between my legs and started stroking my dick. I reached into my dresser, grabbing the lube and a condom, handing them both to the kid. "Fuck yeah. I knew you'd come around eventually. I fuckin' love you so much. I ain't thought of nothing but this for a long time."

He had slipped the condom on and was about to push into me when I stopped him.

"What did you say? You said you loved me? You told me you were over that."

"I... I didn't say I loved you," he stammered. "I said I loved it. I love fucking your ass. That's what I meant." I could tell he was lying.

His hard-on was still pressed against the outside of my asshole, ready to slip inside. I looked into his eyes and finally realized the truth—he was in love with me—Colby had been right.

"You do love me, don't you, kid? Tell me the truth."

He looked incredibly sad, and I knew the answer before he said it.

"Yeah, Flesh. I love you. I love you so much it hurts."

"Why did you lie?"

"I wanted so bad to be able to be with you again. I figured if I said I didn't love you, you'd chill out."

"And you've wanted to be with me this whole time, huh? Even when I was with Colby, you wanted me."

"Please, Flesh, let me fuck you. Let me show you how much I love you."

"Sex isn't love, kid. Sex is sex. I could let you fuck me, and it would just be a fuck. I don't love you, kid. Not like that. Not like you want me to."

I started to pull away, but he tried to hold onto me, he even tried to get his cock into me. I could have easily used my strength to make him stop, but I didn't want to hurt him any more than I already had.

"Kid… Gabe… stop."

He looked at me imploringly.

"Please, Flesh. Even if it's the last time, let me be with you this one more time."

"I can't do that. It would be leading you on."

He let go of me, and I pulled away from him. He stayed resting on his knees, his hard-on going limp.

I pulled on a pair of sweats and walked behind Gabe. I put a hand on his shoulder.

"I'm sorry, Gabe. I don't want to hurt you, but I don't love you, and I never will. I care for you a great deal, and I want to be friends, but you might not be able to handle that."

"You in love with the lawyer?"

"I don't know. I don't really know what love is. But I do know that I have very strong feelings for him. But I don't know if those feelings are enough to make a relationship work."

"I'm sorry, Flesh."

"It's okay, Gabe. Just go home and be with Violet and Victor. If you want love with a man, you'll find it. But don't mistake gratitude for love."

Gabe got dressed slowly, like he was hoping I would change my mind. When he was finally dressed, he stepped to the door and looked back at me.

"You gonna be okay, kid?" I asked.

"Yeah, I'll be okay."

Chapter Twenty-Five

I MOPED around for awhile before working on getting my life together.

I joined Lex for Thanksgiving. Kenny had invited a poker buddy. His name was Ryan Young, and he was a good-looking man in his late twenties. He was a few inches shorter than me, with dark hair and piercing gray eyes. My gaydar went off right away, and the way he looked into my eyes and smiled made me think I was right.

"You meet any guys lately, Cristian?" Lex asked me halfway through dinner.

I looked at her, more than a little confused. Lex and I talked all the time at work about the men I had, or hadn't, met.

"Umm, no," I answered.

Dinner was quiet for a while before Kenny asked Ryan a question.

"Ryan, are you dating anyone? I bet hot guys throw themselves at you all the time, huh?"

He smiled; he had a cute, toothy grin. "No, I'm not dating anyone right now."

A few more minutes of silence.

"Cristian, Kathy Griffin is going to be in town next week. You planning on going?" Lex asked.

"Probably not," I replied.

"What about you, Ryan? You want to see Kathy Griffin?" Kenny asked.

Ryan looked at me, and we both smiled.

"No," he replied. "But I was thinking of going to see Bette Midler or maybe Liza Minnelli."

I laughed so hard I almost snorted beer through my nose. Kenny and Lex didn't quite get the joke.

"We get it, guys," I said. "I'm gay; Ryan's gay. This is a set-up, right? You want us to go out."

"Well, we just wanted to make sure you both knew the other was available," Lex said.

"I knew the moment he walked in," Ryan said.

"Me too," I admitted.

"You did? How?" Kenny wondered.

"Gaydar," Ryan and I answered almost in unison. Everyone laughed.

"But how did you know you were both single?" Lex asked.

"You wouldn't be trying to set us up if we weren't both single," Ryan answered.

"Can we move on now?" I asked.

AFTER the meal, we all sat down in the living room. We talked for a while before Lex excused herself to clean up in the kitchen. Kenny, Ryan, and I continued talking, but soon Kenny left the room. He claimed he was going to help Lex, but I was pretty sure the real reason was to allow Ryan and me to talk privately.

We sat only a foot away from each other, and I enjoyed looking into his gorgeous eyes. It turned out Ryan and I had more than being gay in common, we also had similar jobs. Ryan had been a cop and was now a correctional officer at Nevada State Prison in Carson City.

"I never wanted to be anything but a cop," Ryan said. "I got my Criminal Justice degree in Oregon and started working for the Portland Sheriff's Office. I worked there for a couple years then worked for the Seattle Police Department."

"I've never been to Seattle," I said.

"It's gorgeous, but you have to put up with rain, lots of rain. I was waterlogged a good amount of the time."

We both laughed. "How long were you in Seattle?"

"Seven years. I relocated to Reno three years ago when I left Seattle."

"Why'd you leave?"

He hesitated before answering. "I got shot. Was hurt pretty badly. Almost didn't make it. Decided it was time to get out of that career." I could tell he didn't want to say any more about it.

"Why Reno?" I asked.

"Justin, the guy I was dating at the time, had family here. He convinced me to get a job at NSP."

"What happened to Justin?"

"Turns out he didn't just have family here, he also had an ex-boyfriend. An ex-flame who's torch for Justin hadn't burned out. And the heat between the two was mutual."

"Why'd you stay in Reno? Don't you have friends or family in Oregon or Seattle?"

"I've got an older sister, but we're not very close. I like Reno, and I've got friends here."

Eventually we were interrupted by Lex. "How's everything going, guys?"

"We're good, Lex," I answered.

"You have any plans?" she asked.

"If you mean a date, no, we haven't gotten to that point yet," I replied.

"Why not?"

"Damn, Lex, we're adults. We can take of ourselves," I told her. She laughed.

"I can solve the problem," Ryan said. "Cristian, would you like to go out on Saturday night?"

"I'd like that," I answered.

Chapter Twenty-Six

RYAN insisted on making the arrangement for the night out since he was the one who had asked me out. He wanted to pick me up, but I wanted to meet him there. I didn't tell him that I wanted to have my own car there in case it didn't work out, and I had to leave.

Ryan chose the Rapscallion Seafood House for our dinner. It had small, intimate booths, top-rate service, and excellent food. I ordered the Crispy Asian Deep-Fried Prawns, served on Asian cole slaw with jalapeño soy ginger garlic vinaigrette. Ryan had Pecan-Encrusted Orange Roughy, served on Jack Daniel's pecan cream sauce with wild rice. He also ordered a bottle of Chianti.

"A white Chardonnay would be a much better choice," the waiter said. "If I can make a suggestion?"

"No thanks," Ryan said. "I'll have the Chianti, please."

"Very well, sir."

"I can't believe the waiter did that," Ryan said. I smiled, but said nothing. If I had responded, I would've told him the waiter was correct, white wine goes much better with fish than a red.

"Kenny told me you just came out of a relationship," Ryan said.

"Yeah." I wasn't sure how much I wanted to talk about Colby.

"Was it serious?"

"Yeah, it was."

"You don't want to talk about him?"

I looked at him and smiled a little bit. "Not really. I'm sorry."

"It's okay, Cristian. I understand. After Justin dumped me, I didn't want to even think about him for a couple months."

"Thanks," I said.

During the meal I kept smelling an odd scent, but couldn't place it. It was like Hugo Boss cologne, but not quite. Probably one of those cheap cologne knock-offs. The scent of Colby's cologne filled my nose, and I thought for a moment he was there. I quickly realized it was my own memory of Colby, not the actual presence. I tried hard to push all thoughts of him out of my mind and concentrate on the good-looking man in front of me.

"Hey, Ryan, have you had any trouble at work because you're gay?" I asked him. In an odd random thought, I realized I always called Ryan by his name. I didn't have a funny nickname for him. I wasn't sure if that was a good thing or a bad thing.

"Of course. But not anything I can't deal with. I just have to be extra careful. I basically choose to stay away from any event that could cause me trouble. Like the women officers, I don't do any of the full-body strip-outs. But I've been involved in physical fights with inmates. Nobody questions my ability to defend myself or another officer just because I'm queer."

"I HAD a great time," Ryan said as we finished our dinner.

"Me too."

"I'd like to see you again, Cristian."

"That'd be cool," I said. "But I make the plans next time."

"Deal."

We ended the night with a quick hug at my car and a promise to call him soon.

AT WORK Monday morning, Lex wouldn't rest until I told her how the date with Ryan had gone.

"It was fine. I had a nice time. No, we didn't have sex. Yes, we have plans to see each other again. Does that answer all your questions? Can we get back to work?"

It was a busy week at work, which helped me to keep my mind off of Colby and how much I missed him. Ryan and I talked every few days, sometimes for a few minutes, sometimes for longer. He was hopelessly addicted to reality shows like *The Bachelor* and *Dancing with the Stars*. Shows that Colby and I used to make fun of. Despite my telling him that I didn't like those shows, he insisted on giving me a play-by-play of the episodes. He also begged me to tell him where we were going on our date. It was obvious he was used to being in control. When it came to sex I most definitely liked not being in control, but when it came to dating, I wasn't so sure. Dating was a completely new experience for me.

I chose the Bliss Nightclub. It was a popular dance club with a big dance floor and a bar with plenty of alcoholic choices. It wasn't a gay bar, but the dance floor had couplings of all kinds—male/female, male/male and female/female. Ryan and I agreed to meet there at eight Friday night. I arrived ten minutes early, but he was already there. He was waiting at the bar talking to a good-looking young guy, but when he saw me, he excused himself from the other guy, who shot me a pissed-off glare.

"How are you doing, Cristian?" he asked as he gave me a small hug. I hugged him back, and it struck me how different his body was from Colby's. Ryan was in good shape but nowhere near as muscular as Colby.

"I'm good. You?"

"Excellent, now that you're here." He grabbed my arm and pulled me to a small table. "What do you want to drink?"

"Jack and Coke." He caught the attention of a waitress and ordered a Jack and Coke for me and an appletini for him. I couldn't think of a more stereotypically gay drink than an appletini. Colby wouldn't be caught dead drinking one of those.

Several men couldn't keep their eyes off of Ryan, but he was oblivious to all of them—all of his attention was turned to me. He was in the middle of a sentence when the DJ started playing a song he recognized.

"I love this song," he said. I don't follow pop music and couldn't say what the song was or who sang it. "Dance with me," he said as he stuck out his hand. I wasn't totally against dancing, but it definitely wasn't on my list of favorite things. But I couldn't say no to the almost pleading look on Ryan's face. He smiled wide when I took his hand and stood up. He practically ran to the dance floor, pulling me along with him.

Once we were on the dance floor, I was surprised about what a good dancer he was, excellent, actually. So he was good-looking, intelligent, honest, nice, and a good dancer. So why wasn't I having the time of my life? He was basically perfect.

We were face-to-face, and he pulled me close to him. He had one hand on my waist as our crotches rubbed together to the beat of the music. Our faces were so close we were almost kissing and our eyes didn't break contact for a while. He turned me around and ground into me from behind.

As I glanced at the people in the club, I froze. It took Ryan a minute to realize I had stopped moving. "Cristian, what's wrong?" He followed my gaze to the person I was staring at.

"Who's that?"

"Colby," I replied.

"Who?"

"Colby, my ex."

"Oh."

"I'll be right back," I said. I walked up to Colby, who was sitting at a table. I sat down.

"Hello, Colby."

"Cristian. How are you?"

"I'm good. You?"

He didn't answer my question; instead he asked one of his own, "You on a date?"

I looked at Ryan. "Yeah. His name's Ryan Young. What are you doing?"

"Annabeth's going to be here in a little bit."

"How are Annabeth and Hillary doing?"

Once again he didn't answer my question, and once again he asked one of his own. "This is the relationship you want, isn't it? Being able to go out with a guy and not have to hide behind a lie. You want to go dancing with your boyfriend."

"Well, yeah. I want that. But I wanted that with you."

Colby was quiet for a minute. He had a look on his face that I couldn't quite read. It looked like a mixture of sadness, uncertainty, and maybe even acceptance. Maybe I was just transferring my emotions to him because I was feeling all of those things. Actually, I was definitely sad and uncertain, but I wasn't even close to acceptance. Neither one of us wanted to say anything. There wasn't anything to say other than good-bye.

"Well, hello there." I looked up and saw Annabeth.

"Hey, Annabeth." I stood up and gave her a quick hug.

"Are things good here?" she asked. I didn't say a word, just looked at Colby.

"Not really," I replied. I turned and walked away but turned around when Colby said my name.

"Good luck, Cristian. I hope you find what you're looking for." I nodded and walked to the table Ryan was sitting at.

"You okay, Cristian?" he asked when I sat down.

"Yeah. I guess."

"You want to leave? We can go someplace else."

"Yeah, I want to go home."

"Umm, okay. We can go hang out at your place."

"No, I need to be alone. I'm sorry, Ryan. Let's try this again tomorrow night."

"Oh, okay. Yeah, we'll talk later." He was disappointed, and I was sorry for that, but I wasn't in the mood for company.

We hugged good-bye, and I took off. I looked back and saw Colby and Annabeth dancing. His eyes met mine, and he shot me a small smile that looked like a final good-bye. I smiled back and left.

THE next day, I called Ryan around noon.

"I'm sorry about last night," I said.

"Don't worry about it. I'll let you make it up to me with dinner tonight. I'll pick you up at seven." I let him be in charge of the date again. We had a good time at dinner that night. We shared a short and sweet kiss good night. He was a great guy, and I wasn't sure why I wasn't having the time of my life with him.

Ryan and I talked almost every day. We went out several times to movies, concerts, dinner, or dancing, but we also stayed in several times. He had a top-of-the-line entertainment system and preferred to watch movies at his place. He had an annoying habit of talking through the entire movie. Not even about the movie, but about a thousand other unrelated things. Colby never did that, when we watched a movie, he and I were quiet through the whole thing. Ryan also forced me to watch an episode of *Dancing with the Stars*, during which he insisted on telling me about everything that had happened during the season.

Ryan was obviously used to being the alpha male in the relationship. He liked to plan and pay for the dates. I didn't mind being doted on, though it was unusual for me. We kissed occasionally, usually nothing more than quick pecks, but at the end of one date he pulled me close and stuck his tongue down my throat. He definitely wasn't the talented kisser that Colby was. I wasn't turned on at all by his French kiss and ended it as quickly and nicely as I could.

I could tell he wanted more. I knew he was ready for sex, but I wasn't. And that was something else that was very unusual for me—not jumping right into sex. Even though Ryan was ready and willing to take the next step, he was being extremely patient with me.

ON CHRISTMAS day, Ryan and I joined Kenny and Lex for a turkey dinner. Afterward, he and I went to his place. We watched *A Christmas Story*, a movie he loved, but I thought was completely moronic. He kept quoting the signature line of the movie: "You'll shoot your eye out." I realized he wasn't so perfect, after all.

We sat on his couch, and he pulled me close and wrapped his arm around me. I could smell his cheap cologne, but tried to ignore it. As he held me, memories of Colby holding me flooded into my brain. Colby's body engulfed mine because of his size and muscle mass. Ryan was in no way out of shape, but his body was worlds apart from Colby's. When Colby held me, I would feel protected, safe from everything out there. I didn't get that feeling from Ryan at all.

Ryan's hands were all over me. He wasn't getting super aggressive, but I knew what he wanted. His hands traveled over my chest, on my legs, and on my crotch. He was rubbing me there, and my body was responding, a natural response to the stimulation.

In a quick movement, Ryan moved, causing me to lie down on the couch so that he was on top of me. I could feel his excitement as he rubbed against me. He kissed me and slipped his tongue in, but I moved away. Instead, he started kissing and biting my neck. I was turned on, but I wasn't into it. I tried to force myself to get into the moment by concentrating on the hot man touching me, but it wasn't working.

He unbuttoned my shirt and kissed his way down my chest and stomach before he buried his face in my crotch. He opened my jeans, reached in, and pulled out my erect cock. He wrapped his fingers around it and started quickly jacking it. Everything felt wrong—his stroke was too quick; his fingers were wrapped too tight; his hand wasn't soft enough.

He let go and started licking my shaft before slowly sliding it down his throat. Again, it just didn't feel right—his mouth felt cold, Colby's mouth was warm, almost hot.

"No, I'm sorry. I don't want to do this." I touched his shoulder.

He sat up on his legs and grabbed my erection. "It doesn't feel like you don't want to do this."

I pulled my legs out from under him and sat up. "I am turned on, incredibly turned on. But this isn't right. There isn't a connection between us. You're a great guy, hot, sexy, great kisser, but there's nothing between us."

"Okay, so what? So we don't have to see each other anymore. But you're turned on by me. You turn me on. Forget about feelings or a connection or whatever. Let's just have sex. Just sex, not love."

"That's the trouble, Ryan. I don't want just sex. I want something more." I stood up and grabbed my coat. "Sorry about this, man. I wish things were different."

"Don't worry about it," he said as he stood up and walked me to the door. "Call me if you ever need anything. Just because this didn't work out romantically doesn't mean we can't still be friends."

"I'd like that," I replied. We hugged, and I stepped out into the cold night air. The wind was chilly and whatever excitement remained in me was quickly cooled off.

When I got home I watched the old *Miracle on 34th Street* on Turner Classic Movies. I knew the movie was one of Colby's favorites and wondered if he was watching it at the same time.

I took the choice to not have sex with Ryan as proof of maturity. Visiting the bathhouse didn't even hold the slightest appeal. I realized it had been three weeks since I had any kind of sexual release. For sure the longest I had ever gone since I was a teenager.

Chapter Twenty-Seven

ON NEW YEAR'S EVE, I was alone in my apartment when there was a knock on my door. I was surprised at who I saw through the peephole—Colby.

I opened the door. "Hey, big guy. Come in. What's up?"

"I wanted to say Happy New Year."

"Happy New Year to you too," I replied. We both stood there for a minute before I spoke. "Sit down." We sat quietly for a minute.

"How's it going with the guy you're dating? I don't remember his name."

"Ryan. We're not seeing each other anymore."

Colby looked up at me, meeting my gaze. "What happened?"

"We wanted different things," I said cryptically. Part of me wanted to keep the real reason from him, but I decided to be honest. "He was almost perfect. Ryan's a nice guy, smart, and down to earth."

"Sounds great. So what happened?"

I hesitated for a moment before answering. "He wasn't you." He looked at me, and I could see the hint of a smile on his lips.

We both turned our attention to Dick Clark on TV. Everyone was getting ready for the big countdown.

"I told Constance I'm gay," he said. I wasn't sure if I had heard right.

"What?" He smiled as he looked at me.

"I said, I told my boss I'm gay."

"When?"

"The day after I ran into you at the club."

"That was weeks ago, why didn't you tell me?"

"I didn't do it for you. Well, I didn't do it just for you. I did it for me too. I realized being out was important not just for our relationship, but for my own life as well. I was tired of being in the closet and of hiding who I really was. So I decided to do it and face whatever consequences happened. I thought maybe you had moved on, and I had lost you forever. I'm happy I did it. I'll still be happy even if you tell me you don't want to be with me."

I was speechless. I wasn't sure what to think or do. All I could do was stare at him.

"Say something, Cristian."

"I don't know what to say."

"Okay, I understand. I'll leave." We both stood, and he started walking to the door.

"Wait," I said. He stopped and turned around to face me. I grabbed him and pulled him into a passionate kiss just as the ball dropped on TV. He returned the kiss, and our tongues connected.

"Yes," I said when we stopped kissing.

"Yes what?"

"Yes, I want to be with you. I don't really know what love is, big guy. But I have very strong feelings for you. You make me feel better than I ever have in my entire life. I want to see where this goes." He buried his face in my neck, and I felt a few tears trickle down. He wrapped his arms around me.

"I love you, Cristian. You don't have to say it back, but I want you to know how I feel. I am madly in love with you."

"That means a lot to me. It really does."

"Does that mean you're going to give us a chance?"

"Yeah," I whispered.

I grabbed his hand and dragged him into the bedroom. We kissed and groped and tore each other's clothes off. I lay down on the bed.

"Make love to me, Colby."

"Thank you."

"For what?"

"For calling me Colby."

I smiled and said it again. "Make love to me, Colby."

Colby got to his knees on the side of the bed and pulled me close to him. Pushing my legs into the air, he buried his face in my ass. I felt a soft kiss on my hole, and I melted at the touch. I grabbed my legs, lifting myself so Colby could have easier access. He spread my cheeks apart, and his tongue licked at my hole before it pushed against me, trying to get in. I moaned and that drove Colby on, pressing his face deep in between my cheeks, trying to get his hot tongue as deep as it could go. He retreated and gave me quick bites on my ass before licking under my balls while grabbing hold of my shaft. He stroked it perfectly, just like I remembered it.

I lowered my legs as he licked my prick, paying extra attention to the head, licking the ridge. He kissed the tip before slowly swallowing me to the base. It amazed me that he could take me all the way down his throat without gagging, but he did it easily. His mouth was warm and welcoming, and I was so glad this was where we were at that moment.

He grabbed the lube and squeezed some onto his fingers and rubbed my asshole. As he started to suck me again, one finger slipped into me. He swallowed my shaft, as the finger penetrated me. The finger slid in and out, rubbing my prostate as his warm mouth slid up and down. Everything felt so… perfect. Not just the sexual act, though that was awesome, but being there with Colby and sensing his motions, feeling his love. Another finger slid into me, and I felt like I was going to burst. I grabbed Colby's head.

"Colby, babe, please. I want it. I need it."

He withdrew the fingers and stood up.

"Scoot back on the bed," he said, and I did. He lubed up his cock and crawled between my legs. He lay down on me, trapping our cocks together, and kissed me hard. I grabbed his face and held him against me. I loved the feel of his strong body against me. I felt loved, protected, and safe.

"Please, babe," I whispered in his ear.

"You want it that bad?" He smiled at me.

"Yeah, I need it. I need you in me. It's been so long."

I felt his cock on the outside of my hole. I pushed out as he pushed in, and he slipped in quickly. I gasped at the intrusion, welcome and desired as it was. He didn't move, leaving just the head in me. He watched me as my body adjusted and accepted him. He slowly slid in, our eyes never breaking contact, until he was totally buried in me.

"You're so big," I said, barely able to talk.

"Same as before," he laughed.

"I don't know. It feels bigger. It's been so long since we've done this. It feels different."

He slid in and out of me, and leaned down to kiss me. I grabbed his ass cheeks, urging him to push harder, deeper. I avoided touching my own erect shaft because I was afraid one touch would send me over the edge. I was leaking precome into a pool on my belly, and I knew my cock would be especially sensitive.

Colby pushed in and pulled out of me, giving me short strokes and long strokes, quick jabs and slow thrusts. For the first time in my life, I truly understood what making love was. I moved my hips, urging him on, flexing my sphincter to apply pressure to his cock.

"Oh, baby. You feel so good," Colby moaned. "I missed you so much. I love making love to you. I love being with you. You turn me on so much." The sweet nothings spurred me on even more, and I bucked my hips more.

"Oh, damn, Cristian. You're gonna me make me come. Your ass is so sweet. I can't hold back anymore."

"Do it, babe. Give it to me."

He buried himself deep in me again and again, and I could feel him getting close. With a final thrust, he went as deep as he could go, and I felt him expand even more.

"Ohh, ohh yeah," he grunted. His body went limp, and he lay

down on me. He was breathing deeply. I loved the feel of all of his weight pressed down on me. He stayed buried in me for a minute before he slid out. I could feel his cock against me and could feel he was only partially soft. I was still rock hard, of course.

He put his arms on either side of my head and asked, "You want me to suck you off?"

"I've got a better idea. You're not gonna go totally soft, are you?"

He laughed. "No, I'm ready to go again. You want me to fuck you again?"

"Yes, but something different."

He looked at me slyly. "What do you mean?"

I grabbed hold of him and rolled him over onto his back with me on top. I straddled him and leaned down to kiss him. "Sex for me has always been about not being in control. That's the way it's always been. I was taught I was there to submit and do what I'm told. But right now, I want to be in control."

"I'd love that, baby."

"I want you to fuck me in this position," I said. "I want to ride you. But first let me explain something, but please don't ask me any questions.

"When I was young, too young for what happened, I was told it was my duty to please him. He forced me to ride him, and while he was in me, he would slap me and punch me. He'd call me names and make fun of me. That's why this position brings back memories. Images which are hard to push away."

"You don't have to do this, Cristian."

"I want to."

I lubed him up, positioned myself and slowly sat down, taking him all the way in. When he was buried all the way, I sat there, closed my eyes, and tried to clear my mind. Those old memories took control of my brain, and I couldn't turn them off.

I felt Colby's hands on my face. "Look at me, baby. Concentrate on me. I'm not him." I opened my eyes and looked at his beautiful face and body. Colby was right; he wasn't the man from my past, not even close.

The memories disappeared. All I could feel, all I could see, was Colby. I stared into his eyes as I rode him, letting the feelings take me over. His hands were on my face, my back, my chest, my arms. My own hand encircled my shaft, but I stroked slowly so I could make the moment last as long as possible. I sat back, using my legs to move up and down until my legs began to cramp. I leaned forward, putting my hands on either side of his head as I gyrated my hips, feeling his rod deep inside of me. I felt all of him throughout my entire body. I had closed my eyes again, but the old memories didn't return, and when I opened my eyes Colby was still watching me, his gaze reaching into my soul. I kissed him, gently at first, then harder as our lips parted and our tongues touched. My shaft was trapped between my stomach and his. As I rocked, I not only felt his cock in me, I also felt the friction of my cock rubbing between our sweaty bodies.

As I looked into his eyes and saw the love, I couldn't hold back any longer. "Ohh, Colby," I cried out, erupting with such intensity that I almost blacked out, shooting my seed between us. I lay down on his chest and tried to get my breath back. One hand rubbed my back while the other ran through my hair.

"Baby, that was wonderful," he whispered into my ear. I tried to move but couldn't. My body wouldn't cooperate. Every muscle I had was sore. "I can't move," I said, laughing into his ear.

"Then don't," he murmured back. Between his soft voice in my ear and the gentle massaging of my back, I closed my eyes. I didn't intend to do anything more than rest for a second, but I found myself succumbing to the peace I felt and went to sleep.

FORTY minutes had passed when I woke up. Colby's arms were still wrapped around me, and I thought he was awake. The rhythmic cadence of his snoring told me otherwise. I didn't want to wake him, but my legs and arms were cramping. I slowly rolled off of him, trying not to wake him. It didn't work; as soon as my body was off him, he woke.

"Where you going, baby? I liked having you on top of me." He rolled over and snuggled up against me. We were both sticky from sweat, but I loved the feel of him against me.

"I really need to shower," he eventually said. "I feel nasty." He stood and walked to the bathroom. This time when my head told me to do something, I listened. I followed Colby into the shower.

"Wow," he teased. "Another rule broken. By the time we're ninety, we might manage to break them all."

"Well, one of my rules is to never have sex with anyone over the age of seventy."

He tickled me, then grabbed the soap and washed my back. We took turns washing each other, stopping often to kiss.

After the shower we climbed into bed. I spooned against him and realized how much I had missed the feel of his body against mine.

Something occurred to me. "How did she react?"

"What?"

"Constance. How did she react to you telling her that you're gay?"

"At first she was in shock and kept babbling about the clients we could lose," Colby said, smiling. "But then she started thinking about all the new clients we could bring in. She talked about doing a major marketing campaign to bring in gay-friendly businesses."

I laughed. "So she wasn't as angry as you thought she would be?"

"No, but there will be some clients who will be angry and might seek representation elsewhere. Constance is convinced any clients we lose can be replaced through the new queer campaign."

"I knew it would work out."

"Happy New Year," he whispered into my ear.

"Happy New Year," I replied.

Chapter Twenty-Eight

LEX and I started working on a case of a single mother who had been killed. The case took a lot of my time, but Colby and I managed to spend a lot of our time together. We spent most of our nights together, sometimes at my place, but mostly at his, and there were plenty of nights we spent alone. I didn't know about him, but I usually ended up wishing we were together. I had to force myself to sleep alone, without his warm body next to mine.

I can't explain why I chose to insist I needed my space. I didn't need it. I didn't even want it. I figured I should know how to be alone because sooner or later I was going to lose Colby. After all, there was no way he would put up with me forever.

With everything that happened with Colby, I had put my concerns about who really killed Sanchez behind me. I hadn't even thought about it until something happened, bringing it back to the forefront of my mind.

In the middle of February, after a quick lunch with Colby, I had just returned to the precinct when Simpson pulled me aside.

"What's up?" I asked.

"You know that hooker I arrested a while back? The one you said had information on another case?"

I actually had to think about it for a minute before it connected who he was referring to—Kismet.

"Yeah, what about her?"

"She's dead."

"What?"

"A kid found her body in an alley this morning. She's been dead a couple days."

"Cause of death?"

"It looks like a massive drug overdose."

"Thanks, Simpson. I appreciate it."

I knew Kismet had a drug problem, and it wouldn't have surprised me if that was what killed her. But I couldn't stop thinking about her fear that someone was out to get her. I also wondered how Moxley was connected. The package still bothered me, and I really wanted to know what was in it.

While thinking about the package, I recalled the return address was Pioche. I did a quick search and found a few people with the last name of Sanchez living in Pioche. I made a few phone calls. I reached two people, and neither one knew a Ricardo Sanchez. There were three unanswered calls, and I left messages for all of them.

I was about to keep digging when Lex grabbed me and said we had to talk to a possible witness of the single mother murder. The next day, there was a message for me. It was from a man named Manuel Sanchez. He said he was Ricardo Sanchez's brother. I immediately called him back.

"I don't know how I can help you. I thought my brother's murder was solved," Manuel said.

"That's true, I'm just tying up a few loose ends. Did you send a package to your brother a short time before he was killed?"

"Yeah, I did. I'd forgotten about that."

"What was in the package, Mr. Sanchez?"

"A journal. Ric always wrote in journals. It was a journal from when he was young, before he went to prison."

"Did you read any of those journals?"

"No, sir. That was his business, and I figured it was better if I stayed out of it."

"Okay, Mr. Sanchez. Thank you for your help. If you think of anything else, please call me."

"Yes, sir. I will."

I hung up, even more positive there was something in those missing journals that I needed to see.

On a hunch, I pulled the evidence from Ric's murder and got out the journal. I noticed that even with the pages recovered from O'Reilly's place, there were still some pages missing. I had to wonder what was on those pages and if it was connected to the journals taken from Ric's motel room. An idea popped into my head. When I saw Simpson, I called out to him.

"Yeah?" he asked.

"Do you have any idea where Kismet was staying?"

He pulled out a notebook and flipped through a few pages. "The Gospel Mission on Record Street."

"Good, thanks."

I got in my car and headed for the Reno-Sparks Gospel Mission. I found Rich Redding, the executive director of the shelter. He was a friendly, amiable, middle-aged man who seemed to know every person being housed there. I asked him if he knew Kismet.

"Yeah, I knew her. Her real name was Kimberly. She'd been living here for six months. She was part of our drug-rehab program, and she was doing excellent."

"She was clean?" I asked.

"Yeah, Kimberly had made a great deal of progress in her time here."

"It appears she died of a drug overdose."

"It's possible. Anything's possible. But I never would've thought she would slip. She had talked about making so many mistakes in her life and her plans to make things right."

"Any idea what she meant by that?"

"No, but she did give me something to keep until she was ready."

"What was it?"

"A notebook. I didn't read it."

"Can I see it, Mr. Redding?"

"Sure, follow me."

We walked into his office, a sparsely decorated room with a computer that appeared to be more than twenty years old. He opened a safe and pulled out a notebook.

"Can I have this? I think I may be able to finish what Kismet couldn't."

He handed it to me. "I hope you do, so Kimberly's spirit can rest in peace."

I was walking back to my car when Lex called me. We had to deal with an emergency—a hostage situation involving a man who had confessed to killing the single mother. I shoved the notebook into my glove box and focused on the task at hand.

I didn't get home until late that night. I had decided to spend the night alone. It had been a bad day, the suspect had killed himself in front of his seven-year-old daughter, and I didn't feel like dealing with anybody. I was in my apartment when I remembered the notebook in my glove box. I ran downstairs, got the notebook, and returned to my apartment to read it.

THE journal had starting and ending dates. The first date was months before the murder that got Ric sent away. The earliest entries talked about sex with Pryor. Apparently, even back then, Pryor liked the rough stuff. He liked giving it as well as receiving it. Ric was totally head over heels in love and talked about Pryor's promises of forever love, always being together, and their plans for moving when Pryor went to college. He affectionately called Pryor "Joey."

I skipped ahead to a spot that had been tagged with a yellow sticky note. There was a gap of about a week between entries. This entry, the last entry in the notebook, was dated two days after the death of the old woman:

JOEY and I had been sneaking into the old Harbridge House for months. Everyone thought the Harbridges had died years ago. Old Man Harbridge had died in the house, and after that, the old lady had left town to live with her kids. She hadn't been seen in two or three years, so everyone figured she was dead too.

It was private and secluded so we didn't have to worry about getting caught. We used the master bedroom on the second floor. We had blankets, sleeping bags and porn mags stored there. Of course, we always brought lube with us.

We attacked each other right away that day, and I pounded his ass as he screamed and moaned. Joey was moaning so loud we didn't hear the door open or the footsteps up the stairs, but we did hear the scream at the doorway. I turned and saw Old Lady Harbridge standing in the door, her hands at her opened mouth.

She screamed at us, calling us filthy little rats. She said we were evil and were going to hell for sodomy. We both jumped up, still naked, and started begging her to not say anything. We said we were sorry, and we just wanted to leave.

She said she was going to tell everyone that we were disgusting little perverts. Joey lost his temper and chased after her as she started going toward the stairs. He grabbed her at the top of the stairs and told her that she wasn't going to tell anyone.

She slapped him and told him to get his disgusting hands off of her. Joey totally lost it and pushed her down the stairs. We both watched in shock as she stumbled all the way down the stairs.

When she landed, she was in this weird position. Her neck was at this freakish angle. We knew she was dead and started flipping out. We both got dressed and ran out of there. We had to step over her body when we left.

We realized later that we left everything there we had brought. We had left the bags and the magazines and empty pop bottles. All of that stuff could have our prints on 'em. We knew there was no way we could get away with it.

Joey has a scholarship for college and has his entire life ahead of him. I got nothing. I'm not as smart as Joey and don't have the opportunities he does. He would lose those opportunities if he went away for this stupid thing.

So I'm going to make a sacrifice, my life for his. I'm gonna confess to the crime. I'll do the time, and when I'm out, Joey and I will be together. It's what I have to do to protect the man I love.

KISMET must've read the notebook and learned Pryor killed the old lady and let Ric take the fall. Then the bastard turned his back on him. That would explain Kismet's fear—she was afraid Pryor would come after her if he knew she knew his secret.

I honestly didn't know what to do with the new information, but I knew someone who might—Colby. Despite the late hour, I called him.

"Hey, Bello. What's up?" he answered.

"I know it's late, big guy. But I need to talk to you about something."

"What is it?"

"Can I come over?"

"You don't ever have to ask that," he answered. "See you when you get here."

Colby was waiting at the door when I got there. I told him about Kismet's death, the notebook she had, and what I read in the journal. Colby was as stunned as I was.

"A while back, Kismet said O'Reilly couldn't have been the man she saw because the man she saw had a freshly shaved head. O'Reilly never shaved his head."

"Her word couldn't have been trustworthy."

"Yeah, I know that. But it adds to what we know now."

Colby finished my thought. "It's enough to question everything."

We sat silent for a minute.

"Let's start with getting the journals analyzed. Dated, handwriting analysis, all that. It's possible this notebook is a forgery," Colby said.

"Yeah. But I don't think it is."

"I don't think so, either."

I VISITED a lab tech named Sophie. She was a petite woman in her fifties with long gray hair, and the absolute best at her job. I asked her to analyze the journal entries and come up with an approximate date they were written.

"I also need you to compare the handwriting in this journal to the writing of Sanchez's we found at the murder scene. I need this to be discreet, Sophie."

"No problem, sweetie," she told me as she pecked me on the cheek. "Don't forget, sweetie, my son is a doctor and very handsome. I can hook you up anytime."

"How could I forget? You remind me every time I see you."

We both laughed.

"It's about time for you to settle down and find someone."

"I may already have," I said before I realized it.

She looked at me and smiled. "But is he a doctor?"

"He's a lawyer."

"Well, if you ever get tired of him, let me know."

"I think he'll get tired of me long before I get tired of him."

COLBY and I waited anxiously for the results to come in, but I knew better than to rush Sophie. Two days after giving the items to her, she was waiting at my desk to talk to me when I arrived.

"The handwriting matches, no question about it," she told me. The date she gave me for the journal also matched the timeframe for the murder. It was all legit. I called Colby and told him what Sophie found out. We decided to discuss it that night.

"What're we going to do with this info?"

"We only have a few choices," Colby offered. "We can use the media to expose Pryor as the real killer of the old lady."

"Pryor's name is already mud," I said. "All that would do is stir the water a bit more. He's already in prison. I want something that'll connect Pryor to Ric's murder."

"I agree, but I don't know how to do that."

"Me, either," I said.

We talked for hours, but no decision was made. Colby and I dozed off on the couch and eventually climbed into bed and fell asleep.

I TALKED to Lex about what I had learned, but she couldn't offer me any advice.

"The notebook wouldn't be enough to convict Pryor of the murder, and even if it was, so what? He probably wouldn't get more than five years for an accidental murder."

For the next several weeks, I tried hard to find more of the missing pieces that I knew were there.

It was almost the end of March when a few more pieces fell into place.

CHAPTER TWENTY-NINE

I WAS finishing up the paperwork on an easily solved hit-and-run vehicular manslaughter when I saw a familiar face come into the station under arrest—Moxley. The ultimate mullet gave it away: no hair on top and long stringy hair down his back.

Moxley's eyes met mine, and he smiled a sly little grin. He was taken into an interrogation room, and the arresting officer came out. He was a drug cop by the name of Deene.

"What's he being arrested for?" I asked him.

"Guy's been running one of the largest drug rings in the state. He's going down. For a long time."

Deene and his partner, McGill, returned to the interrogation room a few minutes later. Thirty minutes later, Deene was standing at my desk.

"Moxley insists he ain't talking until he talks to you."

"Me?"

"Yeah, you. What the hell do you got to do with this guy? He a rump rider too?" His intention wasn't to be rude. He liked teasing me about being gay.

"Shut up, fuckhead." I smiled at him. "I don't know why he wants to talk to me. I won't if you don't want me to. I don't want to step on your feet."

"Nah, it's cool. Do what you can."

I went into the room with Deene.

"No, I talk to Flesh alone, or I don't talk at all."

I nodded to Deene and McGill that it was okay. I could handle it.

"What do you want from me, Moxley?" I asked when we were alone.

He looked at me and laughed quietly.

"Remember that beating me and my buddies gave you?"

"Yeah, I remember." How could I forget? It was after the beating that Colby and I began this thing I guess you could call a relationship.

"I know something that you wanna know."

"And what would that be?"

"That red-headed cop ain't the one who really killed that queer guy at the motel."

"You mean Ricardo Sanchez?"

"I guess. I don't worry about remembering names, especially names of queers." He laughed like he was trying to goad me, but it wasn't going to work.

"How do you know O'Reilly didn't do it?"

"Cuz I was there that night. I was hired to watch the motel room."

"You were there when Sanchez was killed?"

"Yeah, I was hired to take care of everything. Well, everything but the murder itself. He wanted to take care of that himself."

"Who hired you?"

He cackled. "You think I'm gonna tell you without some kinda deal?"

"I'll be back," I said.

I pulled Deene, McGill, and Lex into Brunson's office. I told them what Moxley had told me. "Do we want to give up a major drug charge on the chance that he can lead us to the real killer? Which case is more important?" Deene asked.

"It's not about what's more important, Deene," Lex said.

"Well, yeah it is," he replied. "Murder is a big deal; I'm not saying it isn't. But it's one murder. You put this guy back on the street and he peddles his shit again and there will be more deaths."

"I see your point," Brunson agreed.

I was beginning to think we were at a stalemate when Lex spoke up. She turned to Deene.

"Do you think you could find some more charges to hang on Moxley in the next few days? Like trafficking or attempted murder or something like that."

"Yeah, if we were allowed to spend all our time on it. Why?"

"Why don't we offer Moxley a deal on these specific drug charges if the information he has pans out? But when he is released on those charges, we arrest him for the other stuff."

"A double cross?" Brunson asked.

"Yeah?"

"Go for it," the chief said.

Deene and I spelled out the deal to Moxley, of course leaving out the double cross we had decided on. Moxley wasn't the smartest guy—the hair cut was proof of that. After everything was ironed out, Lex and I sat down to take Moxley's statement.

"Pryor hired me," he said. I wasn't extremely surprised, at first.

"I figured that hypocritical, homophobic son of a bitch was behind this," I said.

"Not that Pryor," Moxley corrected.

"What?"

"The son, not the dad."

"Junior?"

"Yeah. I been working for him for a year or so. Little jobs like following his father or other things. This time he hired me to tail Sanchez. He said Sanchez had some dirty little secret of his dad's, and he wanted to take care of him. That night, I told him you had been there, as well as those other two cops.

"He was pretty happy to hear you had been there. He said he could take care of two things at once: killing Sanchez and framing one of his father's faggot lovers. The kid had been taking care of his father's indiscretions for years. A lot of them he could pay off, but you were one he knew was trouble. "

"Did he know about his father hiring O'Reilly and Curtis to pay Sanchez off?"

"Yeah. He took the money with him after he killed Sanchez."

Minutes later, an arrest warrant had been issued for Joseph Pryor Jr. Of course, Brunson told Lex and me to arrest the guy. On the way, I made a quick call to Colby.

"I'm on my way to arrest Junior. I got evidence that says he's the real killer."

"That's great, Cristian. Be careful."

"I will. Don't worry. We'll celebrate tonight." I hung up my cell and got my head into the case.

As Lex and I walked into Pryor Ministries, several other cops surrounded the building. She and I walked into the sanctuary, but he wasn't there. We were heading to the offices when we ran into Madeline Pryor.

"What are you doing here?"

"Actually, Mrs. Pryor," Lex told her, "we're here to arrest your son."

She was visibly shocked. "My son? Joseph? What, ruining my husband's life wasn't enough? Now you have to ruin my son's life too?" Her comments were directed right at me, and she stared at me with an icy cold glare.

"I didn't make your husband queer; God did that."

She hit me with a sharp slap across the face.

I rubbed my face and smiled. "As for your son, he's a killer, and he has to pay for his crimes."

"Where's your son?" Lex asked.

Madeline Pryor looked toward the offices then motioned down the hallway in the opposite direction. "He's in the children's chapel."

Lex laughed. "We'll go this way," she said, and we started

moving toward the offices.

When we were a few feet away I heard Madeline punching buttons on a cell phone. I was heading back in her direction when I heard her speak.

"Baby, it's time to go."

She had already hung up by the time I got to her and had grabbed the cell.

"Where is he, Mrs. Pryor?"

"You'll never find him."

"You're under arrest for obstruction of justice." I snapped cuffs on her and started reading her the Miranda rights. Lex appeared a few seconds later.

"Cris, what're you doing?"

"She called Junior and told him to run. He's gonna go into hiding cuz of her."

We hauled Mrs. Pryor into the precinct and told the chief what had happened. She lawyered up right away, and her shark of a lawyer was there within fifteen minutes. We put a trace on the number she had called but found the cell phone at Junior's place. He had ditched it and taken only a small amount of clothes. We put out an immediate APB.

Mama Pryor was tight-lipped, she wouldn't say a thing, and her lawyer had her out of the precinct in less than two hours. I didn't hold out much hope that we would be able to pin anything on her.

Colby and I didn't exactly celebrate that night. I was pretty upset, and he did his best to make me feel better. Actually, he did make me feel better—by slowly sliding his shaft in and out of me until I came hard and loud. After a quick cleanup, I was asleep with his arms wrapped around me.

JUNIOR'S picture was splattered across the papers. First the stories were about Junior's sudden disappearance, then word got out that he was a murder suspect. Brunson ordered a critical review of all the evidence that had linked O'Reilly to Sanchez's murder. It wasn't easy, but we did find proof that Junior had managed to orchestrate it. Apparently, when he failed to frame me for the murder, Junior had to come up with a different plan. When O'Reilly started losing it, Junior made the evidence point to him.

I remembered when I first met Junior. He was just re-growing his hair after shaving it. He must've shaved it when he killed Sanchez to make himself resemble me.

For weeks, we spent all day every day looking for leads on Junior's location. Then we all spent less and less time on the case. If there were any leads to be found, we couldn't find them. I started to accept the fact that Junior wouldn't be caught; he had probably left the country.

CHAPTER THIRTY

I WISH I could say that I started to lighten up with Colby, but I didn't. I wanted to break a few of the rules, but I had broken so many, the idea of breaking more scared me too much. One night, Colby told me about his family. His grandfather, Theodore Maddox, had been a pharmacist who had turned a chain of pharmacies into a large pharmaceutical company. Colby's father, Theodore II, made Maddox into an international pharmaceutical company.

"My oldest brother, Ted, runs the company with Dad," Colby told me. "My oldest sister, Melody, is a doctor."

"Wow, a lawyer, a doctor, and a businessman. Bet your folks are proud of their kids."

"Yes, they're pleased with us three. But my younger brother is another story."

"What's his story?"

"Danny never had any focus, and he's always been the baby. Mom babied him and always made excuses for him. He never learned responsibility and probably never will. He's nineteen and still lives at home, doesn't work, gets whatever he wants, whenever he wants."

"What about your parents, still happily married?"

"Yes, more than thirty years now."

"A marriage without problems?"

"I never said there weren't problems. But they worked through any problems they had."

"What about you?" he asked me.

"What about me?"

"I'd like to hear about your family?"

"I don't have a family. Not anymore. Don't forget rule number six."

"Okay, Cristian, that's fine for now. Someday, I'll need you to open up, at least a little bit."

"I'll try."

Chapter Thirty-One

IN LATE April, Lex and I had to testify in court. After all day in court, I was finally able to check my phone messages. The first was from Colby. He was excited and out of breath.

"I got a lead on Junior, Cristian. It's unbelievable what I found out. I'm going to fire off an e-mail to you explaining it all. I'm going to check it out right now. I'll call if there's any other news."

It was 4 p.m., and he had left the message at 9 a.m. I hurried back to the precinct to check my e-mail. Among the dozens I had, I found the one from Colby:

I WAS looking into the Pryor's history when I came across Madeline Pryor's maiden name—Newgad.

The name doesn't mean anything to you, I'm sure, but it does for me. For years, I've been representing a man named Dick Hartell and a group called The Historical Donner Trail Committee. The committee has been fighting for years to reopen a historical stock trail that has been closed since nearby land was bought from the railroad by a local couple: Hank and Georgie Newgad. The Newgads believe it is their right to close a public road and have constructed barricades to keep people out. They don't live on the land but do have a few cabins there.

Hank Newgad is Madeline Pryor's brother. The land up there is extremely isolated and would be the perfect spot for Junior to hide out for awhile. I'm heading up to the Cisco Grove Campground on Donner

Summit. I'm not sure what the weather is like up there. I might need to rent a snowmobile or something like that.

I didn't call anyone because I'm not sure the Pryor's don't have any other cops on the payroll. I don't trust anyone but you and Lex. I'll call you as soon as I get there. Don't worry I'll be fine.

COLBY'S e-mail had been sent right after the phone message. He should've arrived on Donner Summit hours ago. The fact that he hadn't called me made me nervous. A few more unanswered calls to Colby's cell made me even more nervous. I found the address to the Cisco Grove Campground and headed up that way.

The snow had hit hard that winter, but it hadn't snowed recently. The snow on the sides of the roads was a couple of feet deep, but the road itself was clear. When I arrived at the campground, I headed to the check-in. I described Colby and asked if he had been there that morning.

"Yeah, he was here," the middle-aged lady answered. "Asked a few questions about the old Donner Trail, rented a snowmobile, and headed up there."

"What time was that?"

"'Bout ten this morning."

"I need a snowmobile and the direction he was going."

"You only got an hour or so of light, young man. You don't want to be heading up there now."

"I don't have a choice. Police business." I flashed her my badge. She grabbed a rental form, and I filled it out while she got a machine ready for me.

She told me the direction Colby had gone, and I headed up. The snow was frozen hard and the air was turning into a bone-chilling wind. I hadn't even thought about getting warmer clothes.

I found the machine Colby had rented parked in front of a large barricade. Must have been the barricade the Newgads had put up. I could see footprints from the snowmobile to a spot in the fence I could climb through. I followed the prints, but it wasn't long before I lost the trail. The wind had blown some of the loose snow around—enough to obscure Colby's tracks. I decided to follow the old stock trail, assuming that's what Colby would have done. Night began to settle in, and soon the only light I had was the glow of the moon.

I considered turning around and going back before I got lost in the wilderness. I hated the idea of waiting until morning to look for Colby, but dying up here wouldn't do him any good, either.

That's when I heard a noise, a small motor—like a generator. I followed the noise before it shut off. I found a small cabin with a generator out back. I didn't see any movement, but I was sure Junior had to be around somewhere. I crept up to the cabin and was about to peek in a window when a bullet whizzed by my head, embedding itself into the cabin. Ducking to the ground, I crawled to the side of the house and peeked back around before another bullet flew by. Junior was standing twenty feet away, hiding between two trees, holding a hunting rifle.

"Give it up, Junior," I yelled at him. "You're done for. You're going down."

"No way, Flesh. I'm taking you out once and for all. You're going to die now, just like your boyfriend."

Colby! I pulled out my gun and fired off a shot at Junior. It missed by a mile, that's what happens when you let emotions get the best of you, and you don't bother with a little thing like aiming.

"You bastard. If you killed him, I will personally make sure you pay."

He laughed loudly. "How sweet. Such concern for your faggot lover."

I was about to fire off another shot, but I held back. I had a limited number of bullets and couldn't waste them. I also knew that trying to win a firefight at night was a hopeless cause. It would be a standoff that would just wear me out.

As much as I hated the idea, I turned from the cabin and started to run. I heard Junior pushing through the trees behind me, but I didn't stop until I couldn't hear any noise behind me. I climbed to the top of a small hill where I had a limited vision around me and sat down. I had a good enough sense of direction that I could make it back to the cabin, but I was sure at first light Junior would be coming after me. I needed a place to sleep for the night.

I wondered if what he had said about Colby was true—was he dead? I put my hands to my face and tried to hold back the tears. I couldn't, and I started to sob at the idea of Colby no longer being around. It was a selfish cry. I wasn't thinking about other people, his family, or the clients he had helped. I was thinking purely about myself and how empty my life would become again without him there.

I finally got control of myself and started following the rocks, looking for a place to bed down. My cell wasn't getting any service where I was, so I knew I was on my own. Ten minutes later, I smelled something—smoke. Maybe campfire smoke. Following the smell, it led me to an open doorway into the mountain. I assumed it was an old mining shaft and stepped in. Without the moon, it got pitch black, but I felt my way along the walls. Suddenly, something whacked me across the head. I fell to the ground and slipped into darkness.

I WOKE up ready to fight, but it wasn't Junior standing over me. It was Colby.

"Cristian, are you okay?" He was touching my face.

"Colby?" I was sure I was hallucinating from the hit on the head. "What the hell?"

"I thought you were Junior. I hit you over the head with a branch."

I looked at him and then around me. There was a small fire that lit up the area. I sat up too fast and got a little woozy, but Colby helped me stand, and we moved to the fire.

"What happened?" I asked him. "Junior said you were dead."

"He thinks I am. He shot me in the leg." I looked at his leg and saw he'd created a makeshift bandage. "He shot me, and I fell down a ravine. He thought I was dead, but I was playing possum. I waited until he left, then crawled up, found this place, and decided to settle in.

"I knew you'd come after me, but I thought you'd be smart enough to wait until it was light out, not rush in when it was dark."

I looked at him sheepishly. "I couldn't wait."

"Is anyone else coming?"

"I didn't tell anyone I was coming."

He looked at me like I was stupid.

"What were you thinking, Cristian?"

I started to get defensive. "I was thinking you needed me. I was thinking you might get into some trouble, and I didn't want to lose you. Not after everything." He pulled me into a hug and kissed me on the cheek. "I love you, Colby." The words came out of my mouth before I even realized what I had said. We were both stunned.

"What?"

"I said I love you. Don't ask me to say it again."

"I love you too."

We lay down in front of the fire with his arms wrapped around me, and we dozed off. I woke up an hour or so later. Colby was shivering uncontrollably.

"I can't get warm," he told me.

"Strip," I ordered.

"Now isn't the time for sex."

"Normally, I'd say it's always the time for sex. But that's not what this is about. We can share body heat. That old myth is true. Get naked."

He started to strip, and I did the same. I lay down next to him, pushing him closer to the fire. I pulled our clothes over top of us as makeshift blankets and pressed our naked bodies together. Soon we were both asleep again.

I actually slept pretty well, considering the circumstances. I woke up as the sun started to rise. I let Colby sleep a bit longer after I dressed, then woke him.

"You need to head back to the campground," I told him. "Go find help."

"Come with me. Don't worry about Junior."

"No, I can't let him go. Besides, I need to make sure he doesn't follow you and finish you off for good."

"I don't like this idea. You could get hurt."

"But I won't. I've never really looked forward to the future before. But I do now, because of you. I'm not gonna lose that now, big guy."

He pulled me into a kiss. We lingered in each other's arms before saying good-bye and setting out in opposite directions. I headed for the cabin, taking it slow. Then I stopped, a new idea forming in my head.

I went back to the mine shaft. The entrance to the shaft stood out from the mountain by about three feet and was about five feet wide. I got the fire started again, feeding it lots of weeds and roots to ensure that there was plenty of smoke billowing out of the shaft. The roof of the entrance was covered with snow and fallen branches. I pulled myself up and dug under the snow and branches, hiding myself, while still being able to see what, or who, was coming.

It was cold under the snow, and I had to focus not to start shivering and lose concentration. I didn't figure it would take Junior long to follow the smoke. I counted on two things with him: he was stupid, and he thought I was stupid. He wouldn't stop to question why the fire was so big.

I heard him coming before I saw him. He was carrying his hunting rifle and was heading straight for the shaft. I readied myself, and as he stepped a few feet into the tunnel, I stood, then swung down into him, knocking him to the ground.

He dropped the rifle, and I managed to grab it, but before I could aim it at him, he tackled me to the ground, and we started to wrestle over the gun. He was on top of me, trying to choke me with the rifle, while I was pushing up on the gun.

My pistol was in my pocket, but I couldn't let go of the rifle to grab the pistol. He was stronger than I gave him credit for, and I'm sure he was thinking the same of me.

Junior let up for just a second to readjust his weight to bear down on me even harder, and I took advantage of that split second. I kicked up with my feet, throwing him into the air. As he was in the air, I pulled the rifle to the side so he flipped to my side, landing on his back.

I flipped over as well, taking the rifle with me and landing on top of him. The air had been knocked out of him, and he didn't have time to respond. I took the butt of the rifle and whacked him across the head, knocking him out.

Then I lost it—totally and completely. I couldn't think of anything but the things he had done. Killing Ric, framing me, hiring O'Reilly, hurting Gabe, shooting Colby.

In that moment, I hated that man so bad I wanted to kill him. I wanted him to pay and to suffer. I whacked him across the face with the butt of the rifle, then slammed it into his ribs. Even unconscious, he made grunting noises. Seeing nothing but red, I threw the rifle to the ground and started using my fists. They slammed into his nose, his face, his chest, and his ribs. I heard ribs snap, and I knew they were broken, but I couldn't stop. I didn't hear the snowmobiles coming up, and I didn't hear the voices telling me to stop. But I did feel the hand on my shoulder, the soft gentle feel of a woman's skin.

"Cris, stop. It's over." It was Lex, and I knew she was right. It really was over.

I crawled off of Junior. He was cuffed and taken away. Lex pulled me into a hug. At first I just stood there as she hugged me, my arms at my side, but soon my arms went around her, pulling her close to me, hugging her like I had never hugged a woman before.

When I finally had enough control to talk, I asked, "How did you know to come here?"

She smiled at me. "I know you pretty well, Cris. I woke up with a feeling that you needed help. I tried to call you. When you didn't answer, I went to your place, then Colby's. When I saw both of you were gone, I knew something was up.

"I got on your computer and found the e-mail from Colby. I

convinced Brunson I needed a team to come up here."

"How'd you get into my e-mail?"

"I know your password, Cris. Sex69."

I laughed at her. "Colby okay?"

"Yeah. He's at the campground getting medical treatment for the bullet and hypothermia. He'll be fine."

We stood there for a moment longer.

"You know I would've killed him?"

"Yeah, Cris. I know. And I don't think anyone would've blamed you if you had. But he's going to go away. Imagine a good-looking guy like him in prison. There's going be a lot of big inmates loving him."

We both laughed.

"Sweet justice for a homophobic prick like him."

I hopped on the sled with Lex, and we drove to the campground. Junior had been officially arrested and was being taken away in an ambulance as I arrived. I made my way to the ambulance where Colby was.

"Hey there, big guy." I smiled at him.

"Bello! You're okay."

"I told you I would be." I climbed into the ambulance and gave him a kiss. The EMT looked a little shocked, but not offended.

"He needs to go to the hospital to be checked out by a doctor," the EMT said. "He'll be fine, I'm sure. You can ride with us, if you want."

CHAPTER THIRTY-TWO

BY JUNE, Junior was wearing prison blues at Ely State Prison, Nevada's maximum security prison. He had taken a deal to avoid the death penalty, but he would spend the rest of his life behind bars.

Junior was doing time not just for killing Sanchez and framing me, but also for arranging Kismet's murder. Moxley had confessed to drugging Kismet, but it was Junior who had told him to do it.

Rich Redding was happy to hear that Kismet, Kimberly, didn't succumb to drugs. He was able to find her daughter and told her that her mother had been turning her life around when she died.

The elder Pryor also had time added to his sentence. The notebook was enough proof to convict Pryor of the decades-old murder. He was hit harder than I expected—he was given an additional fifteen years.

A few days after Junior was sentenced, Colby and I took Gabe and Violet out to celebrate an important event. Gabe had decided twenty years old wasn't too late to get his GED, and we were celebrating the fact he had passed his final test. They had also started stepping away from the gang life, so far with good results. Gabe even had plans for college. He wasn't sure what he wanted to do for a career, but at least he was making plans for the future.

THINGS weren't perfect for Colby and me, but they weren't bad, either. Even though I had told Colby I loved him on Donner Summit, it was hard for me to say the L-word again.

"How come you don't tell me you love me?" he asked me one time.

"I do. I tell you all the time."

"No. If I say it to you, you say me too or same here or ditto."

"You know I do, Colby."

"Yeah, you say that too."

"It's hard for me to say it," I admitted. "It doesn't mean I don't, but it's difficult. I can't explain why."

"How about we make a deal?"

"What you got in mind?"

"You say the words at least once a month."

I laughed. "It's a deal. I love you. There, I'm done for a month."

"Why do you have to be such a dick?" he teased.

"It comes naturally."

He grabbed my sides and started tickling me. Yeah, he had figured out that I was ticklish, too, and loved to torture me. We tickled and grabbed each other as we wrestled around on the floor. We stopped with him on top, and we started kissing.

"Wait, Colby. I have something to tell you."

"I know you love me, you don't have to say it again, not right now, anyway."

"No, not that. I'm gonna tell you something about me you don't know. But it's all I'm gonna say for now. Please don't ask me any questions or dig for further information. I'll say more later, when I'm ready."

"Okay."

"My parents are still alive, still married. I have a younger brother."

He looked at me for a minute, making sure that was all I was going to say. When he was sure it was, he leaned down and kissed me gently on my lips.

"Thank you, Bello."

ETHAN STONE lives in Nevada. But not Reno or Las Vegas. There are other cities there, you know. Where he lives, gambling isn't on every block, just every other block. He has been obsessed with two things in his life: books and all things gay. After spending years trying to ignore the voices in his head, he finally decided to sit down and listen to them. What he discovered was a perfect union of his two obsessions. Ethan has a day job that pays the bills. He wears a uniform to work, and he looks damn sexy in it.

You can contact Ethan at ethanstone.nv@gmail.com and visit his blog at http://www.ethanjstone.blogspot.com. You can also find him on Facebook.

More Mystery Romance from DREAMSPINNER PRESS

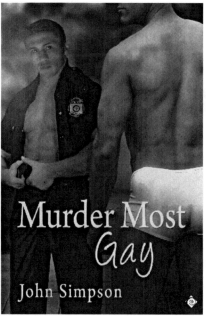

http://www.dreamspinnerpress.com

Lightning Source UK Ltd.
Milton Keynes UK
UKOW03f2303100913

216967UK00014B/398/P